CONSPIRACY IN BOLOGNA

NICO ARGENTI SERIES #4

KEN TENTARELLI

copyright © 2022 Kenneth Tentarelli

All rights reserved. No part of this publication may be reproduced or used in any manner without permission of the copyright owner except for use of quotations in a book review.

This is a work of fiction. Names, characters, places, and incidents are a product of the author's imagination. Locales and public names are sometimes used for atmospheric purposes. Any resemblance to actual people, living or dead, is completely coincidental.

ISBN: 978-1-7331773-9-9 (ebook)

ISBN: 979-8-9856624-0-5 (paperback)

ISBN: 979-8-9856624-5-0 (hardcover)

Also by Ken Tentarelli

The Laureate: Mystery in Renaissance Italy

The Advisor: Intrigue in Tuscany

Assignment Milan

Rebels in Pisa

MAIN CHARACTERS

<u>Nico's Family</u>

    Nico Argenti - Graduate of the University of Bologna law school. Member of the Florentine Security Commission.

    Alessa - Nico's adopted sister

    Donato - Nico's cousin. Owner of the Uccello, the finest restaurant in Florence.

    Joanna - Donato's wife

<u>Nico's Colleagues</u>

    Massimo Leoni - Decorated soldier. Member of the Florentine Security Commission.

    Vittorio Colombo - Peerless investigator. Member of the Florentine Security Commission.

Scala - Chancellor of the Florentine Republic. Overseer of the Florentine Security Commission.

Other important people

Patrizu Nieddu - Petty criminal /con man.

Luigi Attendolo - Mercenary captain

Ercole Strozzi. - Wealthy Florentine exile

Cardinal Capranica - Papal authority in Bologna.

Matteo Fontana - Papal prosecutor in Bologna.

Giovanni Bentivoglio. - Patriarch of Bologna's leading family.

Livio Paltroni – Manager of the Bardi bank in Bologna.

Gerhard Ritter – Student at the University of Bologna law school.

Allard – Professor at the University of Bologna.

Gasparo - Boy abducted by mercenaries

MAP OF ITALIAN STATES

Italian States in year 1465

1

Florence, Italy April 1465

A sharp sound in the quiet night startled the sandy-haired boy. He sat up abruptly. Perhaps he had heard another child coughing or calling out in his sleep. He glanced down the rows of beds, expecting to spot a restless form among the line of sleeping children, but darkness hid any hint of movement. The orphanage packed all the young children, more every year, into one enormous room. With so many children, he could hardly see to the far end of his row, and this room held only the younger children. The older children were segregated from the young ones, with the older boys in one room and the older girls in another.

The boy anticipated a second disturbance, but when none came, he leaned back and closed his eyes. He was almost asleep when he heard another sound. This one was softer, farther away. It had the cadence of people talking. It couldn't be the nuns because they retired to their quarters after compline prayers, except for one who passed through the room periodically to check on the children. He looked toward the doorway. In the darkness, he could barely make out its squarish frame in the corner of the room. From the doorway, he guessed, he might be able to hear whether the sounds were truly voices or just wind blowing in through an open window.

He swung his legs over the side of his bed. His was only a small cot, yet his feet did not reach the floor. He slithered, lowering himself slowly until his toes felt the cold stone floor below. He paused, standing beside the bed. When he was sure his movement had not disturbed any of his neighbors, he stepped quietly on the balls of his feet to the doorway.

He was sure that the sounds were voices, but they were too faint to distinguish any words. Curiosity pulled him through the doorway and into the hall. Light spilled into the hallway from a room at the far end of the corridor. He crept forward until he heard a clipped phrase, "This one is big for his age," and a responding grunt. The speech was rough, too rough to have been uttered by one of the nuns. He heard several more indistinct exchanges and then a final statement. "Our business is done until you have another one."

A large shadow followed by a second smaller one flowed out of the lighted room and into the hallway. A moment later, two figures followed the shadows into the hallway. Fearing discovery, the boy pressed himself flat against the wall, praying that the darkness would hide him. He held his breath. The only sound now was his beating heart. He caught only a glimpse of their faces before the figures turned away and headed toward the building exit. The larger person was a man whom the boy did not recognize. With him was Armando, an older boy liked by all the young children, and his friend. *Why is Armando going out at night? Where is the man taking him?*

The man placed a hand on Armando's shoulder. Reassurance or pressure?

2

"Another child is missing."

Alessa's words caught Nico with a honey roll raised nearly to his lips. He set the pastry down on his plate, looked up at his sister, and echoed, "Another child? Missing?"

Alessa came to the table and sat across from Nico. "Ah, Nico, I mentioned the missing children at dinner yesterday, but your mind was filled with visions of Bianca. It had no room for any other thoughts. That happens every time you return from visiting Bianca in Siena."

Nico's expression shifted from puzzlement to a guilty smirk. "Well, it's been a year since I last saw her."

"A year?" Alessa laughed. "You weren't even away in Milan for a month, and you visited Bianca just before you departed for Milan. You were told when you accepted a position on the Florentine Security Commission that assignments could take you away for extended periods."

"Calendars aren't the only way to reckon time, sister. Aristotle said time depends on the motion of matter. And for me, time moves quickly when I'm with Bianca, and slowly when we're apart." Nico winked. "A month can seem like a year." He held out his hands, palms up, in resignation. "But I'm listening now; tell me about the missing children."

"Maria visits the orphanage every week. On each of her recent visits, another child has gone missing."

"Maria? I have not heard her name before. Who is she?"

"Maria lives nearby. Every day we walk to the central market together. Men are fortunate. They have many opportunities to talk with other men, but women have few chances to meet with other women, so I welcome our time together walking to and from the market. We always shared pleasant news, until recently." Alessa shifted uneasily in her chair. "Maria is deeply troubled. She says it feels like her own children are being lost."

"What does she do at the orphanage? Does she go there to help the nuns?"

"She's a midwife who is often called upon to deliver the illegitimate children of wealthy men." With bitterness in her voice, Alessa continued, "Despite having wives and mistresses, some men feel the need to prove their manhood by impregnating their slaves and servants. Those men don't want the children, so they have the babies taken from their mothers at birth and sent to the orphanage. Since Maria is the midwife, she is the one who brings the unwanted infants to the orphanage."

Nico winced. Seeing his revulsion, Alessa said, "It happens. You know it happens."

"Yes, I know it happens." Nico shook his head. "But it's despicable."

"The mothers are prevented from caring for their children, but Maria never forgets them. She goes to the orphanage to visit the children she has delivered. She's been doing this for many years."

"And suddenly children are disappearing?"

"Yes, that's what Maria said. Whenever children are placed with a family as an apprentice or a servant, Maria hears news of the placement before the children leave the orphanage. But lately children have vanished without a word."

Nico ran a hand through his hair. "Someone must know what is happening to the children. Has Maria asked the nuns about the disappearances?"

"She spoke with a nun who claimed she didn't know what became of the children. Maria saw that her question made the nun uneasy, so she didn't ask any further." Alessa looked directly at Nico. "Will you speak with Maria? Then you can ask at the orphanage. You're a lawyer, so you know how to ask the right questions."

Nico leaned back in his chair and laughed. "I've always found it difficult to resist your pleas when you fix me with your big brown eyes. Now you bolster your request by praising me with words. How can I possibly refuse?"

Alessa smiled. "Thank you, dear brother. I told Maria you would help."

Nico's eyes narrowed. "You already told her that I would inquire at the orphanage?"

"I knew you'd be as troubled as I am."

Nico rose from the table, paced across the room, then turned back to face Alessa. "Both of my parents were taken by the plague in my ninth year, and I still miss them greatly. At least I had nine years with them. You were torn from your family at a young age, so you understand the loss. We are fortunate that we were brought together in a caring family. What must it be like for children at Ospedale degli Innocenti who don't even know their parents?"

Alessa closed her eyes while recalling an image of her family, her mother, father, and younger brother happily together in their tiny Moroccan village. A moment later, she returned to the present and said, "Maria often helps her husband at the bakery. If she is at the bakery this morning, you can speak with her there."

Nico took a bite of the honey roll and licked a wayward dab of honey from his finger. "Upon our return from Milan, Chancellor

Scala graciously allowed Massimo, Vittorio, and me a four-day holiday...."

Before Nico could finish his statement, Alessa interjected, "Which you spent in Siena with Bianca."

"Yes," Nico grinned. "But now that my holiday is finished, I must see whether Chancellor Scala has a new assignment for the Florentine Security Commission. If he doesn't have a new assignment for us, I may be able to meet with Maria later today."

3

Every time Nico crossed the piazza to the Palazzo della Signoria, he glanced upward to admire the building's stately facade topped by the tower that had held the city's first community clock for more than two centuries. A sudden hush spreading across the piazza interrupted Nico's reverie. He turned and joined the others, captivated by the sight of two distinguished-looking men escorting a younger man toward the palazzo. The escorts wore dark-colored silk tunics favored by bankers. The young man contrasted with them in his stylish pale green tunic adorned with silver buttons and silver embroidery at the collar.

Nico recognized the young man immediately as Lorenzo de Medici. Although only sixteen years of age, Lorenzo was well known and admired by everyone in Florence for the services he rendered to the republic, most recently as an attaché to the Kingdom of France. Nico stepped aside and as the entourage passed, the young de Medici's eyes locked with Nico's and Lorenzo gave a slight nod. Was it a simple courtesy or a gesture of recognition, or did it signify that the powerful young de Medici might know of Nico Argenti?

Nico waited until Lorenzo and the bankers disappeared into the palazzo before entering himself. Whispering among bystanders in the hall to his left told Nico that Lorenzo had gone in that direction toward the meeting rooms. Nico took the quiet corridor to his right that led to the chancery offices. He stopped at the largest room in the chancery wing, the nexus where clerks received reports and dispatched orders to Florentine diplomats.

The chancellor and his staff supervised the activities of all Florentine embassies. Chancery clerks recorded reports received from ambassadors and envoys. Those describing routine matters were sent to the chancery annex, where they were filed in the annex's massive archive. Those requesting assistance or information were routed to the responsible government department. Any reports raising concerns that might bear on the well-being of the republic were delivered directly to the chancellor. If Chancellor Scala perceived even the slightest possibility of a threat, he forwarded the report to the Florentine Security Commission for Nico, Massimo, and Vittorio to investigate and take appropriate action.

Nico spotted Massimo across the room, where he and a clerk were engaged in lively conversation. When Massimo noticed Nico, he gave the clerk a friendly slap on the back and moved to greet his fellow commissioner. "When I last saw you, you were charging off to visit with your woman in Siena," Massimo teased.

Nico laughed. "You know better than to call her my woman. She is her own woman and don't let her hear you suggest otherwise. Even you, a decorated soldier, would be wise to avoid her reproval."

"Ah, you need say no more. I have learned through painful experience to avoid the rebukes of strong-willed women." Then, laughing, Massimo added, "Yet it is a suffering not entirely without stimulation."

"It was generous of Chancellor Scala to allow us holiday time after our assignment in Milan." Then, to shift the focus from himself, Nico said, "And you, my friend, were you drawn back to Pavia by the woman you described as seasoned?"

"Were Pavia not so distant, I surely would have sought her fragrance. Instead, my holiday was spent at the army base outside the city. As an army officer, I'm permitted to reside at the base. It is a benefit that lets me avoid the outrageous fees charged for apartments in the city. Once each month, card players hold a bassetta tournament. I used the opportunity to relieve some brash recruits of their excess florins."

Nico feigned surprise. "Are you claiming that you endured five days without the company of a woman?"

"Days, yes," Massimo laughed. "The challenge was deciding how to divide my nights between two lovelies, a charming green-eyed Sicilian and a compliant Florentine beauty." Massimo sighed. "Like all others, this holiday was too short."

"For me too," Nico agreed. "Did the clerk know whether we have a new assignment?"

"No, he doesn't, but Vittorio may know. The clerk said Vittorio was here earlier."

As the two men spoke, they climbed to the palazzo's upper level, where a storage room had been converted into the security commission office. Two modest tables and a few chairs were all the room could accommodate without being overcrowded. The men had added small accessories to make the room more comfortable and useful. Nico had brought a lantern with a highly polished reflector to supplement the daylight that entered through two small windows. Immediately upon entering the room, they noticed the latest addition, blue cushions donated by Vittorio, to pad the hard wooden chairs.

Vittorio, the Guardia investigator assigned to the security commission, stood facing a wall filled with columns of notecards. In his hand were several more cards that he intended to add to the display. Each column held cards related to a matter of concern. On each card was a pertinent item gleaned from dispatches sent to the chancery. The arrangement of cards on the wall let the men organize information received from Florence's many embassies.

Vittorio acknowledged Nico's and Massimo's arrival with a quick nod and pointed to papers strewn across a table. "Those are dispatches that arrived while we were on holiday. I already read the reports from our embassy in Rome." He held up the note cards in his hand. "And these are the issues I found in those reports."

Massimo asked, "Are we to expect problems from His Holiness?"

"Not according to these reports. The Vatican has its full attention focused on troublesome lords and princes in the south. The information in these dispatches concerns business dealings in Rome, some of which might impact Florentine merchants."

Nico said, "The Papal States cover a wide territory. If the Vatican has its full attention turned to the south, it may be neglecting its northern states. That neglect could conceivably become a problem for us." Massimo and Vittorio stared at Nico as they absorbed his conjecture.

Massimo and Nico divided the unread dispatches between them. Like Vittorio, they recorded items of interest on cards, which they pinned to the wall. Soon the three men were standing and facing the array of notecards. Vittorio pointed to one column, then tapped one of the cards. "This note from the embassy in Venice is disturbing. It says that a wealthy Florentine exile who had been living in Venice has disappeared, but it doesn't give the exile's name or tell how he disappeared."

Nico said, "Wealthy exiles have been trouble in the past; that's why the embassies keep watch on them. The report deserves further investigation."

Massimo gestured to the stack of papers on the table and said, "There are no recent reports from Siena or Austria. The couriers bringing those documents aren't expected to arrive for several days."

"That will give me time to explore a possible problem here in Florence," Nico said. Massimo and Vittorio turned their attention to Nico, who continued, "A midwife who regularly visits the Ospedale degli Innocenti claims that children are disappearing from the orphanage."

Massimo said, "That doesn't seem like a problem for the Florentine Security Commission."

The perplexed looks of his fellow commissioners caused Nico to add as an excuse, "It might be nothing, but I promised my sister I would inquire at the orphanage."

4

When Nico and Alessa arrived at the bakery, Maria was taking rolls from a tray and putting them into a cloth sack. Behind her, her husband was retrieving another tray from the oven. Warmth from the oven and the heady aroma of yeast filled the air. Upon seeing Nico and Alessa, Maria set the sack down on a counter and pointed to a small table in a corner of the shop. When the three were seated, Alessa made introductions; then she said, "Maria, tell Nico what you have seen at the orphanage."

With trembling hands, Maria began, "Every time I am at mass, I pray for the infants I brought to the orphanage. I pray too for the mothers who still suffer the loss of the children they carried." She tensed and rubbed her hands together. "And may the Lord forgive me, when I leave the church I curse the men who forced the mothers and children apart.

"I visit the children often to let them know that someone cares. I have no children of my own. The law says…" Maria paused; then looked up at Nico. "You are a lawyer, so you know the law. It says that all unwanted children have a place at Ospedale degli Innocenti until their fourteenth year. When they reach fourteen years, girls are to be placed as servants with families, and boys are to be apprenticed in shops and mills."

"From what Alessa has told me, I understand you have reason to think this is not happening," Nico said.

"For the girls, it still happens, but for the boys, I am not sure."

"What have you seen that gives you concern?"

"When a girl's time comes, the sisters find a family to take her. They make sure it is a good family, so the girl does not become a slave or a whore. The sisters help the girl gather her clothes and her few meager possessions. It is a sad day because the girl leaves the only people she has known, but it is a happy day too because she is starting a new life."

"Is it not the same for the boys?" Nico asked.

"In the past, yes, but no longer. On my last visit to the orphanage, I arrived in late morning after the children had finished their morning chores. When their chores were done, the boys like to play ball in a field behind the building. I try not to have favorites, but there is one boy, Armando, who is special. He is big, strong, and always happy. The other children like him because he is kind and willing to help the younger ones.

"I walked out to the ball field expecting to find Armando, but he was not there. The other boys said he was not with them at breakfast. I thought perhaps he was sick, so I went inside to the infirmary. When I learned that he was not there, I asked Sister Leona about him. She could not face me. She cast her eyes down and told me Armando was gone. She said that I should not ask further; then she turned abruptly and walked away."

"Did you ask one of the other nuns?"

"No, I was too upset by Sister Leona's reaction to my question."

"What age is Armando?" Nico asked.

"Thirteen years," Maria replied. "He will be fourteen next month. I am certain because I was the midwife who helped birth him. He was born on Pentecost."

Alessa sat quietly listening to the exchange as Nico said, "There must be someone who knows what happened to Armando."

Maria replied, "Ospedale degli Innocenti has an administrator. He must know, but it is not my place to question him."

Finally, Alessa spoke. "You told me that Armando is not the only missing child."

"He is not. Two other boys also went missing suddenly."

"Boys," Nico echoed. "Are only boys missing? What about the girls? Are any girls missing?"

"No, only boys."

Nico said, "Tell me about them."

"One is named Claudio, and the other is Beppo. Two fine boys. Both are about the same age as Armando. They are not my children... I mean, I didn't deliver them, so I don't know much about them."

Nico folded his hands, looked down at them for a minute, then looked up at Alessa. "I will need a pretext, a reason for asking questions of the orphanage administrator."

"Can't you say it's an official inquiry?" Alessa asked.

Nico shook his head. "No, security commission members don't have the authority to question Florentine citizens. Only members of the Guardia can do that."

Alessa smiled. "I'm sure your legal mind will discover a reasonable excuse."

5

Ospedale degli Innocenti was located near the center of the city, so Nico had often walked past the attractive building. Never had he failed to admire the exquisite portico and facade designed by Filippo Brunelleschi, the same architect who had engineered the magnificent dome of Santa Maria del Fiore cathedral. What always surprised Nico was the size of the building. *"Could there be so many orphans in the city of Florence that a building two levels high and stretching the full width of a piazza is needed to house them?"* he thought.

As soon as Nico entered the anteroom, a young boy approached him and smiled. Like the other children within Nico's view, he was barefoot and wore a rough brown wool smock. He said nothing but beckoned Nico to follow and led him to a large common room where people were busily preparing food for *pranzo,* the midday meal. A few of the workers were nuns, but they were outnumbered by laypeople, mostly women. Nico recognized one of the women as a member of his parish, and he recalled that members of the church's Society of San Michele volunteered at the orphanage.

Before Nico could approach the woman, a man came from

behind. Nico's stylish tunic suggested that he hadn't come to help with the meal service. The man asked, "How may I help you?"

"I wish to speak with the administrator."

With a sheepish grin, the man said, "He prefers to be called the rector." He shrugged and pointed to a doorway. "Through that doorway, go to the left at the second hallway. His office is at the far end."

Following the man's directions, Nico passed through a long corridor. Its walls, perhaps once white, had discolored to the pale gray color of a lightly overcast sky. Their only decoration was a painting hung at the intersection where Nico turned left. The depiction of Saint Francis feeding birds appeared to be the product of an apprentice who would never become a master. The administrator's office was at the end of the second hallway in a section of the building far from any noise or activity. The administrator was a big man with broad shoulders, rough hands, and thick wavy hair. A book sat open on his desk, but instead of reading, he was gazing through a window that looked out to Piazza Santissima Annunziata. He was captivated by a sight in the piazza and failed to notice Nico standing in the doorway until Nico knocked.

After an awkward "Huh?" the administrator collected his thoughts and asked coarsely, "What do you want?"

"I am Messer Nico Argenti. I have been retained by a furrier who wishes to apprentice one of the boys at the orphanage."

The administrator's face brightened. "I am the rector of Ospedale degli Innocenti. All of our boys are well disciplined and hard working. I am sure many of them would be pleasing to your client." The administrator paused a moment before adding, "I trust your client is aware that it is customary to make an offering to support the work we do here in the name of our Lord."

"I assure you that my client is an honorable and generous man. He is a member of the furrier guild, and his family has a long record of service to our republic." Nico paused to compose his thoughts before continuing. "A boy named Armando was recommended to my client as an especially strong and capable child who could perform the tasks of an apprentice furrier. And we understand this boy is of an age that it will soon be time for him to leave your charge."

"Armando?" The rector mused. He reached behind, pulled a paper from a shelf, set it on his desk, and scanned a list of names. "Ah, unfortunately, Armando is no longer with us. But do not be concerned; we have many other strong and capable boys who can serve your client's needs. Come, let me show you."

The administrator rose and moved toward the door. Nico stood immobile, folded his arms across his chest, and frowned. "My client asked specifically that I obtain the boy Armando. I do not have the latitude to consider other children. Can you tell me where Armando has gone?"

"To a farm."

"A farm?" Nico echoed. The administrator's answer surprised Nico because most children were apprenticed to mills and shops in the city. "Which farm?" Nico asked.

"I don't recall the name of the farm, only that it is a farm in the Chiana Valley."

Feigning surprise, Nico said, "The Chiana Valley is far from Florence. Is it common for children to be placed so distant from the city?"

"I can't say why people come here looking for children, but we have so many children that we do not limit their placement. Perhaps there are no orphans in the Chiana Valley." The administrator showed his growing impatience with Nico's questions by moving toward the door. "If the child Armando is your only interest, then I cannot help you." He brushed past Nico, saying, "You must excuse me, Messer Argenti. I have duties to perform."

6

Early the following morning, Nico's cousin Donato hired a horse and wagon, and the two men set out for the Chiana Valley. Farms in the fertile valley supplied vegetables, fruits, and grains to Donato's Uccello restaurant. Every spring, Donato visited the farmers to bolster their relationships. That gesture and the gifts he brought for the farmers' wives and children guaranteed that the Uccello always received top quality produce. Nico wanted to assure Alessa, Maria, and himself that Armando was in a safe place, so he had decided to accompany Donato.

The two men rode along the ancient Roman road, the Vecchia Aretina, that followed the Arno River from Florence toward Arezzo. A full day of riding took them to the hilltop hamlet of Laterina. Hundreds of years past, the villagers of Laterina built fortifications to protect themselves from roving bands of brigands. Since then, travelers took comfort in the safety of the town's inns. The next morning, Nico and Donato continued along Vecchia Aretina as it turned south and entered the broad Chiana Valley. Although the sun had not yet risen above the distant Apennine peaks, farm wagons laden with goods filled the road en route to Florence.

Nico said to his cousin, "Thank you for adjusting your schedule so you can come with me to look for the missing orphan."

"I welcome the opportunity to get away from the city." Donato chuckled. "And if I didn't support you, I would surely suffer Alessa's wrath."

"Have you ever been to Ospedale degli Innocenti?" Nico asked.

Donato replied, "I've passed the building many times, but I've never been inside. Is the interior as stunning as the exterior?"

"No, it seems that Brunelleschi devoted his creative touch to the exterior. What struck me most, though, were the throngs of children. I never realized that Florence had so many orphans. There must be hundreds of them."

"Poverty is one reason. The poor cannot provide for all their children," Donato explained. "Also, many children are orphaned when their parents succumb to disease and the plague. The Ospedale takes in all the unwanted without explanation or consequence and the city provides for the children's welfare."

"I wonder if other cities have as many orphans as Florence?" Nico mused.

Donato turned the wagon from the main road onto a dirt path leading to a distant farmhouse. In a field to their left, a group of men was harvesting an early crop and in the field to their right, other men were pulling up weeds. "The pickers are collecting beans," Donato observed.

Nico scanned the fields, searching unsuccessfully for Armando. The earthy smell of fertile soil gave way to the sweet smell of hay as they neared the farmhouse. Donato guided the wagon to the side of the house, where the farmer's wife was washing clothes in a large metal tub. After they exchanged greetings, she directed him to the barn where her husband was repairing a plow.

The farmer paused as the two men approached, then gestured to the twisted plow blade in front of him. "I thought I could fix this, but it calls for a blacksmith." He set his tools aside and greeted his two visitors.

Donato introduced Nico. The men spent several minutes discussing crops and farm life, then Donato said, "My cousin is looking for a boy from the orphanage in Florence."

The farmer looked at Nico, who explained, "I was told that a boy was taken from the orphanage to work on a farm in this valley. The boy's name is Armando."

The farmer shrugged. "The farms in this valley are far from Florence. I'd be surprised if one of us went all the way to Florence to find workers." He paused and brushed his hair back before continuing. "But I can't say. Women talk with other women about such things. Ask my wife."

While Donato continued talking with the farmer, Nico walked back to the farmhouse. Two toddlers and a dog ran past him and around the side of the house. The farmer's wife had left the washtub and was walking toward the house when she saw Nico. She said, "The clothes need to soak. Would you like to come inside for a cool drink?"

The morning air still felt brisk to Nico, but he accepted that the woman, who had been working since first light, felt the need for refreshment. Nico followed her into the kitchen, where the woman reached down to grasp a basket sitting in the corner of the room and, in one smooth motion, lifted it and set it on a table. The unexpected movement woke the basket's occupant, who opened his eyes and stared up at Nico. "He is my youngest," the woman explained as she ladled water from a wooden bucket into two mugs and offered one to Nico.

Before taking a drink from her mug, she checked whether the infant needed his cloth changed. Nico stood silent, not wanting to disturb her until she said, "We can talk while I tend to this one."

"Your husband said you might know whether a boy named Armando from the orphanage in Florence is working at one of the farms," Nico said as he watched her removing the baby's wet cloth.

"You saw two of my other children playing with the dog outside. Three older ones are working in the fields."

"All boys?" Nico asked.

"On the farm, there is no difference between boys and girls. Our daughter guides the plow as well as any boy, and our sons have their times milking cows."

Nico studied the farm wife for the first time. She was hardly older than he; maybe even younger. Her hands were red and raw from the lye in the washtub, and her face, once pretty, showed the effects of many hours laboring under the hot sun.

"The other farms are the same," she said. "Farm women are as fertile with children as our land is with vegetables and grain. We have no cause to fetch orphans from Florence."

After leaving the first farm, Nico accompanied Donato to four other farms that supplied produce to the Uccello. Each repeated the belief that Armando had not been placed on a farm in the Chiana Valley.

Nico and Donato ended their day at the inn in Laterina. After freshening up, they met in the inn's small dining room, where they enjoyed a simple pasta dinner. As the server cleared plates from the table, Nico sipped a glass of digestivo, then said, "The administrator at Ospedale degli Innocenti must have been mistaken about Armando being placed on a farm in this valley. The farm must be elsewhere."

Donato's eyes narrowed. "Or Armando is not on any farm. What do you know about the administrator? Could he have misled you intentionally?"

Nico stroked his chin and recalled how the administrator's brusque response was when asked about Armando's placement. "What reason might he have to mislead me?" Nico wondered aloud.

7

In mid-afternoon, Nico and Donato returned to Florence. Rather than continue to the Uccello with Donato, Nico got off the wagon at Piazza San Lorenzo and walked along Via San Gallo to the chancery annex, the repository of all Florentine Republic records. Sounds of the city were left behind in the annex's main cataloging room, where clerks and notaries worked diligently and silently to catalog newly arrived records from the republic's many commissions and agencies.

The annex's senior notary recognized Nico immediately. He rose from his desk and wended his way across the room, past other busy notaries, to greet the visitor. "Messer Argenti, how may we assist you today?"

"I am seeking information about the administrator, or rector as he prefers to call himself, of the Ospedale degli Innocenti."

The notary responded without hesitation. "If you can tell me the administrator's name, I can search the index. It will list all documents where he is cited."

Nico's shoulders slumped. "I do not have his name."

The notary's eyes brightened, reflecting the pride he felt in the cataloging system used at the annex. "The records can be searched in other ways. Ospedale degli Innocenti is the responsibility of the Officials Over Orphans commission. That commission oversees all aspects of the orphanage. We can search the commission records. They should include an account of the administrator's appointment."

He led Nico to a smaller room behind the cataloging room. "This room contains the index of all documents in our archive." He scanned the shelves, eventually pulled out a thick folio, opened it, and read, "The Officials Over Orphans commission records are in aisle seven on the second level."

Nico followed the notary up to the building's second level, past several aisles containing shelves filled with folios, where he pointed to a low shelf. "That shelf contains all the documents created by the Officials Over Orphans commission." He bent down to scan the documents on the shelf. "Some commissions generate many documents. Apparently, that is not the case with Officials Over Orphans. The commission was formed nearly two decades past, yet all their official records do not fill a single shelf."

He selected a few of the most recent folios and carried them to a desk at the end of the aisle, where light entering through a window afforded good visibility. Together, the men searched through the documents. Midway through the second folio, the notary declared, "Nieddu. The administrator's name is Patrizu Nieddu. This document states the commission appointed Signor Nieddu as the administrator of the Ospedale degli Innocenti."

"When was the appointment?" Nico asked.

"This document is from February one year past."

"Is there any information about Signor Nieddu? Does it say how he came to be appointed?"

"No, but now that we have his name, I can search the index to find all other documents in which he is mentioned."

"While you search the index, I'll continue looking through these folios. I'm curious to know what led the commission to appoint Signor Nieddu as the orphanage's administrator."

The notary nodded and returned to the index room on the first level. Several minutes later, he reappeared. "The index lists only one other citation for Signor Nieddu in another Officials Over Orphans document."

Nico held up the folio he had been reading. "Yes, this one. It says there were two applicants for the administrator position, a schoolteacher and a dockworker named Nieddu."

"A dockworker?" the notary said with surprise. "Why would they have chosen the dockworker rather than the teacher? It seems unlikely that a dockworker would be qualified to manage an orphanage."

"I agree," Nico replied. "Unfortunately, as you observed, the commission doesn't keep copious records. This document says only that the teacher withdrew his application from consideration. The commission felt pressure to appoint someone to the post quickly, so they chose the only other applicant, Signor Patrizu Nieddu."

The two men looked at each other, both surprised that the documents contained no information about the new administrator. "A dockworker," Nico muttered as he handed the document to the notary.

∽

The next morning found Nico along the Arno River, where barges were being loaded with bundles of silk and wool garments. The barges would take the Florentine products to Pisa, where sea-going vessels would then transport them to destinations throughout Europe and Africa. Nico pulled up the collar of his mantello to shield him from the stiff breeze blowing along the water. He sat on a boulder at the river's edge and watched each barge in the queue advance in turn to the wharf, where the dock supervisor barked commands to the laborers. Following the supervisor's instructions, the workers carried boxes and crates from a nearby warehouse to the barges. Each barge captain made sure workers placed the cargo so that its weight was distributed equally on the deck. The workers had no chance to rest. As soon as one barge was loaded, they began loading the next in line.

After the last barge departed, the laborers scattered, many heading toward their second job of the day. Loading barges was hard work, but the meager pay was not sufficient to support a family. The men would return later in the day to unload barges arriving from Pisa with English wool fleece and other raw materials to feed the Florentine mills. The dock supervisor stayed at the wharf to tally his lists of barges loaded and goods shipped.

Nico approached the supervisor. "Excuse me, signore, there was a man called Nieddu who worked here one year past. Did you know him?"

The supervisor threw up his hands. "Eh. Men come and go. I can't remember them all." He moved away from Nico, then he stopped and turned back. "Neiddu could be Sardinian. There was a Sardinian. He no longer works here. I know nothing of him. The docks are where foreigners look for work when the first come to Florence. It's hard work, so most don't stay long. They look for other work, easier work.

"All the foreigners keep together. One of them who has worked here the longest is a Tunisian. He might know about the Sardinian."

"A Tunisian?" Nico repeated.

The supervisor pointed to a tavern on a street angling away from the river. "Later, after they unload the barges from Pisa, many of the foreigners go there. Maybe you find the Tunisian there." The supervisor shrugged and walked away.

∼

Boisterous outbursts reached Nico in the street before he entered the tavern. He pulled the door open and was struck by the rank odor of dried sweat. The young, athletic, well-dressed lawyer didn't fit with the muscular dockworkers dressed in dirty, stained clothes. For an instant, Nico might have considered turning around and leaving, but his presence did not register with the men seated at the tables. They continued their loud conversations and their drinking, oblivious to the newcomer.

At the serving counter, the barkeep didn't approach Nico; he merely aimed his persistent scowl in Nico's direction. "Beer," Nico called, loudly enough to be heard over the din.

The barkeep filled a mug, set it down within Nico's reach, and took the silver coin that Nico had placed on the counter. That mug was the most expensive beer Nico had ever purchased because the barkeep did not return the excess payment. Nico decided that his generous payment entitled him to ask a question. Before the barkeep moved too far away to hear, Nico called out, "I am looking for one of the dock workers, a Tunisian. Is he here?"

The barkeep took a step backward, suspicious of the well-dressed stranger. He jerked his arm up with his hand extended in the direction of one of the tables. Conversation stopped, and the men looked up at the stranger as Nico approached the table. "I am looking for the Tunisian."

A man with dark skin and a craggy face looked up at Nico through narrowed eyes. At length, he asked, "And who are you?"

"I am Nico Argenti. I'm looking for information about Signor Nieddu?"

"Who?"

"The Sardinian."

The Tunisian thought for a moment, then muttered, "Ah, Patrizu." He picked up his mug, took a long draw, held it out, and said, "It's empty."

Nico nodded, and the two men went to the serving counter where the scowling barkeep refilled the mug. This time Nico paid with a copper coin. The Tunisian took a long drink, nearly emptying the mug, then asked, "What about Patrizu?"

Nico explained his interest in Nieddu. "The dock supervisor said that you worked with Signor Nieddu… Patrizu on the docks. How long did he work there?"

The Tunisian scratched his crotch. "Six months... maybe seven months. I'm not sure. Less than a year."

"Did you know him well?"

"No. We talked when he came here after work. He was always bitching about the hard work and low pay." He laughed. "I don't blame him for that. We all bitch about the work."

"Patrizu worked on the dock, then he became the administrator of the orphanage. That's an unusual step. Do you know if he had any experience as an administrator?"

The Tunisian scoffed, "He told the fools who hired him that he was the manager at a shipping company in Sardinia before he came to Florence." He paused a moment, then laughed again. "That was a pile of shit. He told us that he was a dockworker in Sardinia, the same as here. He said he got caught with the supervisor's daughter in a grain warehouse. He said that's why he left Sardinia. If he stayed, the supervisor would have cut off his man parts."

"Why did he come to Florence?"

"Patrizu took the first ship that would get his ass away from Sardinia. It landed him in Pisa. He said that many ships sail between Pisa and Sardinia. He was afraid that someone on one of those ships might recognize him if he stayed in Pisa, so he took a barge upriver to Florence.

"He got a job at the dock. There are always jobs for dockworkers to load barges. It bothered him whenever he saw rich men walking the streets of Florence. He said he'd find a way to become a rich bastard himself."

"How did he know that the orphanage needed a new administrator?" Nico asked.

"Someone must have told him."

"As the administrator of the orphanage, Nieddu is responsible for the welfare of helpless children."

"Children?" The Tunisian sneered. "I wouldn't trust him with my dog. If the fools in charge of the orphanage had checked, they never would have hired him."

"Did he say why he wanted the job at the orphanage?"

The Tunisian looked at Nico, puzzled by why Nico had asked such an inane question. "We bust our asses every day, loading and unloading barges. Who wouldn't want easier work and better pay?"

"Is that all? No reason why he chose the orphanage rather than someplace else?"

"Patrizu never said nothing to me about no orphanage. He wanted a way off the docks. I guess he found one at the orphanage. That's all."

Nico said, "There was another candidate for the administrator job, a schoolteacher. The teacher applied for the job but then withdrew his application. Do you know anything about that?"

"Patrizu never said anything about no teacher." He shrugged. "Maybe Patrizu told the teacher it would be safer if he kept teaching." He took a step back and folded his arms across his chest. "Why are you asking about Patrizu? What's he done?"

Rather than respond to the questions, Nico said, "I've kept you too long from your friends. It looks like you could use another refill." He laid a coin on the counter and signaled the barkeep to fill the Tunisian's mug.

8

Nico, Vittorio, and Massimo sat together in the Florentine Security Commission office on the upper level of Palazzo della Signoria. The three commissioners had been called by Chancellor Scala to analyze dispatches received from the Florentine embassy in Venice.

Vittorio picked up one of the reports that had been brought to the commission office by a chancery clerk. He scanned the pages until he came to the item that Scala had marked and read the item aloud. "A member of the Strozzi family has been living in Venice since the family was exiled from Florence. While in Venice, he tried to engage others with grievances against Florence. Unable to garner strong support in Venice, he recently left the Venetian Republic." Vittorio looked up from the page. "The report does not give his destination."

Nico said, "The Strozzi family were bankers whose wealth exceeded even that of the Medici. Eventually, they tried to wrest control of the government from the Medici, but their attempt failed and Cosimo de Medici had the entire family exiled."

"I don't recall that incident. When was that?" Massimo asked.

"It happened more than two decades past, so I don't recall the incident myself either, but my uncle told me about the exile. He said that some of the family members went to Naples and Vincenza, where they continued to prosper and earn respect as bankers. Two of the brothers fled to Venice, where they continued the family's feud with the Medicis. They tried to find others in Venice who share their contempt of the Medicis. Now it seems like they failed to gain support in Venice, so they're looking elsewhere. My uncle said that when the Strozzi family left Florence, they took all the funds from their banking business, so they can certainly afford to recruit followers."

Vittorio glanced down at the page in his hands. "This report from our ambassador in Venice doesn't mention a destination. It just cautions Florentine officials to be on guard."

"It would be foolish for the brothers to return to Florence at this time since the Medici are still in power," Massimo opined. "They'd have more success finding supporters in a nearby duchy or one of the Papal States."

The three commissioners searched through dispatches from other Florentine diplomats looking for any other mention of the name Strozzi. After an hour, Massimo stood and suggested that they take a brief recess. He left the room and began pacing the hallway. Nico stood and stretched while watching Massimo make three complete circuits of the hallway. When Massimo returned, he grinned and quipped, "Nico, have you solved the mystery of children vanishing from the orphanage? Or did they suddenly reappear? Young boys can be clever when they want to disappear. I once hid for an entire day to avoid having to muck out a stable."

Rather than comment on Massimo's tale, Nico turned serious. "I went to the orphanage and asked the administrator about one of the children, a boy named Armando. He told me that Armando was placed on a farm in the Chiana Valley."

Vittorio's brow furrowed. He said, "The Chiana Valley is a fair distance from Florence. I'd be surprised if orphans were sent there."

Nico turned toward Vittorio. "My cousin Donato and I visited five farms in the valley. The people there share your belief. None of them ever heard of boys from the orphanage being placed on farms in the Chiana Valley."

Massimo, now serious, said, "Might he have mistakenly said Chiana Valley? There are farms in other valleys."

Nico shook his head. "I doubt that the administrator's error was merely a mistake. From a document in the chancery archive, I found that he was appointed to the administrator post only a few months past. Before that, he worked on the docks."

Vittorio raised an eyebrow. "From the docks to orphanage administrator. A most unlikely move."

"I agree. I went to the docks and spoke with one of the other dockworkers who said that Nieddu, that's the administrator's name, came to Florence after being forced to flee from Sardinia. He said that when Nieddu applied for the administrator position, he told the Officials Over Orphans that he had been the manager of a shipping company in Sardinia. If it is true that he lied to the Officials, that would be a violation of the law."

"You have only a dockworker's word that Nieddu lied. You don't know that for certain," Vittorio said. "From years of investigating crimes as a member of the Guardia, I've learned that witness testimony is often fabricated. I advise you to rely only on factual evidence."

Nico nodded, "Yes, all I have is his word, so I don't intend to bring an accusation to the Officials Over Orphans. However, I do plan to inquire of the shipping companies in Sardinia asking whether they employed a manager named Nieddu.

"I'm most concerned about the children," Nico continued. "Nieddu told me Armando had been placed on a farm in Val di Chiana, and I am certain that claim is not true. Nieddu told me about the farm after consulting a paper listing, so his statement can't be attributed to a memory lapse."

Massimo asked, "Do you have reason to believe the administrator is mistreating the children?"

"Or that he's selling them into slavery?" Vittorio questioned.

Vittorio's comment startled Nico. "I don't know what he's doing, but the children are Christians; if he is selling them into slavery, it would be a violation of the law."

"If not slavery, then what other purpose?" Massimo wondered.

"I'm going to visit Nieddu again to confront him about Armando." Nico looked directly at Vittorio and asked, "I could benefit from the discernment of a keen investigator. Would you be willing to accompany me?"

"I can join you," Vittorio replied. "Realize though, since you are not formally accusing him of a crime, my role will be limited."

"I understand you cannot act in an official capacity, but merely having a member of the Guardia present may loosen his tongue."

*

Later that day, Vittorio followed Nico into the orphanage and through the corridors that led to the administrator's office. Unlike Nico's last visit, no children greeted him in the anteroom, but young voices reached him from elsewhere in the building. At the Saint Francis painting midway along the corridor, Nico and Vittorio turned left and were surprised to see the administrator walking directly toward them. When Nieddu saw the two men, he pressed himself close to the far walls so he could pass them without stopping. Nico stepped to the side, blocking Nieddu's path and called out, "Signor Nieddu!"

Nieddu grunted, "I'm attending to business now. Come back tomorrow if you want to speak with me."

Nico dismissed Nieddu's protest. "You told me that Armando went to a farm in Val di Chiana. That is not so."

Nieddu raised an arm, ready to push his way past Nico. He stopped when he eyed Vittorio, reaching out to intercept him.

Seeing Nieddu appraising Vittorio, Nico announced, "This is Guardia inspector Colombo."

Mention of the Guardia froze Nieddu. He turned, pointed to a nearby room, and said, "In there."

The three men moved into a small storage room. A bucket set in one corner filled the room with the stinging odor of lye. Vittorio lifted a cloth from a hook and draped it over the bucket to contain the vapor.

"I've done nothing wrong," Nieddu whined.

"Armando. Where is he?" Nico demanded.

Nieddu leaned back against a shelf stacked with towels. He looked down at the floor and coughed to clear his throat. "My job is to place the orphans. A man came. He wanted boys. Armando went with him."

"You told me that Armando went to a farm."

"There are so many orphans, I can't remember them all. The man who took the boy said something; maybe he said farm. I forget."

"The other boys. Did the same man take other boys?" Nico asked.

Nieddu nodded.

"Girls? Does he also take girls?" Vittorio asked.

Nieddu looked up and faced Vittorio. "No. No girls. He wants only boys, strong boys."

Despite the cloth covering the lye bucket, its offensive odor still filled the room. Nico pushed the door fully opened and moved to stand in the doorway.

"Does he pay for the children?" Vittorio asked.

"Yes, he pays." Then Neiddu added quickly, "Payment is to the orphanage, not to me." Vittorio noticed Nieddu's neck twitch, an indicator of lies that Vittorio had seen many times. Nieddu might be misappropriating the orphanage's funds but lacking testimony from the man who made the payment, it would be impossible to prove him guilty.

"How many boys has he taken?"

"Three."

"Will he come again?" Nico pressed.

Nieddu wrung his hands together, hoping he could avoid answering, but upon seeing Vittorio's scowl, he said, "He sent a message that he will come again tonight for another one. He comes when the nuns are at compline prayers, so they don't see him."

From the corner of his eye, Nico observed Vittorio raise a hand, flatten the fingers, and slowly move the hand up and down. It was a gesture that Vittorio had taught him, one used by members of the Guardia. It signified they should end the interrogation because they had learned all that the suspect, in this case Neiddu, could tell them. Nico responded with a slight nod.

To Nieddu, Nico said, "Don't tell anyone that we talked." As Nico turned and walked out of the storage room, he began formulating a plan.

Nieddu watched Nico and Vittorio until they reached the end of the corridor. Then he headed back toward his office to devise a plan of his own.

9

Bologna

The manager of the Bardi bank branch in Bologna, Marco Paltroni, spent weeknights in his apartment in the city. On weekends, he found relief from his hectic job and the city's noisy throngs at his villa in the foothills south of the city. The villa was his solitude. Other weekend escapees from turbulent city life pretended to farm or spent their weekends tending tiny vineyards; not Paltroni. He could occupy himself for hours by absorbing recent translations of the wisdom of ancient Greek philosophers or watching hawks circling in the blue sky. An elderly couple who lived nearby served his mundane needs: the man cut firewood and made repairs when needed, and the woman prepared his meals.

Paltroni sat on the terrace, enjoying the early morning sun. His nose was buried in a collection of doctrines written by an ancient Athenian philosopher, when he glimpsed movement on the road, a carriage coming toward him. He set the book down and watched the elegant coach, expecting it to pass by on the road, but instead it turned onto the dirt path that led to his villa. When the coach reached the villa, the coachman opened the door and helped his passenger step out. The man brushed a thread from his embroidered silk tunic. His narrow face, high cheek bones and close-set eyes gave Paltroni no clue to his identity. "I am Ercole Strozzi," the man announced.

The name sounded vaguely familiar, but Paltroni couldn't recall the context until Strozzi added, "You received funds from my account in Venice and a list of items I require."

The statement refreshed Paltroni's memory. A large sum had been transferred to Bologna from the bank branch in Venice. The courier who delivered the account transfer also delivered a series of requests on behalf of the account holder, Ercole Strozzi. The bank prided itself on providing exceptional services for its clients, especially its extremely wealthy clients, but expecting accommodation from a bank officer outside of normal business hours was unreasonable. Calling upon the bank manager at his home was outrageous.

"This is my home," Paltroni protested. "Today is the sabbath, the Lord's day. Go to the bank tomorrow."

Undeterred by Paltroni's objection, Strozzi climbed onto the terrace. "My presence in Bologna must go unnoticed. The message sent to your bank made that clear."

"I do not have the message or any papers with me. Everything is at the bank."

"My most immediate need is for lodging. Have you found a suitable villa outside the city, one that is private and with discreet servants?"

Realizing that he wasn't going to dissuade the intruder, Paltroni growled inwardly, then said. "There is a villa north of the city that was once owned by one of Bologna's most powerful families. That family fell into a feud with another, each seeking to crush the other. Their violent acts eventually landed on other prominent citizens. Nearly all the family members were killed in an uprising after one of them murdered Bologna's chief magistrate. The others were driven out of the province. Their villa has been unoccupied since."

Strozzi chuckled. "Rebels against the state. How fitting. You know how to find the villa?"

"It is about an hour..." Strozzi raised a hand to interrupt the bank manager.

"The driver needs the directions. Tell him, not me." Strozzi said in a condescending tone.

Paltroni gritted his teeth. "Wait here." He went into the house and returned with paper and ink. He scratched out a simple map, then climbed down from the terrace and walked to where the coachman was wiping dust from the carriage.

Strozzi followed Paltroni and fidgeted impatiently until the bank manager finished giving directions to the coachman; then he asked, "Has the captain arrived in Bologna?"

Paltroni balled his hands into fists. "My staff at the bank has been working on fulfilling your... demands. Come to the bank tomorrow and they can tell you what progress they've made."

Strozzi shook his head vigorously. "No, no, that's unacceptable. I need privacy. As I said, I don't want to be seen in Bologna. I can't go to the bank; you must send your people to the villa." Without waiting for a response, Strozzi turned away and climbed into the carriage.

"Insolent bastard," Paltroni muttered to himself as he watched the carriage drive away.

10

As administrator of Ospedale degli Innocenti, Patrizu Nieddu had the respect, or at least the deference, of others at the orphanage. When in a kind mood, he treated those around him as underlings; at other times, he dismissed them as fools. Perquisites of his position included an ample salary, meals, and living accommodations in a quiet wing of the building. His first dinner in the common room with noisy children proved to be intolerable. "How can anyone stand these noisy creatures?" he complained to the nuns. Henceforth, he had meals delivered to his office or his quarters by a nun. At least the nuns were quiet and did not pry into his affairs.

Despite the rules prohibiting alcohol, Nieddu kept a bottle of wine in his desk; however, beer was his drink of choice, and he couldn't conceal a beer keg in his room, so he satisfied his thirst through daily visits to The Lame Horse tavern. The nuns believed that his times away from the orphanage were spent at a nearby parish church, an illusion that Nieddu fostered by carrying rosary beads conspicuously in view whenever he left the orphanage.

The small dingy tavern drew only a few locals as regular patrons. That suited Nieddu because he went there to drink, not to engage in conversation with drunks or moochers. Another advantage of The Lame Horse was its proximity to the orphanage.

The buyer had approached him for the first time one afternoon. Nieddu never asked how the buyer had found him or how he knew that Nieddu would be amenable to his proposal. The chance to profit while expending little effort was all that mattered to Nieddu. Since then, whenever the buyer was in Florence—for business known only to him—he contacted Nieddu at the tavern to learn whether any boys were available.

Nieddu sat at his usual table. The tavern's only other patrons were two old men, regulars, playing cards at a table across the room. Nieddu had already emptied one mug and was midway through his second mug of beer when the buyer entered. His broad shoulders filled the doorway. He had thick black hair, a weathered face, and a purple scar across the back of his right hand. The sound of his hard leather boots striking the wood floor alerted Nieddu, who turned to see the buyer tell the barkeep to bring two mugs of beer to Nieddu's table. The men waited until the beer arrived before either spoke. The buyer took a slug, then asked, "Any boys this week?"

Nieddu ignored the question. He leaned forward, rested his elbows on the table, and spoke in a low voice. "There is a problem. A lawyer came looking for one of the boys, the one called Armando. I told him that Armando had been placed on a farm. I thought that would satisfy him, but the bastard went to farms looking for the boy. Can you believe that? He rode all the way to the Chiana Valley, looking for the boy. Of course he didn't find the boy, so he came again asking mores questions. This time he brought a member of the Guardia."

"Why is he interested in that particular boy? Is there something special about him?" the buyer asked.

"No, he's no different from all the others. I don't know why the lawyer cares about him." Nieddu wiped a bead of sweat from his brow. "There are supposed to be records of where the children are placed. If the lawyer goes to the officials who oversee the orphanage, and they come looking for records, they won't find any for the boys who went with you." Nieddu thought about his growing succession of lies: he had told the Officials that he had been a manager in Sardinia; he told the lawyer that payments for the children went to the orphanage, and he said that Armando had been placed on a farm. The lies were catching up to him. He muttered, "The lawyer won't give up. I can't take the risk that he'll keep asking questions. I have a problem."

The buyer rubbed his beard stubble. With a dispassionate voice, he said, "I agree. You have a problem."

In an unsteady voice, Nieddu said, "I haven't had time to think of where I'll go, but I can't stay in Florence."

Nieddu's predicament meant an end to the source of boys from Florence, and that created a problem, but only a minor problem. There were other sources of strong boys. The buyer leaned forward, picked something from his teeth, then said, "There are always other opportunities."

Nieddu stared intently at the buyer, wondering whether the statement was meant for his ears or whether the buyer was speaking to himself. The goddess Fortuna had brought Nieddu to the orphanage in Florence. He had wanted only to escape from hard labor on the docks when he heard by chance that the orphanage needed an administrator. Except for the noisy children, being the administrator of an orphanage had advantages: the pay was good, the work was effortless, and the position gave him status. But now he need not go to another orphanage; he could go anywhere that fortune beckoned.

His experience in Florence, although only for a short time, would be a benefit if he were to apply for a position at another orphanage. He remembered once hearing the name of an orphanage in Naples, a city that had always intrigued him. In Sardinia, sailors often told stories of the good times and available women in Naples. He tried to recall the name of its orphanage, *Santissima*....

"Bologna," the buyer barked, startling Nieddu and disrupting his thought. "Bologna has an even bigger problem than Florence with exposed children. 'Exposed' is what they call orphans in Bologna.

The orphanage in Bologna is Ospedale degli Esposti, the hospital of the exposed."

"Does that orphanage need an administrator?"

"That's not a concern. Our patron is wealthy and money buys influence in Bologna." The buyer leaned back in his chair and folded his arms across his chest. "There are other opportunities besides orphanages. You're an ambitious buck. Our patron might find something else for you. When can you leave for Bologna?"

The barkeeper placed two mugs on the table. Nieddu lifted one and took a sip. He always savored his first beer of the afternoon. "Nothing keeps me in Florence. I can leave in the morning."

The buyer wrote the name of an inn. "Take a room at the inn when you get to Bologna. Someone will contact you."

11

The following morning, as Alessa prepared to go to the market, Nico came into the courtyard. "Nico, tell me! What happened at the orphanage last night?" Alessa implored. She set down the basket she had been holding and stood motionless, eager to learn what Nico had learned about Armando.

Nico looked somber as he replied, "When Massimo and I headed to the orphanage, the clock at Santa Maria del Fiore cathedral confirmed that we would reach the orphanage before the bells sounded compline prayers. That was the time when the buyer was expected to arrive. When we reached Piazza Santissima Annunziata, the fading light cast long shadows that put the piazza in darkness."

Alessa rolled her eyes. "Please dear brother, I'm not in need of a folktale. Just tell me you caught the person who has been taking the boys."

Nico smiled, "In good time, dear sister. We believed the buyer would enter through the main entrance, but Massimo suggested that we walk around the building to check whether there were any other entrances. We did find two other doors, one at the rear of the building and one not far from the administrator's office. We separated so I could observe both the main entrance and the side door, while Massimo watched the rear door. We positioned ourselves in the shadows to keep from being seen. I tensed when the compline bells sounded. I scanned the piazza and the nearby streets, expecting someone to walk toward the orphanage. But no one came."

Alessa crossed her arms and shifted her weight from one foot to another, her impatience growing.

"Minutes later, on a street to my left, I saw shadows wavering in the darkness. I was able to see a figure coming toward the piazza. I was ready to step out of my hiding place when he crossed the piazza, but instead, he turned away from the orphanage and headed toward Piazza San Marco."

No longer able to bridle her curiosity, Alessa interjected, "Nico, withhold the details and tell me, did you apprehend the man? Will I be able to tell Maria what happened to Armando?"

Nico held his arms out, palms up. "I am sorry, but no one came. We waited for what must have been a half hour before Massimo came around to where I was standing. Either the buyer changed his mind or Nieddu warned him not to come."

Alessa slumped down onto a bench.

Nico rested a hand on her shoulder and said, "I too am disappointed. We tried to find him, but we failed. I'll pay another visit to Signor Nieddu and I'll bring Massimo with me. I'm sure Massimo can persuade Nieddu to tell the truth."

"I hope so," Alessa said. "Maria and I are going to the market. She'll be pleased to hear that you're making an effort to find Armando."

Nico watched her leave, then followed the aroma of freshly baked breakfast rolls to the kitchen. Donato and his wife Joanna had already eaten and were clearing the table when Nico declared, "My nose is detecting something tasty."

"There are onion rolls warming by the fire and almond butter on the sideboard," Joanna smiled as she brushed past Nico and said,

"Alessa is going to the market, so I'm taking my dear child to his tutor this morning."

Nico opened the cloth covering the rolls. "Three," he said to himself, then asked Donato, "Has everyone else already eaten?"

Donato laughed. "Yes, those rolls are for you. Joanna knows you like her cheese and onion rolls, so she made a larger than normal batch."

"Are you leaving as well?" Nico asked.

"Yes, I'm going to the dock. A barge is scheduled to arrive this morning with fruit from Sicily. I want to get the first pick of the produce for the Uccello's spring menu."

Nico was slathering the last onion tart with almond butter when the house servant came into the kitchen and handed him a message from Chancellor Scala requesting that Nico meet with him at a trattoria in the Santa Maria Novella district. Although Nico was unfamiliar with the trattoria, he did know the location, a small street close to the Arno River. He knew the street because it was near *il Pennello*, a tavern with cheap beer favored by Nico's friend Sandro Botticelli and his fellow artists. Nico left the note opened on the table so Alessa would see it when she returned and would know his visit to Signor Nieddu at the orphanage would be delayed.

12

As Nico passed through Piazza Antinori on his way to the trattoria, a voice called to him from behind. "Is that you, lawyer?" Nico turned to see Massimo approaching and paused until Massimo came alongside.

"Did you also get a message from Chancellor Scala?" Massimo asked. "Perhaps he has another assignment for us."

"That's my impression too, although the message had no details. I'm curious why we are meeting at a trattoria rather than at the chancellor's office."

Shortly, the Arno River came into view. The men turned right at San Salvatore church. Massimo scanned the church's plain gray facade and said, "The chancellor must have a reason for meeting with us in this neighborhood. It lacks the elegance of his office in Palazzo della Signoria."

"The chancellor has spoons in many pots, so it's impossible to guess his purpose," Nico replied. "The message I received didn't say who would be attending, but since both of us were summoned, I suppose Vittorio will be there as well."

They turned right again onto the narrow street that held the

Mangia con Luigi trattoria. Although it was too early for *pranzo*, the mid-day meal, the door to the eatery was unlocked. Inside, two lone patrons, Chancellor Scala and Vittorio Colombo, sat at a table in a rear corner of the room. The aroma wafting from the kitchen hinted that preparations for the daily luncheon fare were underway.

As the men approached the table, Scala pointed to the platter of antipasti in front of him and said, "Luigi is in the kitchen. If you would like something to eat, ask him for another plate." Nico and Massimo declined the offer and took seats at the table. Scala spread his hands and said, "It is unfortunate that your holiday could not have been longer." Then, looking directly at Nico, he added, "I'm sure you would have welcomed more time in Siena." Eager to learn the purpose of the meeting, Nico's only response was a thin smile.

Scala perceived the men's curiosity, so he dropped the small talk. "Two disturbing reports have reached me in recent days. The archbishop called upon me yesterday to relate information given to him by a monk. The monk had been administering the sacraments in outlying villages when he learned that some villages had been attacked by rogues."

"The attackers, were they bandits?" Massimo asked.

"I don't know," Scala replied. "The archbishop had only vague information. He said the villages were north of the city in the Apennine foothills and that more than one village had been attacked. He didn't know the names of the villages."

Nico said, "Bandits usually prey on small towns and estates in the countryside where there is value to plunder, but villagers are poor. There is little to gain by attacking villages." He paused for a moment before adding, "Doesn't the military have patrols in the foothills to protect the villages?"

Massimo knew how army patrols were assigned, so he responded to Nico's question. "Villages in the Apennine foothills are close to the borders of Modena and Bologna. Raiders can easily come across the border, attack a village, and then retreat." With scorn evident in his voice, Massimo added, "Officially, our military is not permitted to cross borders into neighboring states, so it's easy for bandits to escape from our patrols."

"These raiders are confiscating more than goods," Scala said. "What alarmed the archbishop is that children were taken from the villages."

Nico tensed. For the second time in hours, he was being told about children being displaced. A coincidence? Nico wasn't a believer in coincidences.

Scala looked across the table at Nico and Massimo. "I believe the Florentine Security Commission should investigate this situation. I would like you to travel to the villages and learn more about the raiders. Find out who are they and why they are taking children."

Nico said, "Do you expect us to pursue the raiders? Massimo has the experience and training to do so, but I...."

Scala interrupted. "No, I don't expect you to pursue the bandits. As you said, it is not profitable for bandits to attack poor villages and abduct children. They must have another purpose. I feel that the bandits might have said something during the raids that would indicate their motive. By speaking with the villagers, you may be able to discover that motive. Knowing their motive will tell us how to deal with the situation."

Nico and Massimo looked at each other; then both nodded.

Scala continued, "You can begin by questioning the monk, the one who reported to the archbishop. Unfortunately, he is secluded in a silent retreat and will remain sequestered until after vesper prayers. You may speak with him then."

Massimo turned to Nico. "While we are waiting for the monk, we can ask at the army base whether any of their patrols have encountered the raiders. Even if the patrols have not met the raiders, they may have heard rumors about them. The army thrives on rumors."

Next, Scala turned to face Vittorio and said, "Now let's discuss another matter. You read the report about the Strozzi brothers that came from our envoy in Venice. Members of the Signoria who have seen that report fear that the brothers might have gone from Venice to Ferrara or Modena to gather support for an action against Florence. Lord Este rules Ferrara and Modena and he is no friend of the Medici. Members of the Signoria fear that the Strozzi brothers might convince Lord Este to mount an attack against Florence.

"The envoy who represents Lord Este has an office in this part of the Santa Maria Novella district; that is why we are meeting here. I intend to ask him whether the Strozzi brothers have taken up residence in Ferrara or Modena. Signor Colombo, you are an experienced investigator with a keen ability to sense whether people are speaking truthfully and whether they are withholding information. I would like you to join me when I meet with the diplomat."

The usually reserved Vittorio gave a quick nod but said nothing.

∽

A plaque emblazoned with the House of Este's silver crowned eagle on a field of blue hung beside the main entrance to the building that held the offices of diplomats representing Ferrara and Modena, two states ruled by the House of Este. A servant escorted the visitors to an anteroom where a burly man stood across the room, rigidly straight, with his arms folded across his chest. With narrowed eyes, he assessed the two men. In a bitter voice, he said, "One of you must be Chancellor Scala. I've served as Lord Este's envoy for more than a year, and this is the first time I've been called upon by any official of the Florentine government. Since your government has advanced no hospitality in all that time, I assume your presence has another purpose."

"I am Chancellor Bartolomeo Scala." Gesturing toward Vittorio, Scala said, "And this is Signor Vittorio Colombo, a member of our security commission. I regret that we have not met previously, and I beg forgiveness if my government has not been properly attentive. I will see to it that our lack of cordiality is rectified."

Scala allowed time for the envoy to respond, but when he said nothing, Scala continued. "Ten years past, members of the Strozzi family were exiled from Florence following their violent bid to undermine the Florentine government. Two members of the Strozzi family fled to Venice, where they've been recruiting support for an attack against Florence. Their efforts failed to gain them the aid they sought and recently they left Venice."

"And you have come to me because you believe they are in Ferrara or Modena?"

"We must consider all possibilities."

"I know nothing of these men," the burly man said with indifference.

"Might they be in Modena or Ferrara in hiding?" Vittorio asked.

"Who can say? It is not difficult for men to hide. Can you be certain they are not hiding in Florence?"

Realizing that the conversation was not productive, Scala said, "If you hear of any members of the Strozzi family arriving in Modena or Ferrara, my government would appreciate being informed." Scala turned to leave. Vittorio followed behind him and offered a final comment. "Ferrara has strengthened its relationship with Venice, making it easy for men to travel between those two states."

"Some republics are more amicable than others. Ferrara values its alliance with Venice," the envoy said through clenched teeth.

13

Nico and Massimo walked across the city through the San Lorenzo neighborhood toward the army camp located a short distance outside the city walls.

They passed through the wall at the Porta Faenza gate, where a queue of wagons waited for approval to enter the city. Nico watched as two tax collectors lazily inspected the cargo of one wagon. Finally satisfied that it contained only non-taxable farm produce, they signaled it to proceed and turned their attention to the next wagon in the long line. Farmers shared with each other complaints about the tax system that had them wasting time each day sitting in lines.

Outside the gate, two heavily traveled roads extended north toward the towns of Pistoia and Faenza. Massimo led Nico past the line of farm carts to a smaller, less busy road that veered off and wound through a grove of trees. In a short distance, it ended at a vast open expanse that held the army camp.

"This camp is much smaller than the army camp in Milan," Nico observed.

"That's because Florence maintains a much smaller army. Our

republic prefers to hire mercenaries whenever it needs a large military force to defend its interests."

The stiffness in Massimo's speech prompted Nico to reply, "The Signoria believe that having a small army preserves the treasury, but you seem to disapprove."

"Florence is far wealthier than Milan, yet we behave like poor cousins. The problem with mercenaries is that they have no loyalty. They change sides without warning or apology whenever they're offered a larger purse. One day the citizens of Florence may regret the Signoria's frugality."

Nico did not rebut Massimo's assertion. The men walked on in silence until they reached the guard post at the camp entrance. Massimo waved a greeting to the attendant, a corporal who recognized Massimo by sight. Inside the camp, Massimo pointed toward a small structure ahead. "We can begin there. That building is where documents are stored. It will have maps showing the villages and roads in the Apennine foothills."

The camp lacked the frenzy of the army base that Nico had visited in Milan. The few soldiers who were moving between buildings sauntered casually. There were no lines of men marching in precise formations, nor cavalry units practicing drills.

When they reached the document building, Massimo pushed open the door and stepped inside. A sergeant seated behind a desk looked up from the paper he was reading. He smiled broadly and said, "Massimo, are you here to start another card game? Didn't you lift enough silver from the new recruits during the bassetta tournament? They claim to have not even enough soldi for beer and they swear their card-playing days are finished."

Massimo scoffed, "It's the usual complaint of the defeated, but by the next tournament, their purses will again be heavy with silver." He rubbed his hands together. "And I will be ready to relieve them of their coin."

After Massimo introduced Nico, the sergeant scanned the visitor from his carefully brushed hair to his fine leather shoes. Then he turned to Massimo and said, "A lawyer. Hmm. You should bring him to the next tournament. All lawyers have purses bulging with silver. A few hands of bassetta could lighten his load. You would be doing him a service."

"Perhaps I'll do that, but we have come for a serious purpose. There's been a report of disturbances in villages near the border beyond Prato. We would like to see a map of that area."

"Disturbances? I've heard nothing of any disturbances." The sergeant spread his hands, gesturing to his surroundings. "But my time is spent in this catacomb of paper, so I hear little." Then, with a flash of remembrance, he added, "You are assigned to the security commission. That is why you are concerned about the disturbances."

"Yes, and Nico is also a member of the commission. We have been charged to find whether there is substance to the report."

The sergeant retrieved a rolled paper from one of the shelves that lined the walls of the room. He unrolled the sheet and spread it across a table. "The army doesn't have an official cartographer. This map was pieced together from sketches made by cavalry officers who led patrols through the mountain foothills. It is the best map we have of the border area."

Nico leaned down and studied the drawing. He traced a finger along one of the roads. "The roads look like stripes. They all run nearly parallel from the high mountains until they reach the towns of Prato and Pistoia."

"Yes, that is so," the sergeant replied. "The roads follow the courses of rivers flowing down from the mountains. The rivers tend to remain parallel until they reach flat terrain."

"This map shows no roads cutting across from one river valley to another," Nico observed. He looked up, hoping the sergeant might have insight beyond what the map showed, but the sergeant merely shrugged.

Massimo, who was gazing at the map, said, "Also, the map doesn't show the location of the northern borders."

"It's not always easy for the cavalry patrols to find the borders," the sergeant replied. "A portion of the border between Bologna and Florence follows the Reno River. The Reno is a major river, so it's easy to find the border where it follows the Reno. Elsewhere, the border is defined by small streams and mountain peaks."

Nico interjected, "Even trained surveyors often have difficulty distinguishing one landmark from another. Remember what happened with Cospaia."

Massimo and the sergeant looked at each other with blank expressions. Finally, Massimo turned back to Nico and asked, "What happened at Cospaia?"

"A treaty between Florence and the Papal States specified that a particular stream was to form the border between the two territories, but surveyors had difficulty identifying the stream. Each side drew its maps using a different stream. The town of Cospaia lies between the two streams; consequently, neither side claimed the town. The result is that today Cospaia is an independent republic."

Massimo raised an eyebrow. "You must have learned that fact at the university."

"Yes, that and others. Boundary disputes were a favorite topic of law school lecturers. Borders are erased whenever there is a conflict between states. Then, when new treaties are negotiated, diplomats call upon lawyers to help define the new borders. Some lawyers spend their entire careers establishing borders and resolving border disputes."

"I knew there was a purpose to wars," Massimo quipped. "They keep the lawyers busy."

The sergeant wondered, "Do you suppose there are disagreements about our borders with Bologna and Modena?"

"I would be surprised if there weren't," Nico answered. "But if the disagreements are in the mountains and don't include any villages, then they are of little consequence."

Nico quickly sketched a copy of the map, then Massimo thanked the sergeant for his help and stepped toward the door. "Nico, we should see the captain responsible for patrolling the border. He may have heard reports of problems in the villages."

Massimo led Nico to a large building near the center of the camp. Flags flanked the building's entrance. One was the white flag bearing the red iris that represented the Republic of Florence. The second flag was the red and white flag of the Florentine Army. Inside, a corporal directed them to the office of the patrol captain.

Massimo explained to Nico, "We are fortunate to find the captain in his office. He often goes out on patrol with his units. He says that joining the men on patrols helps him to assess his men's efficiency. He is known among his cohorts as The Hunter because he is the one who dispatches patrols to hunt bandits and criminals."

The Hunter was seated behind a desk when Nico and Massimo arrived at his office. His head was inclined forward. One hand twirled aimlessly in the air, and he muttered softly as he studied the document lying open on the desktop. A brown dog lay curled up on the floor near his feet. Three chairs intended for visitors were precisely spaced and squared, facing the desk. The desktop was clear except for the single document. A cabinet along one wall held folders arranged in carefully aligned stacks. Two books bearing the Florentine Army insignia sat side-by-side atop the cabinet.

Lines at the captain's eyes and on his brow were the only indication of the captain's age. Unlike others of his rank, he had the build of a younger man and he lacked the girth of men who spend their days behind a desk.

The dog's tail thumping against the side of the desk announced the arrival of Nico and Massimo. The Hunter looked up with steely eyes to appraise the two men standing at his doorway. "Sergeant Massimo Leoni, if I recall correctly."

"Yes, captain," Massimo responded as he stepped into the office. "And this is Messer Nico Argenti. We are assigned to the Florentine Security Commission, and we've been asked to verify a report of attacks on villages in the north."

The captain motioned for the two men to be seated. "I've not been told of villages being attacked. Who told you about the attacks?"

Nico answered, "A monk administering sacraments to villagers made a report to the archbishop when he returned to Florence. Massimo and I have not yet interviewed the monk, so we have no details about the attacks."

Massimo added, "We came here to ask whether your patrols are aware of villages being harassed by bandits."

Directing his words to Nico, the captain said, "As Sergeant Leoni knows, we have only three patrols along the entire Apennine frontier. We rarely encounter bandits on the move. Our successes come by locating their camps and confronting them when they are unprepared."

Nico raised an eyebrow. "Are three patrols adequate to safeguard the entire border?"

Massimo smiled in anticipation of the captain's answer.

The Hunter exhaled forcefully. "Adequate? No." He tapped his fingers on the desk. "Lately, wealthy businessmen traveling on horseback between cities have become the favorite targets of bandits, so our patrols concentrate on the busiest roads. Smaller roads rarely see a patrol. Today, one of our patrols is on the Via Flaminia Minor because it is the most traveled road between Florence and Bologna. We send patrols to that road nearly every day."

Nico recalled, "I traveled that road many times myself when I was attending the University of Bologna and I was accosted only once. Two derelicts driven to thievery by hunger and poverty demanded money. I took pity on one of them. He reformed and is now in the employ of my cousin. I'm not sure what happened to the other one."

"You were fortunate. Other travelers have been assaulted on that road by violent rogues. Three weeks past, one of my patrols came upon a merchant who had been robbed, beaten, and left bleeding at the side of the road. Even though we patrol the Via Flaminia frequently, bandits still manage to find targets."

"Bologna is one of the Papal States. Does the Papal Army patrol its section of the road?" Nico asked.

"No, unfortunately, they do not. The Papal Army is busy taming renegades in the south. It rarely comes north. Bologna maintains a security force, but it operates only near the city. The Bolognese countryside is a refuge for bandits and even rogue bands of mercenaries. However, if villages are being attacked, I may need to revise my patrol deployments. When will you be speaking with the monk?"

Massimo replied, "He is in a silent retreat today. We can't meet with him until late afternoon."

"I'd like one of my men to join that meeting. If the monk's report is correct, I may need to change the deployment of my patrols."

Nico nodded his consent and Massimo said, "The archbishop has arranged for the monk to meet us at the diocese office after vesper prayers. You can have your man join us there."

∽

Nico walked from the army base to Casa Argenti, the house formerly owned by his uncle Nunzio and now owned by his cousin Donato. Nico had lived there ever since his parents' death when he was taken in by his uncle.

Nico's growling stomach told him it was past the usual time for a midday meal. He had intended to have lunch with Alessa, but she had already eaten. Fortunately, the kettle she left hanging in the fireplace held a generous portion of pea soup. He placed a few lengths of wood in the fireplace, stoked the dull red embers into flame, and hung the kettle over the fire. Alessa took a pinch of spices from a paper cone and added them to the pot. Then she picked up a wooden spoon and began stirring the soup. "I found these spices at the market this morning. They're not as pungent as the ones in Morocco, but I think you'll like their flavor."

Alessa had been born in a small village in Morocco where she lived with her mother, father, and younger brother until seven years past, when she was abducted by slave traders and sold to the captain of a Neapolitan merchant vessel. Donato saw the quick-witted slave girl while on a business trip to Naples. He purchased her from the sea captain, brought her to Florence as a free citizen, and welcomed her into the Argenti family, where she became like a sister to Nico.

"Alessa, did you see the message from Chancellor Scala that arrived this morning?" Nico asked.

Alessa looked up from the soup pot. "Yes, I saw the message, but it said only that the chancellor wanted to meet with you. Is he sending you on another mission?"

"A monk who had been ministering to people in mountain towns to the north reported to the archbishop when he returned to Florence. He said that some villages had been raided by renegades." Nico decided not to mention that children had been abducted. "The chancellor asked that Massimo and I investigate the matter. We will be meeting with the monk in the afternoon, so I will not be able to return to the orphanage today."

Alessa slumped upon hearing that Nico's investigation of the orphanage would be delayed. "I understand," she uttered softly. When the soup began to bubble, she carried the pot to the table and ladled it into a bowl, which she set in front of Nico.

To keep Alessa from dwelling on her disappointment, he steered their conversation with a series of questions about her morning activities: Did she meet anyone else at the market? Had river barges brought any fish from the boats at Pisa? What spring vegetables were the farmers selling? Was cousin Donato at the market buying produce for his restaurant?

14

The archbishop had arranged for Nico and Massimo to meet with the monk after vesper prayers at the archdiocese offices. Nico paused briefly as he walked past the cathedral to watch the workmen who were cleaning the doors of the baptistery. They worked carefully, using soft cloths to avoid marring Ghiberti's bronze doors acclaimed by many as one of Florence's finest art treasures.

The archbishop's palazzo sat directly across Piazza San Giovanni and faced the baptistery. Nico walked to the rear of the palazzo to a separate gray stone building that housed the archdiocese's administrative offices. As he entered the narrow street behind the palazzo, he spotted Massimo and another man standing outside the building's entrance. The man stood taller than the average Florentine, almost as tall as Massimo. He shared Massimo's high cheekbones, square jaw and deep-set eyes.

"Nico," Massimo called. "This is Sergeant Spinelli. He is the army's representative." Then to the sergeant, Massimo said, "Nico Argenti is the lawyer assigned to the Florentine Security Commission."

Sergeant Spinelli and Nico greeted each other by gripping wrists. "You are not in uniform," Nico observed.

"Weapons are not permitted in the city, and I feel uncomfortable wearing my uniform unless I have my sword at my side." Spinelli flashed a grin. "I'd feel only partially dressed."

They moved inside the office building, where a priest led them to a small chapel. Friar Alberto, the monk who had reported the raids on villages and the abduction of children to the archbishop, sat alone in the dark space lit only by votive candles. An undyed wool robe covered his ample frame. His hair, in need of brushing, hung to his shoulders. On his feet were sandals of loosely woven straw. The men paused in the doorway, hesitant to disturb the friar's prayer. However, their footsteps echoing through the quiet hallway as they approached had alerted him to their presence. He rose, turned, and beckoned them through the vestry to a small sitting room, its musty air and dust suggesting that the room was rarely used. Friar Alberto sat on a chair and looked up at the men, who remained standing. "The archbishop said you wish to speak with me."

Massimo looked to Nico who began, "We understand that while you were administering sacraments in towns near the Bologna border, you were told about raids on some outlying villages."

Alberto nodded, "Yes, that is so."

"Did you speak with people in those villages?"

"No, I didn't visit the villages myself. I reported what I was told by monks at the Santa Maria Abbey in Montepiano. Monks from that abbey administer to those in the outlying villages. Men from one of the villages told the monks about the raids."

"Which villages were raided? Did they tell you the names?"

"No, I didn't ask their names, and they didn't say. I stopped at the abbey only briefly to pass along greetings to the abbot from the archbishop. I was eager to return to Florence, so I didn't stay for long. However, while I was there, I noticed the monks were very upset. When I asked what was troubling them, they told me about the raids and said that the bandits had taken children during the raids. They said villages had been raided before, but never before were children taken. The children are the reason why I mentioned the raids in my report to the archbishop."

Nico recalled that only boys were missing from the orphanage. He asked, "Was it only boys that were taken?"

"I heard them mention boys, but I didn't ask any further. It's possible that girls were also taken. I'm sorry I can't tell you more."

Massimo said, "I'm not familiar with Montepiano. Where is it?"

Friar Alberto closed his eyes as he pictured roads in his mind, then replied, "It's north of Vernio. About four miles north." The answer meant little to Massimo, as he was also unfamiliar with Vernio, but he saw a flash of recognition in Sergeant Spinelli's eyes.

"Is there anything else you can tell us?" Nico asked.

"No, nothing. I am sorry. I had only brief conversations with the monks." With that, the friar excused himself to return to his prayers, blessing the men as he left.

Nico unfolded the map sketch he had drawn at the army base. He touched a finger to the map. "Here is Vernio. It's not far from Prato. I don't remember seeing Montepiano on the map that I copied."

Sergeant Spinelli looked up from the map and said, "Vernio is not part of Florence or Bologna." Spinelli's statement surprised both Nico and Massimo. The sergeant continued, "Vernio is part of an independent territory between Florence and Bologna. Have you heard of the Bardi family, the bankers?" Spinelli waited for Nico and Massimo to acknowledge that they had heard of the Bardi family before he added, "Many years past, the Bardi family purchased a vast expanse of land in the mountains. Their purchase includes the town of Vernio and several villages. The area is a profitable source of lumber. Loggers harvest trees in the mountains and float logs down the Bisenzio River to the lumber mills in Prato.

"I know about their land because the Bardis are Florentine citizens. They wanted the Florentine militia to patrol and secure their land, but the Signoria refused to let patrols go outside the republic.

We send patrols on the road along the Bisenzio River north of Prato, but we go only to the border. We don't go onto the Bardis' land."

"Do the Bardis retain a private military force to secure their land?" Nico asked.

Spinelli shrugged. "I don't know."

Nico studied his map, then frowned in disappointment. "This sketch isn't helpful. It doesn't show the border between Florence and the Bardi lands, nor does it show Montepiano or other villages in the area."

Massimo rubbed his chin. "We don't know the names of the villages being raided and we don't know whether they're in the Florentine Republic or on Bardi land."

Nico stated what all three men were thinking, "There's only one way to find out."

15

The men returned to the army base, where Sergeant Spinelli asked the stable master to ready horses for them. He advised Massimo and Nico, "It can be cold in the mountains. We should dress warmly."

At his quarters, Massimo donned a gray wool cloak and heavy leather boots. After strapping on his sword, he said to Nico, "Now let's get something warm for you to wear."

Massimo led Nico to a row of buildings near the center of the army base. "Rostelli is the *Sarto* here at the army base. He provides our clothing. I'm sure he can find a warm cloak for you."

Rostelli, a chubby man who looked more like a friar than a soldier, hummed as he stitched a clasp onto a leather belt. He looked up when Massimo entered his workshop and called out, "Rostelli, this is Messer Argenti. He'll be accompanying me on a patrol in the mountains, so he needs warm clothing." Massimo indicated the cloak he was wearing. "A heavy cloak like this one."

Rostelli set aside the belt he was repairing, stood, and circled Nico. "Yes, I can find something in his size. One moment," he announced as he shuffled out of the room. Moments later, he returned with three wool cloaks draped over his arm. He held one cloak out in front of him, looked again at Nico, and said, "No, not this one. Too small." He discarded that cloak onto a table and held out the second. "Yes, try this one," he said as he handed it to Nico.

Nico wrapped the cloak around his shoulders. The sleeves reached to Nico's fingertips. "This one is a bit too large," Rostelli laughed, "but it will keep you warm. You can roll up the sleeves if you must. Now boots. If you are going on patrol, you must have boots. Give me one of your shoes." Rostelli appraised the shoe Nico handed to him, then left the room a second time.

"After you are properly dressed, we can visit the armorer to get you outfitted with a weapon," Massimo suggested.

Nico declined the offer, saying, "Someday you can teach me to use a sword, but for now, little would be gained by my having one." He laughed. "You'll be safer if I am not waving a blade in your vicinity."

"Every man should know how to use a blade. Mastery of the sword is just one of the many skills you are missing. It is not too late for you to join the army," Massimo teased. "I'm going to help ready the horses. Join us at the stable when you are finished here."

Rostelli returned, carrying Nico's shoe in one hand and a pair of leather riding boots in his other hand.

He handed the boots to Nico and watched as Nico pulled them on. "Do they fit? If not, I have others." Nico assured him that the boots fit perfectly.

Rostelli said, "You and Massimo are simpatico. How long have you known each other?"

"We met less that one year past, but we've worked together closely since then. Massimo has become a good friend."

"You couldn't have a better friend. I've known Massimo since he was a youngster. I'm the one who convinced him to join the army."

"All I know is that he is a decorated soldier." Nico's lips curled into a smile. "And that he likes women and gambling."

"He was decorated twice for bravery on the battlefield," Rostelli corrected. "There are men at this base who owe him their lives."

"I once asked him if his father was a soldier. All he said was 'no,' but the way he said it told me that he didn't want me to probe further."

"His father was a vile man who found his only pleasure in a bottle. He would have his first taste of grappa before breakfast each morning and finish a bottle by noon. He made his poor wife suffer. His drinking got worse until one day he just disappeared. Thank the Lord that Massimo was able to protect his sister from the beast."

"Massimo has a sister?" Nico asked incredulously.

"She's married now… to a carpenter. I'm not sure where they are living."

"And his mother? What happened to her?"

"When her husband vanished, she took the girl and went to live with her brother. He had a farm in the Chianti region. She may still be there… I don't know. Massimo got an apprenticeship with a stone mason until he was old enough to join the army."

Nico said, "Massimo never spoke about any of this."

"His childhood was not pleasant, so I'm not surprised that he doesn't speak about it."

Now dressed for cold mountain weather, Nico joined Massimo and Sergeant Spinelli at the stable. They mounted up and set out on the well-traveled road through the broad valley from Florence to Prato. Shortly before reaching the city, they crossed a bridge over the Bisenzio River that flowed alongside the road to the town.

Sergeant Spinelli led them into Prato through the Fiorentina gate and through the Corridore del Cassero, an enclosed walkway built many years earlier so Florentine military troops could enter and leave the city without being seen. The corridor ended at a castle in the city center. From there, they followed the sergeant through the town, past the duomo to the Travaglio gate where they took the road heading north along the river.

An hour later, they passed through the hamlet of La Dogana. Spinelli pointed ahead and said, "There the river bends to the right." Then he pivoted and pointed to a mountain peak. "That peak is

Poggio Caprile. That river bend and the mountain peak mark the end of Florentine territory; beyond is the land owned by the Bardi family."

"Will you be leaving us here?" Nico asked.

"No, I'll come with you to the abbey at Montepiano, but beyond this point, I'll do so as a traveler, not as a member of the Florentine military."

At the town of Vernio, the river Bisenzio made a sweeping turn away from the road. Massimo stopped his horse and called to Sergeant Spinelli. "I'm curious to know if there is a military presence in this town."

Spinelli replied, "Yes, it would be interesting to know whether the Bardis have enlisted a mercenary unit for protection." The two army officers dismounted, left their horses with Nico, and walked around the periphery of the town.

When they rejoined Nico, Spinelli said, "There's no sign of a military force in the town." He pointed to a building on a hill overlooking the town. "That is the Fortress of Vernio. At one time, it served to defend the town, but many years past, its fortifications were dismantled. Now it's a castle belonging to the Bardi family; however, I doubt that any members of the Bardi family have ever stayed there. It has none of the elegance of their palazzo in Florence."

As they rode on, Nico asked, "If the Florentine army doesn't patrol as far as Vernio, how did you become familiar with the castle?"

"Our patrols don't come into this area routinely, but there are exceptions. Once we chased a smuggler who thought that he would be safe by fleeing across the border. He's now in prison in Florence," Spinelli reported happily. "If the Bardis do have a military force, and it is not in town, it might be at the castle."

At the turnoff to the castle, Massimo dismounted. He unfastened his sword and handed it to Nico. "Spinelli and I will walk to the castle. It's best if we're not armed, so we don't appear hostile."

"Be quick," Nico pleaded. "If anyone is accused of being a

belligerent, it will be me standing here with three horses and two long swords."

After a short climb to the top of the hill, the two soldiers reached a stone archway that opened into a courtyard enclosed by the castle wall. Spinelli peered through the opening. "The castle looks deserted."

Massimo walked around the side of the building to a large field. "The grass is matted and there is fresh horse shit," he observed. "Soldiers or mercenaries camped here recently."

From the corner of his eye, Massimo spotted a young boy at the edge of the field. The boy walked slowly, looking at the ground as though searching for something. At the far end of the field, the boy reversed direction. When he spotted Massimo, he tensed and turned to flee. Massimo yelled, "Don't be afraid. I just have a question." He advanced slowly toward the boy with his hands out, palms up, in a non-threatening manner. "There were men here recently. Do you know them?" Massimo asked.

Still unsure whether he should run, the boy replied in a quivering voice. "There were soldiers here, but I know nothing about them."

"Were they part of a military unit or were they mercenaries?" Massimo's question confused the boy. He stood open-mouthed but did not respond.

Spinelli stepped next to Massimo and asked, "What are you searching for?"

The boy held out an arrow and a metal cup. "Soldiers always leave things behind. Sometimes I find coins."

Massimo studied the arrow, but neither its feather fletching nor its barbed arrowhead revealed a clue to its origin. "Do the soldiers come here often?" he asked.

"Not these men. I have not seen them before."

Massimo peppered the boy with questions: how many men were there? Where did they come from? Where did they go? How long did they stay? Did you hear any names mentioned? Did you see their leader? What did he look like? The boy's limited answers gave them limited information. Spinelli examined the metal cup that the boy had found. "This cup is engraved with the initials of its owner. Armies provide identical equipment to each man. Most likely, this cup belongs to a mercenary."

16

The air grew cooler as Nico, Massimo, and Sergeant Spinelli ascended the winding road toward the village of Montepiano. Twice they were forced off the road by wagons piled high with newly cut logs. At Vernio, the logs would be launched into the river and floated to the mills at Prato. The men rode in silence until Spinelli in the lead said, "There's a break in the forest ahead. It could be Montepiano."

The mountain pass they had been following opened to a large valley. A cluster of small wooden houses at the near end of the valley marked the village center. Other houses were set on farms scattered throughout the area. The three men dismounted. Massimo and Spinelli remained with the horses, while Nico approached the nearest house and knocked on the door.

His knock was answered by a woman who cracked the door open just enough to peer out at Nico. She tensed upon seeing that the caller was a stranger. A young girl clinging to her mother's skirt looked out as well. With chocolate brown eyes and ginger brown hair, the girl appeared to be a miniature version of her mother. Her warm smile showed that she had not yet learned to be wary of strangers.

"Scusa Signora, can you direct me to the Santa Maria abbey?" Nico asked in a soft, almost melodious voice.

"You came from Vernio?" the woman responded tentatively.

"Yes."

"Continue on the road. In a short distance, you will see a stream to your left. Follow the stream until you reach the lake. From there, you will see the abbey's bell tower in the distance." Nico thanked the woman, returned the girl's smile, and turned to rejoin his companions. The woman continued watching. Her eyes tracked the three strangers until they rode out of sight.

Nestled against the hills at the valley's end was a modest sandstone church with a stone bell tower that rose above one end of the building. Massimo pulled the door open, and three men stepped inside. Cool air radiating from the thick stone walls enveloped them. Both walls of the long, narrow nave were adorned with frescoes. In the dim light, Massimo stood facing one of the paintings, a larger-than-life-size image of a saint. "I'm always amazed when unimposing churches in tiny towns and villages have such beautiful paintings," he remarked.

Nico, always ready to tease his friend, asked, "Have you visited many churches?"

Massimo winked at Spinelli, then turned to Nico and replied, "I've seen more naves than any priest."

Massimo's response made Spinelli grin. He understood Massimo's innuendo, but before Nico could make sense of it, their banter was interrupted by the creak of the door and a monk entering the church. Sunshine streaming through the open doorway bathed the frescoes in light, making the colors even more luminous. Massimo, overwhelmed by the sudden glow of the paintings, took an involuntary step backward. The monk left the door ajar to let the sun highlight the paintings.

The monk's gray hair matched the color of his Vallombrosian Order robe. He was bent-over and walked with short quick steps to where Massimo was standing. "Beautiful, isn't it?" he said, with obvious pride. "He is Santo Cristoforo, the patron of travelers." He waited a few minutes while they admired the painting, then said, "Come, let me tell you about the others."

The monk led the men through the church, describing each painting in turn. They ended at the stone altar, which held the remains of the church's first abbot, where the monk then described at length the Vallombrosian Order and the history of Montepiano. Finally, the monk paused and Nico found an opening to speak. "We have come here to speak with the abbot about a report of raids and abductions in the nearby villages."

The monk looked up at Nico. "Ah, we get many pilgrims who come here to witness these beautiful paintings, but I could tell that you men are not pilgrims." He glanced at Massimo and Spinelli. "Pilgrims don't carry weapons." He turned back to Nico and said, "I am the abbot."

Nico said, "A priest from Florence, Friar Alberto, visited here recently. When he returned to Florence, he told the archbishop that the monks here at the abbey had spoken of raids and abductions in nearby villages. The archbishop was disturbed to hear about the raids and that children had been abducted."

The monk's eyes widened. "The Archbishop of Florence sent you?"

Nico responded evasively, "The archbishop asked that the matter be investigated."

The monk sat on one of the benches and looked up at Nico. "There are four other members of our order here at the abbey. Like me, they are old, too old to make regular visits to the villages, but the villagers are always welcome here. They come here for marriages, baptisms, and funeral services.

"One week past, a family came to the abbey from Case del Monte, a father, mother, and two children. The father said that their hamlet had been raided by bandits who took food, horses, and two young boys. The mother feared that if the bandits returned, her children might be taken, so the family fled their home."

"What happened to the family? Where are they now?" Nico asked.

"They stayed here at the abbey for one night; then they went to Vernio. The father has relatives in Vernio, a brother, I think."

Spinelli asked, "Have you heard of other villages being raided?"

The abbot shook his head. "No. Praise God, I have heard of no others."

The Florentines shared a look, and without speaking a word, they agreed on their next move. Speaking for the three, Nico asked, "Can you tell us how to get to Case del Monte?"

"You came through the pass from Vernio?" The three men nodded. "Continue on that same road. Soon you will be in the village of La Storaia. There you will see a logging road to your right that will take you to Case del Monte."

"Is it far to Case del Monte?" Nico asked.

"Not far, but the road winds along the mountainside. It will seem far."

17

Massimo leaned back in his saddle and inhaled deeply. "The abbot was right about this being a winding road. I keep watching that peak ahead and we don't seem to be getting any closer to it."

Spinelli said, "I've been watching it too and I agree. If we are circling around the peak, we must be close to the border with Bologna. We may have already crossed over. Without knowing the landmarks, I cannot tell."

Two deep wheel ruts suggested that the road was used by wagons heavily laden with logs. Initially, it seemed that the road twisted haphazardly, but it soon became clear that the route had been carefully planned to maintain a consistent grade. Except for open areas where trees had been cut, the road was barely wide enough to accommodate wagons. Nico hoped they did not encounter any wagons coming toward them.

Smoke rising ahead from a chimney was the first indication that the men had reached Case del Monte. A woman near one of the houses heard their approach. "Riders! Riders!" she shouted as she raced inside and fastened the door. Other women, upon hearing her warning, gathered their children, bolted for their houses, and locked themselves inside.

The hamlet consisted of fewer than two dozen simple wooden houses, each separated from the next by a small vegetable garden. By the time the men dismounted, no villagers were in sight. Spinelli said, "This must be Case del Monte. The raiders have made everyone fearful of all strangers."

Massimo said, "It's an understandable reaction." Then he grinned at Nico and said, "Lawyer, now is the time to use your silver tongue. Convince these people that we mean no harm." As Nico walked toward the nearest house, Massimo, still grinning, added, "You not only have a lawyer's tongue, you look less menacing than the sergeant and me."

Turning his head over his shoulder to reply, Nico jested, "You mean I'm the most handsome."

Massimo laughed and kicked a spray of dirt in Nico's direction, but it fell far short of its mark. Nico approached the closest house. Although he had seen a woman run into that house, his knock on the door brought no response. He called out, "We are not bandits. We mean you no harm. We only want to talk." His petition drew no response.

Nico opened his mouth to say, my companions are soldiers, they are members of the Florentine army, but he held those words. Instead, he paused, rubbed his chin, and then said, "The abbot at Santa Maria Abbey in Montepiano gave us directions to your village. We were sent by the archbishop of Florence to investigate the raid by the bandits."

After a long moment, a thin voice from inside the house said, "The men are working. You can talk with them when they return."

The day had many hours remaining until dark, so the men might continue working for hours and Nico did not want to wait until they returned, so he asked, "Where are the men? We will go to them."

"On the road up the mountain," the woman said, unwilling to say more even from behind a locked door.

Only two roads extended from the village: one had brought them from Montepiano and the other wound its way higher onto the mountain. The men mounted their horses and headed up into the forest. They had ridden only a short distance when they heard the sound ahead of a tree crashing to the ground. After rounding two more bends in the road, they spotted a crew of axe-wielding men removing limbs from the fallen tree. A pungent pine scent hung in the air. A few of the lumbermen spotted the newcomers, but they did not stop working.

The Florentines watched as the men quickly severed the tree limbs. One of the lumbermen fastened one end of a rope sling to the tree trunk and the other end to the harness of a pair of draft horses. Two men guided the horses as they pulled the trunk into position and dragged it onto a wagon beside two other logs. When the log was secured in place, one of the men climbed onto the wagon and started along the road. The driver stopped the wagon when it neared the three strangers. He faced them, but he said nothing. His rigid posture conveyed that he expected them to explain their purpose.

Spinelli leaned close to Massimo. "They've all become fearful of strangers, even the men."

Using the same approach that had gained a response at the house, Nico stepped forward and said, "The archbishop of Florence is distressed by the recent raids on villages and the abduction of children. We are here at the archbishop's request to investigate the matter. The abbot at Santa Maria Abbey told us that your village was one of those that was raided. I am Nico." Gesturing toward his companions, he said, "Massimo and Sergeant Spinelli."

The driver's expression softened upon hearing Nico's words. "We were working farther up on the mountain when the raiders came. We were too far away to hear them. We didn't know what happened until they had gone and women came from the village and told us. They said that some of the women and children were outside working in the gardens and tending the animals when the raiders appeared. Other women and children were inside, but it did not matter. The bandits searched every house. We never kept our doors locked. The women said that suddenly the bandits were everywhere. They took all the horses except for two old mares. They slaughtered pigs and took sacks of grain."

"Did the bandits… were the women…" Nico let the question hang.

"No, the women were not attacked. One of the bandits grabbed a girl, but the leader made him release her. I don't understand why, but I thank the Lord she was not harmed. Usually men like this…"

All fell silent for a moment, thinking about what might have been. Then Massimo asked, "So, there were only women and children in the village when the raiders came?"

The driver pointed at one of the men in the group that was preparing to fell another tree. "He was in the village, but he is just one man. He could do nothing against armed bandits." Before Massimo could ask, the driver waved his arms to catch the lumberman's attention. He yelled, "Come here! These men want to speak with you!"

A short, barrel-chested man wearing a leather doublet streaked with pine sap came forward. Massimo said, "You were in the village when the raiders came. Can you tell us what happened?"

The lumberman removed his cap. He shifted from foot to foot uneasily as he recounted the incident. "The bandits came out of the woods. They were like a pack of wild animals, yelling and shouting. I think they did that just to terrify the women. I was near the barn unloading a wagon when I saw them coming toward me. I stood waiting for them to stop so I could ask their purpose, but instead of stopping, the rider in front drove his horse into me and knocked me down. One of the other men dismounted, unsheathed his sword, and held it at my neck. He kept me pinned to the ground and told me not to move. I could tell he didn't want to hurt me, but he would have cut me if I had resisted.

"All I could do was to turn my head just enough to see what was happening. Two of the men went from house to house. Some women had locked their doors, but the locks didn't stop those men. Our locks were never meant to stop intruders. I heard about other villages being raided by bandits, so I expected these raiders to take things from the houses, but they didn't. I also thought they would take girls and young women. Thank the Lord they didn't. Later, I learned that they had taken boys. While those men were searching the houses, other men were taking animals and grain. I couldn't see them because I couldn't look in that direction."

Nico asked, "How many raiders were there?"

"I'm not sure. I saw at least twelve or thirteen."

"We were told that two children were taken." Spinelli said.

"Yes, two boys, but I didn't know it at the time. Women were screaming. I could only look in one direction, so I couldn't see everything that was happening. It felt like a nightmare. I didn't know the boys were taken until the raiders had gone. There was nothing I could do." He looked down at the ground and swept his foot slowly in an arc through the dirt. "The women still cry every night. My wife cries too, and we don't have any children. Now, the women are afraid to let their children out of their sight. They fear that the bandits might return. We all have that fear. I can only imagine how terrible it must be for the woman whose son is gone."

The driver looked at Spinelli. "Two boys were taken during the raid, but two days later, one of the boys returned home. One of the bandits rode into the village, carrying the boy on his horse. He left the boy and then rode away."

That unexpected turn rendered the Florentines speechless. The driver continued, "The boy said that the raiders were mercenaries. They wanted only able boys who could fight with them. The boy who was returned has a bad arm. He was born that way."

"They must want only boys who can be trained to fight," Massimo reasoned. "I've never met mercenaries who would send one of their own to free a victim. Most have no feelings. They would just cast the boy out, or worse. It's also strange too that they took no girls." His brow creased in disbelief. "For some of those *pervertiti,* no girl is too young."

Nico asked, "Is the other boy still with the mercenaries?"

"He is." A moment passed before the lumberman added. "It is painful for the boy's mother and father. They used to be happy and cheerful, always with good words for everyone. The mother used to sing to herself when she worked in the garden. Now they keep to themselves, hardly speaking to others." The lumberman moved closer to Nico. In a low voice, he said, "I would never say this to the boy's parents, but maybe he is happy being with the mercenaries. Life in our village is a lonely life for the children. Whenever travelers pass through the village, the children hear stories of excitement and adventure in a world they've never known. I've often heard children wish they could leave."

Massimo asked, "Can we speak to the boy who returned?"

The lumberman looked at the driver, who said, "We can't leave here until the work is done." Then he folded his arms and thought for a moment. "Go to my house. It's the one with the rain barrel near the door. Tell my wife that I sent you."

As the men turned to leave, Nico thought about his map and asked one last question. "Is this land owned by the Bardi family, or is it in the Province of Bologna?"

The driver spread his arms. "God made these trees, and we cut them. Far-off princes and wealthy men can draw lines on maps to say they own the land, but those lines mean nothing here. I don't know who claims this land."

At the house with the rain barrel, Massimo knocked on the door. He called through the locked door and moments later, a robust woman with flour-covered hands lifted the latch and stepped out of the house. She appraised the three men, then said brusquely in a husky voice, "You want to speak with the boy who was returned? I will take you to him."

She walked briskly with the three Florentines following, like a hen leading her chicks. They passed two houses; at the third, she called loudly to the occupants. "The archbishop in Florence sent these men. They have questions about the mercenaries."

A boy, who looked to be about fourteen, opened the door. His mother stood behind him with a trembling hand on his shoulder. Massimo spoke first to the mother. "Don't be afraid. We are gathering information about the raid for the archbishop of Florence." Then, to the boy, he said, "We want to learn about the bandits… the mercenaries."

The boy nodded and followed Massimo, who walked to where Sergeant Spinelli and Nico were standing. The mother remained in the doorway with her eyes locked on the boy and her hand unmoved, as though it were still gripping her son's shoulder.

Spinelli began the questioning. "We are sorry that you were taken. We want to know what happened so we can protect other boys. Tell me, the men who took you, where did they take you?"

The boy's shoulders slumped. "I'm sorry, signor, but I don't know where we went. We rode through the forest on narrow trails, not on wagon roads. All I could see were trees. We rode for a long time. The sun was down when we got to their camp."

"I understand. It's easy to become disoriented when riding through the forest on unfamiliar trails. Why did they let you return home?"

The boy raised his right arm. It extended stiff and straight with no flexing at the elbow. "I cannot bend my arm. People say something is wrong with the bones. I never could bend this arm. The mercenaries said they only wanted boys who can ride and fight with them. I am not able to do those things."

Nico asked, "What did they do when they found out about your arm?"

"The one who first saw my arm wasn't sure what to do. He thought they could find work for me at the camp, but he talked with another man who said their leader only wanted boys who could fight. They weren't sure what to do with me. One of them spoke with the leader. He decided that I should be returned home."

"The other boy, the one they kept, did they force him to stay? Didn't he want to return home?"

"The boy who stayed is my cousin. They told him that they would take him to wonderful cities and would teach him to fight with a sword. He often talked about leaving the village. He listened whenever anyone talked about Florence, Rome, or Bologna. He wanted to see those cities. He asked me to tell his mother and father not to worry about him."

Massimo continued the questioning. "What can you tell me about the mercenaries? How many were there?"

The boy looked down in thought, then said, "I saw at least twenty, but I'm sure there were more. I was only in the camp for a short time, so I didn't see everyone."

"And boys. Were there other boys your age?"

"Yes, I saw at least six. Three of them had swords. One boy let my cousin hold his sword. He laughed and cheered as he waved it in the air."

"Did you learn the names of the boys?" Nico asked, wondering if one might be named Armando.

"No. I wasn't there long enough to hear any of their names."

"What about their leader? Did you see him?" Massimo asked.

"Yes, my cousin and I were together when the leader came to look at us. He said we should be proud to be members of his army. He was big... like you. He wore black leather, and his horse was black too, as black as the night. Hanging from his belt, he had a sword on one side and a dagger on the other side. His men called him captain."

Massimo's eyes narrowed. "Did he wear a ring?"

The boy brightened. "Yes, a big silver ring. How did you know?"

Massimo turned to Spinelli and exclaimed, "I know him! Sword and dagger, black leather, black horse, silver ring; he's Luigi Attendolo. I met him when his mercenary band fought on the side of the Papal forces in Le Marche. I heard that later he had a disagreement with the Papal Army Captain General, so he left Le Marche and came north to join with the Venetians. In Le Marche, he had commanded a force of two hundred men, maybe more." Massimo flexed and unflexed his fingers. "Now he's raiding villages with a few dozen men.

It makes no sense, but Attendolo is no fool. There's a reason he is doing this."

"And he's recruiting children. For what purpose?" Nico wondered aloud.

Massimo pondered Nico's question for a moment, then said, "Attendolo is a clever man. The children may be just for show. The captain who commands the Venetian forces once used a similar ploy to hold a town hostage. He had the town encircled by boys wielding swords and other weapons. The boys' cheeks were smeared with wood ash to mask their youth. The townspeople believed they were surrounded by a mercenary army, so they mounted no resistance. That ruse left the captain free to deploy his strongest forces elsewhere. Attendolo may be preparing to make a similar show of force somewhere."

"For what purpose?" Spinelli wondered. His question went unanswered.

Nico squatted down and faced the boy. "The mercenaries stole food and horses from your village. Is there anything else you can tell us that could help us find them before they steal from other villages and maybe hurt people?"

The boy bit his lip. "No, again I am sorry. Whenever the men talked with each other, they stood together far from us so we couldn't hear them."

His eyes filled with tears as he recalled his experience. He murmured, "If my arm didn't have a problem, I would have been forced to stay with them. I wouldn't be here now."

Nico kneeled next to the boy and rested a hand on his shoulder. "I understand. It is frightening to be taken from your home and family."

As the men returned to their mounts and prepared to leave the hamlet, one of the women walked up behind Nico and said, "I have a daughter. She can cook. She could make you happy and give you many children." Nico walked on, pretending he did not hear.

Massimo leaned close to Nico and grinned. "The woman asked about you. I told her you are a successful lawyer in Florence."

18

The moon shone brightly by the time Nico and Massimo returned their horses to the stable at the army base outside of Florence. Nico dismounted and patted his animal's nose. "You covered many miles today, so I imagine you are more tired than I am." As he flexed his back and legs, he pondered, "I wonder if you're as happy to be free of me as I am to be out of the saddle." Nico handed the reins to a stable boy and turned toward Massimo. "It's too late for the Uccello to be serving dinner, but I know the owner, so I'm sure we can get something to eat there."

Massimo gave Nico a friendly poke. "It may be late by lawyer time, but by army time, the night has barely begun. We can eat here at the base. I won't claim that army food compares with the Uccello's specialties, but I eat here regularly, and I've survived."

Massimo led Nico to a large tent where Nico was surprised to see that it wasn't empty. Two tables were occupied by men having a late-night meal. "I thought we'd be the only ones here."

"These men must have just returned from patrols. Smugglers and thieves don't rest at night, so neither does the army. There are men on patrol at night whenever there is enough moonlight to follow the roads."

Massimo passed by the tables and greeted the men whom he knew. "Tonight's meal is stew," he said as he led Nico to the serving counter, where the chef filled their plates with generous portions.

After they finished eating, Massimo persuaded Nico to join him for an after-dinner glass of grappa. "It will help your digestion," Massimo claimed. They took turns refilling their glasses until the entire bottle of the potent liquid had been emptied. By then, Nico's unsteady balance told him it would be unwise to walk across the city to Casa Argenti. He spent the night in a blanket on the floor in Massimo's room.

The next morning, they went to the captain's office to report on what they had learned about the raids and abductions. Sergeant Spinelli, the soldier who had accompanied Nico and Massimo to the village of Case del Monte, joined the debriefing. Massimo said, "We spoke with people in one of the villages that had been raided. A boy who had been abducted from the village was returned because he had a malformed arm. The mercenaries wanted only boys who could be trained to fight."

"That's not usual behavior for mercenaries," the captain said. "I would have expected them to throw the boy to the wolves."

"Their behavior surprised me as well," Massimo agreed, "until the boy described the mercenary leader as Luigi Attendolo."

The captain said, "If there was ever a civilized mercenary, it is Luigi Attendolo. He earned an honorable record serving with the Venetians and the Papal forces. But perhaps I shouldn't be surprised that he now commands a band of rogues. That seems to happen with all mercenaries, eventually. They trade their scruples for gold. Is the village that was raided in Florentine territory?"

Sergeant Spinelli answered, "I am certain that the village is not in Florentine territory, but we could not determine whether it is in Bardi owned land or in the Province of Bologna."

The captain focused his attention on Nico. "Although the army has no jurisdiction outside Florentine territory, the Florentine Security Commission's authority extends beyond our borders. Whether to pursue Attendolo or not is the commission's decision."

Nico and Massimo shared a look. They were unsure what action they could take, but they were certain that before doing anything, they needed to consult with Chancellor Scala.

∽

At the chancery, a senior clerk greeted Nico. "Buon giorno, Messer Argenti. Chancellor Scala is eager to meet with you but he didn't know when you'd return to Florence. He's at a meeting with the consuls of the silk guild and won't return here until the afternoon. He would like to meet with you and Signor Leoni."

Nico said, "Signor Leoni and I will return later."

As Nico turned to leave, the clerk held out an envelope. "A courier from Pisa brought this for you."

Nico recognized the handwriting as soon as he opened the letter. It belonged to a friend of his in the Maritime Office at Pisa who had inquired into Patrizu Nieddu's former employment at Nico's request.

> Nico,
>
> I asked about Signor Patrizu Nieddu at the shipping companies on Sardinia, as you requested. I found the company where he worked. The owner said that Nieddu had worked for him as a dockworker. Nieddu never held any other position. He was never a manager. I spoke with other officials at that company and none of them had good words to say about Nieddu. They told me that Nieddu was a schemer who always tried to get the easiest jobs, so he would not have to work as hard as the other men. He was forced to flee from Sardinia after seducing a warehouse owner's daughter. The woman's father filed an accusation with a criminal prosecutor. The accusation remains on file, so Nieddu would face criminal

charges if he ever returned to Sardinia. I hope this information is helpful to you.

Your faithful friend, Mario

Nico had suspected that Nieddu had lied to the Officials Over Orphans when he applied for the position at the orphanage by claiming that he had managerial experience in Sardinia. Now Nico had proof of the lie. Apparently, the Officials had been so desperate to fill the vacant administrator position that they did not investigate Nieddu's background as they should have.

Nico considered two options: he could bring his findings to a meeting of the Officials Over Orphans or he could speak privately with one of the officials. If he brought the matter to the entire body, a record would be made of their oversight and that would result in public embarrassment of its members. Nico recalled that one of the Officials' members dined regularly at the Uccello. Nico had met him at the restaurant and judged the man to be thoughtful and conscientious. Nico remembered the man's name, Signor Dagostino, and that he owned a leather tanning business.

Tanning shops were forced to locate far from the city center to keep their offensive odors away from Florence's influential citizens. Nico exited the city through Porta Santa Croce, then headed toward the river. The pungent tannin smell reached Nico long before he reached the tannery. Signor Dagostino's tannery was a long stone building close to the riverbank. Outside his shop, racks held hides drying in the sun. Nico gave thanks that the office was upwind from the drums of foul-smelling liquids. Dagostino looked puzzled when he first saw Nico standing in his doorway, then brightened with a flash of recognition. "You are Nico, Donato's cousin." He motioned for Nico to enter and be seated. "What brings you to this edge of the city? Have you come to purchase leather?"

"No, not today. I have some information to share with you

regarding the administrator at the orphanage." Dagostino's mood lost its buoyancy. He said nothing and waited for Nico to continue. "Signor Nieddu was not truthful when he applied for the position of administrator at the orphanage. Nieddu came to Florence from Sardinia, where he claimed to have been a manager at a shipping company. That was a lie. He was never a manager; he only worked on the docks." Nico held out the letter from his friend. "This letter explains why Nieddu left Sardinia."

Dagostino took the letter, read it, and handed it back to Nico. He lowered his head and said, "We should have done more than just accept Signor Nieddu's claim that he had administrative experience. There were only two applicants and the other one, a teacher, withdrew his application. This morning I received a report that Signor Nieddu is gone. He was not at the orphanage yesterday, and he is not there today. No one knows why he is missing or where to find him."

Nico was prepared to tell Dagostino about the missing children and his suspicion that Nieddu had been selling the children, but that seemed less important now that Nieddu had vanished. "Is anyone searching for him?" Nico asked.

"Who could look for him? The Officials Over Orphans have no resources to find people and we have no evidence that he committed a crime, so we can't bring the matter to the Guardia."

Nico reached into the bag he carried, pulled out the Florentine Security Commission authorization letter, and held it out for Dagostino to read. "I am a member of the commission. If the Officials Over Orphans have no objection, the Security Commission can investigate Nieddu's disappearance." Nico felt a twinge of uneasiness. This was the first decision he had made on behalf of the Security Commission without seeking prior approval from the chancellor.

"Hmmm," Dagostino uttered as he considered Nico's suggestion. "I would have to consult with the other officials, but I see no reason why they would object."

Nico asked for Dagostino's approval only as a courtesy. He knew that the Florentine Security Commission operated with the authority of the Signoria and did not need the approval of the Officials to investigate Nieddu's disappearance.

∼

Nico had learned that orphan children were being sold through his conversations with Nieddu. He wanted real evidence before accusing Nieddu of a crime, and he believed that evidence, if there were any, would be found in Nieddu's quarters at the orphanage. He invited Vittorio as the security commission's experienced investigator to help him look for clues in Nieddu's office and his living quarters. The nun who received the men at the orphanage summoned the abbess. "We are here to investigate the disappearance of Signor Nieddu," Nico explained.

The abbess did not question his authority. She said, "Sister Caterina is most familiar with Signor Nieddu. She delivered the meals to his office."

"He didn't eat in the common room with the others?" Nico asked.

"No, he preferred the quiet of his office." She expressed no opinion, but something in her tone told Nico that she was not pleased with his desire to isolate himself.

While Nico and the abbess spoke, Vittorio observed nuns and children moving throughout the building as they would on any other day. "No one seems disturbed by the administrator's absence," he said.

The abbess glanced at one of the nuns, who was escorting a line of children toward the common room. "The administrator has little involvement with our day-to-day activities. He is more concerned with financial and other matters. The sisters know what must be done to care for the children."

Sister Caterina accompanied Nico and Vittorio to Nieddu's office. Nico and the sister entered the office. Vittorio stood in the doorway, surveying the room, looking for anything unusual or out of place. When he entered, he walked directly to a shelf holding a glass figurine of a dog. He lifted it from the shelf, held it out, and asked Sister Caterina, "Did Nieddu have a dog or an interest in dogs?"

"I never heard him mention a dog," she replied. She turned to see Vittorio holding the figurine, and added, "That didn't belong to Signor Nieddu. That dog and the other animal figures were here before he came. They were left in the office by the previous administrator."

Vittorio gestured toward the shelf that contained several other items. "Which of these belonged to Signor Nieddu?"

Sister Caterina answered quickly. "None of them. They were all here when he arrived."

"So, he took all his personal items with him when he left," Vittorio proffered.

"I don't recall him having any personal items... except for these." She lifted a string of rosary beads from the corner of the desk.

Nico cocked his head. "Was Signor Nieddu devout?"

"Oh, yes. He went to church every afternoon."

"What church did he attend?"

"He didn't say, but every afternoon when he left the orphanage, he carried these rosary beads." Vittorio arched an eyebrow and muttered something to himself.

A shelf behind the desk contained a single folder. Nico opened it and scanned several pages. "When was Signor Nieddu appointed as administrator?" he asked without looking up.

"He has been here almost four months," Sister Caterina replied.

"These pages are records of purchases and information about the children who were released from the orphanage. All the papers in this folder are older than four months. Why are there no records from Nieddu's time as administrator?" Nico asked rhetorically.

"Perhaps he took them with him?" Sister Caterina speculated hesitantly.

"Or he destroyed them," Vittorio asserted in a cynical tone.

Vittorio looked through the drawers of Nieddu's desk and retrieved a nearly empty bottle of chianti. Sister Caterina inhaled sharply at seeing the bottle. Vittorio locked his gaze on her. "Is there a problem, sister?"

Feeling his stare, she said, "We have rules. Wine and beer are not allowed in the orphanage. They would set a bad example for the children."

The office yielded nothing else of interest. Nico asked, "Can you take us to Signor Nieddu's room, sister?"

Sister Caterina led the men a short distance along the hallway to Nieddu's living quarters. "I have never been inside," she said, and remained in the corridor as Nico and Vittorio entered the room.

The sparsely furnished room contained only a bed, a wardrobe, a desk and chair, and a small table. Nico opened the wardrobe. Inside were two well-worn tunics. "He must have taken his clothes. He left only these old things. Clearly, he doesn't intend to return."

Vittorio opened the desk drawer and withdrew a copy of Petrarch's sonnets. With a voice dripping disdain, Vittorio said, "If Nieddu read Petrarch's sonnets, he would be the first dockworker ever to do so. This too must have belonged to his predecessor."

The bust of a Roman dignitary, one whom Nico could not identify, rested on the table in a corner of the room. He reached behind the statue and retrieved a bottle of wine, this one about half full. "Obviously, Nieddu wasn't deterred by the prohibition against wine," Nico announced.

Vittorio walked to the wardrobe and sniffed at a stain on one of the tunics. "Beer," he declared. "Nieddu didn't limit himself to wine."

Nico scanned the room one final time, took a deep breath, and sighed. "I'd hoped we might find a clue to where Nieddu has gone. But all we have are a couple of old tunics, two bottles of wine, and rosary beads. Since he took his clothes and any personal items he might have had, we can be sure he doesn't intend to return."

As Vittorio left the room, he said, "Were Neiddu as devout as he led the sisters to believe, he wouldn't have left the rosary beads."

"I'll visit the nearby churches," Nico said. "If Nieddu really did spend much time at a church, he might have said something to a priest."

Vittorio cleared his throat. "After you visit the churches, try the nearby taverns. I suspect the rosary beads were just a prop to explain his afternoon absences."

Two churches were within a short distance from the orphanage. Nico entered the first church, nearly deserted in the afternoon. A priest sat at a writing desk preparing a sermon. He glanced up when Nico entered. "Yes, my son. How may I help you?"

"Father, I am looking for a man who may have been coming to your church every afternoon."

"I say mass every morning, but most afternoons I work on my sermons, as you can see, or I enjoy a long walk. There are women who say the rosary in the afternoon. Perhaps they have seen the one you seek."

Nico walked around to the church and spoke with the women who said no man came regularly in the afternoon. Nico had a similar experience at the second church. Florence was a city of many churches. Nico could reach three others by widening his search area only slightly, although if Nieddu sought the comfort of God's house every day, he likely would have chosen one of the churches closest to the orphanage.

Rather than visiting another church, Nico acceded to Vittorio's suggestion. He had spotted a small tavern not far from the orphanage. The crudely fashioned sign above its door read The Lame Horse. Two old men were playing cards at a table in one corner when Nico entered. The barkeep sat behind the counter on a chair tilted back and leaning against a wall. He didn't stand, but his eyes followed Nico, curious to learn why a stranger had come into the tavern usually frequented only by locals.

Nico had no desire for a beer, and he was dubious about the quality of the tavern's offerings, but he judged that buying a mug of beer might be the best way to induce the barkeep to answer his questions. Nico placed a high-value coin on the counter as a further inducement.

Nico described Nieddu and asked whether the barkeep had seen him. Nieddu's features were not especially distinctive. The description could have fit many men, so Nico was not optimistic that the barkeep would recall seeing him. After describing Nieddu's physical features, Nico said, "He's a Sardinian," and immediately felt foolish for mentioning the trivial fact.

Perhaps the barkeep saw conversation as an opportunity to relieve his boredom, but to Nico's surprise, the barkeep said, "The Sardinian. Yes, he's been here. The first time he came, that was about four months ago, I noticed he spoke funny, so I asked him where he came from. I'd never met a Sardinian before. He comes every afternoon… well, he did, except for the past two days."

"Was he alone or did he meet with others?"

The barkeep gestured with his thumb. "Mostly, he sat by himself over there in the corner. He would down three mugs of beer, then leave." After a moment, he added, "Sometimes, though, another man joined him."

"Do you know the other man?"

"No, I don't know him, but I can tell you he doesn't live in the city." Before Nico could ask for an explanation, the barkeep said, "He wears heavy boots that clatter on the floor when he walks. Florentines wear soft leather shoes like the ones you are wearing."

Nico considered telling the barkeep the reason he was looking for Nieddu, but the truth seemed too complex, so he opted, instead, to fabricate a reason. "The man I'm looking for owes me a debt. I'd be most grateful to anyone who could help me find him." Nico pushed his silver coin across the bar in the direction of the barkeep.

"He never told me anything." Again, the barkeep pointed to a table across the room. "When the other man came, they sat there. They weren't loud, so most of the time I couldn't hear what they talked about. But the last time he was here, I brought two mugs to the table, and I did hear him say 'Nothing keeps me in Florence. I can leave in the morning.'"

"Did he mention a place? Venice or someplace else?" Nico asked hopefully.

"If he mentioned a place, I didn't hear it. All I heard him say was that he was ready to leave Florence."

Nico left the silver coin and a full mug of beer on the counter when he exited The Lame Horse. Vittorio was correct. Nieddu spent his afternoons at a tavern, not a church. Unfortunately, Nico's conversation with the barkeep did no more than confirm what he already knew: Nieddu had left Florence. It shed no light on Nieddu's destination.

Nico's father had found pleasure in reading the works of ancient Roman writers. As a soldier, he favored the writings of Julius Caesar, but he also read lesser-known writers. Whenever he came upon a piece of sage advice, he shared it with his young son, who recorded it in a ledger. Nico recalled one of those sayings: he conquers who endures. When he first heard those words at the age of seven or eight, he did not know what they meant. "To succeed, you must be persistent," his father had said. Nico told himself, "There must be a way to find Nieddu and the missing boys."

19

"You're too far left. You've got to keep the lines straight," Lapo called to his son.

"I'm trying, but every time the blade hits a rock, it turns to the side."

"You're a plowman now. You've got to work together with the ox. He will keep the plow moving. Your job is to make sure the blade goes straight."

At age thirteen, this was the boy's first time behind the plow. When they reached the end of the row, he let his arms drop to his sides. His muscles throbbed.

Lapo patted his son's head. "You did well. It got away from you only once."

Buoyed by his father's praise, the boy said, "I want to do another row."

Lapo looked back across the plowed rows toward the houses clustered at the village center. As he adjusted his cap, he scanned the other farms that surrounded the hamlet and saw several of his neighbors in their fields. Sunshine, a cool breeze, and friable soil made it an ideal day for plowing.

"What's that?" the boy called.

Lapo turned to look in the direction his son was pointing. A column of dust rose from a trail on a distant hillside. By cupping both hands to shield his eyes, Lapo could discern men on horseback, too many to be local hunters.

"Raiders. Many of them. Get to the house. Warn the others. Run!" Lapo yelled.

Lapo and his son raced toward the village. The boy quickly outpaced his father. Following his father's cue, he shouted, "Raiders!"

Women tending gardens near their homes heard the warning and echoed it to men plowing fields on the far side of the village and children tending animals in pastures. From past raids, the villagers had learned to defend themselves against attacks by bandits. Women and children locked themselves inside their houses while men took up pitchforks and other tools as weapons. One man had become skilled at throwing rocks with a sling, and another was proficient with a bow and arrow.

Lapo glanced over his shoulder as he ran and saw the riders approaching rapidly. He knew the villagers weren't going to reach safety before the riders were upon them. Lapo altered his course toward a nearby pasture where a girl was tending sheep. She must not have heard the warning cries. Lapo grabbed the startled girl, lifted her onto his shoulder, and continued running. When he reached the barn where the villagers stored their farm implements, he set the girl down and told her to run to her home.

From the selection of tools in the barn, Lapo chose a scythe. Back outside, he again looked toward the riders, and this time he stiffened with fear. These were not inept bandits; they were a band of mercenaries wearing leather armor and brandishing swords. Lapo knew that farmers with pitchforks would be defenseless against these trained fighters. When the first of Lapo's neighbors reached the barn, Lapo yelled, "They're mercenaries. We can't fight them. Go to your houses. Better that we lose a few pigs than get someone killed."

Chaos spread through the village, stoked by a cacophony of

conflicting shouts. Some children ran toward their homes, but others remained in the pastures, afraid to leave the animals unattended. Some men ran to their homes, while others headed for the pastures to fetch their children. Women, tense with fear, stood outside their houses waiting for their husbands and children. Antonio, the archer, ran through a pasture toward a nearby thicket with a quiver of arrows on his back, a bow slung over one shoulder, and his young daughter on his other shoulder. He held tight to his wife with one hand and pulled his son along with his other hand.

The band of riders split into groups of two or three as they reached the village. One pair, a seasoned horseman trailed by a recent recruit, rode to a pasture where a girl trembled in fear amidst a flock of sheep. The thundering horses scattered the sheep, leaving the girl exposed. Without breaking stride, the horseman reached down, swept the girl up onto the horse and set her face down across his saddle. He held her firmly with one of his powerful hands and laughed loudly as she kicked her feet, trying to free herself. "This is how it's done, boy," he called to the young recruit following behind him.

"Lock the door," one villager called to his wife and two sons. She pushed the door closed and set the latch. Her husband stood outside the house, preparing to guard it with only a wooden staff. Two riders who had eyed the boys as potential recruits brought their horses alongside the man. One rider dismounted; the other swung his sword and struck the man's back with the flat of his blade. The powerful blow knocked the man down face-first into the dirt.

The man scrambled to turn over, only to find a sword pressed against his neck. "We want the boys," said the one holding the sword. "Tell your wife to unlock the door and send the boys out."

The man growled and feebly spit at his assailant. The mercenary kicked the man, then turned to face the house. "Come out now boys, or when you come out later, you can dig your father's grave."

The man remained defiant, but the door cracked open and two boys looked out from the doorway. "Go back inside," the man yelled at his boys. The boys looked down at their father, a sword pressed firmly against his neck, and they stepped forward hesitantly. The boys were about the same age, but not twins. They were muscular from toiling in the fields and tan from hours in the sun. The mercenary on horseback summoned two of the recent recruits who rode to where the boys were standing. He gestured toward the riders with his sword and commanded the boys, "Get on the horses with them."

The one standing withdrew his sword and climbed up onto his mount. As he turned his horse to leave, he called back over his shoulder to the father, "The boys are part of our family now."

Luigi Attendolo, wearing a silver ring and black leather and riding a black horse, saw Antonio and his family fleeing from the village and gave chase. He tightened the reins to stop his steed when he neared the thicket that shielded the family. He peered into the thick underbrush, but was unable to see anyone. Listening intently, he heard a sharp crack, a branch breaking underfoot. "Come out of there. You can't go anywhere." His demand drew no response.

"Everything you own is in your house." That veiled threat produced a response, but not the one he expected. An arrow flew out from behind a bush and struck Attendolo in the chest. He shuddered, fearing the worst. Fortunately for him, Antonio's homemade bow lacked the power of a military longbow. Attendolo's leather armor absorbed much of the arrow's force. The tip drove through the leather and into his chest, but not deep enough to penetrate a vital organ.

"Bastard," Attendolo shouted; then he gritted his teeth, reached down, and snapped the arrow shaft, leaving only the point and a nub of the shaft embedded. He would have one of his men with medical training tend to the wound when he returned to camp.

Rather than risk a more serious wound, he backed his horse away from the thicket and headed back to the village. When he reached the area where his men were assembled, his lieutenant reported, "Four boys were taken, six pigs were slaughtered, and ten sacks were filled with grain. They are already on their way to camp."

"Very good. Any resistance?"

"None, sir." If the lieutenant saw his leader's wound, he thought it best not to mention it.

From the corner of his eye, the leader noticed that one of his men held a girl down across his saddle. Her legs flailed in the air. Attendolo rode closer to investigate. Seeing that the girl was just a child, he commanded, "Put the girl down."

"I've been a long time without a woman," his man pleaded.

"Then get yourself a proper whore." Attendolo's voice hardened. "My men are not rapists. Put the girl down," he repeated.

Reluctantly, the man withdrew his hand from the girl's back. Freed from the pressure that had been holding her against the saddle, the girl slid down from the horse. Whimpering, tears streaming from her eyes, she bolted to her house. Attendolo surveyed the scene a final time, then said, "We got what we need. It's time to go." He eased his horse to a brisk walk out of the village. His men queued behind him with their booty and captives.

20

In late afternoon, Chancellor Scala returned to the chancery. He was walking slowly, a sign he was tired, when he joined Nico, Massimo, and Vittorio in the conference room. "It's late and we have much to discuss." He gestured to Vittorio. "Tell Signori Leoni and Argenti what we learned in our meeting with the envoy from Modena."

Vittorio cleared his throat. "You may recall that reports from our embassy had alerted us that the Strozzi brothers left Venice, but our ambassador did not know the Strozzis' destination. Our objective in meeting with Lord Este's envoy was to find out whether they had moved to Ferrara or Modena.

"The envoy was totally uncooperative. I might even say defiant. He denied having any knowledge of the Strozzis. Although his answers to our questions were vague, I sensed no indications that he was trying to deceive us. I believe he was being truthful in saying he had no knowledge of the Strozzi brothers arriving in Modena or Ferrara. Of course, his ignorance doesn't mean the Strozzis haven't relocated there. It says only that he is uninformed.

"I raised the issue of Ferrara's relationship with Venice. At that, he began to squirm. He admitted that Ferrara and Venice are strengthening their relationship, but he was abrupt and offered nothing specific."

Nico and Massimo looked at Scala, eager to hear his reaction to the meeting. "I agree with Signor Colombo that the envoy was evasive. Ever since Borso d'Este rose to power, the relationship between Florence and Ferrara has been strained. Earlier today, I discussed the matter with members of the Signoria. They are concerned that Ferrara might not honor our diplomatic credentials, so we believe it would be unwise to send an agent there at the present time. If we get evidence that the situation is deteriorating, we may need to revisit that decision."

Scala paused to entertain questions. There were none, so he continued. "Lord Este's brother commands the military forces. It would be telling if he were to travel to Venice. I have asked our ambassador in Venice to make discreet inquiries about Venice's military activities and to report if any of Este's military delegates appear in Venice.

"Fortunately, we have another possible source of information. Despite our fragile relationship with Ferrara, our silk and wool merchants travel there frequently. They may have noticed unusual movements of army troops, new appointments to the ducal court, or other abnormal activities."

Scala leaned forward and rested his elbows on the table. "Signor Colombo, can you meet with those merchants to see whether they have any helpful insights?"

The characteristically taciturn investigator merely nodded.

"You can begin by speaking with the consuls of the merchants' guild. I have asked them to prepare a list of men doing business in Ferrara."

Scala then looked at Nico and Massimo. "I am eager to hear what you learned about the raids on villages."

Nico gestured to Massimo for him to speak. "We visited Case del Monte, which is one of the villages that was raided. Descriptions we obtained from the villagers led me to realize that the raiders are mercenaries under the command of a mercenary captain named Luigi Attendolo." Massimo noticed Scala's surprise upon hearing the mention of Attendolo. "You have heard of Captain Attendolo?" Massimo asked.

Scala replied, "Yes, but the last report I saw that mentioned him placed him in Venice."

Massimo said, "I had also heard of him being in Venice. I was surprised to learn that he is heading a band of rogues, but there is no doubt that he is the leader. Their description of him was clear. I can't explain why he has become a leader of bandits. He never let his men commit acts of violence in the past.

"This morning I spoke with two army scouts who are certain that Case del Monte is in the Province of Bologna. It is the only raided village known to the abbot at Santa Maria Abbey in Montepiano, but the villagers believe that other villages have also been raided.

"Two boys were taken during the raid on Case del Monte, although one was later returned because he has a deformed arm. Apparently, Attendolo wants only boys who can become fighters, or at least give the impression that they are fighters."

Scala took notes as he listened to Massimo's report. When Massimo finished speaking, Scala gazed up at the ceiling for a moment, then he spoke aloud, as much to himself as to the others in the room, "Officials in Bologna need to be made aware that rogue mercenaries are operating in its territory. Unfortunately, our diplomatic connections to Bologna are painstakingly long. Since Bologna is a province of the Papal States, all official communications to them must go via our ambassador in Rome. I am certain that our archbishop will want to warn the Papal Legate in Bologna about the abductions, but he too has no direct means to communicate with his counterpart in Bologna. Protocol demands that he send all communiques through church officials in Rome."

Scala gazed downward at the tabletop and fell silent while he considered possible actions. Then he rubbed his chin and looked up. "There are times when diplomatic channels are insufficient. Yesterday, I met with officers of the magistrates' guild. There is a promising student at the University of Bologna law school. The guild wants to encourage him to relocate to Florence upon his graduation."

Scala's sudden change of subject surprised and intrigued the others. He never rambled and his words always had purpose. The men listened with rapt attention as he continued. "I can think of no one better to entice him than a recent graduate of that institution," Scala's eyes locked onto Nico. "That ruse will give you a pretense for being in Bologna. Your true purpose will be to learn whether officials in Bologna are aware of renegade mercenaries operating in the province and what action they are taking, if any, to stop the raids."

In his eagerness to return to Bologna, Nico answered Scala's question before the chancellor asked it. "I can leave for Bologna tomorrow."

"Excellent. The name of the student that the consuls wish to invite is Gerhard Ritter. He is one of several Austrian students at the university. Signor Ritter is entering his final term in the law school."

"Gerhard Ritter," Nico repeated.

"And while you are in Bologna, you can call upon the Papal Legate to deliver a message from the Florentine archbishop. It will be a brief unofficial note, just enough to stroke the legate's interest. You can then provide details of the situation. I'll ask the archbishop to write a note and have a chancery clerk deliver it to you."

As they exited the conference room, Massimo stepped close to Nico and quipped, "You'll be on your own this time, lawyer. Are you sure you can get along without us?"

"I survived six years in Bologna, sitting in lectures and taking exams. That experience took concentration and perseverance. I expect this mission will present no hardships that would challenge even a bambino."

"As a student, you spent all your time studying. You may have known a few respectable taverns, but I doubt that you had time to discover the finer pleasures that the city had to offer. Now, if I were there with you...." Massimo let his voice trail off.

Nico responded with just a smile, but as he walked home to Casa Argenti, he reflected on Massimo's question: Are you sure you can get along without us? Vittorio, the Florentine Security Commission's investigator, had a unique ability to seek the truth by interrogating people and uncovering their lies. Massimo had a soldier's instinct for sensing impending harm. In Bologna, Nico would be without his colleagues' skills.

Nico crossed Piazza del Duomo; then turned into an alley next to a cobbler's shop. Midway through the alley, a hand grabbed his shoulder from behind. The unexpected pressure caught him off balance. He spun, and the hand shoved him back and pressed him flat against a wall. "You spoke with Patrizu Nieddu. Take me to him." The voice came from a barrel-chested man with a black beard. He wore a sailor's cap embroidered with the image of a sailing ship.

"Who are you?" Nico snapped.

The assailant ignored Nico's question and repeated, "Take me to Nieddu."

Nico pushed aside the hand that had been holding him. "I can't. Nieddu is gone."

"You spoke with him," the voice insisted.

"I spoke with him at the orphanage. He was the administrator, but he's gone."

The man took a step back and pulled out a fish filleting knife. He swung the curved blade up toward Nico's face and pressed the sharp point against Nico's chin. "Take me there. Take me to the orphanage," the man demanded.

Nico recoiled at the sight of the blade. He thought for an instant of trying to disarm the desperate man, but then thought again, and said, "This way. The orphanage is this way." Nico led the stranger to the Ospedale degli Innocenti.

When they reached their destination, the man scanned the impressive two-level building that spanned the entire width of the piazza. "That is an orphanage?" he said doubtfully. "Florence must be infested with orphans."

Nico led the man to the building entrance, where Sister Caterina welcomed them. The man, keeping his knife hidden, said, "I want to see Patrizu Nieddu. Bring me to him."

In a sympathetic voice, the nun said, "I'm sorry, but Signor Nieddu is gone."

"Gone where?"

"He did not say. He didn't even tell us he was leaving, he just disappeared."

The man pulled Nico to the side, away from the doorway. In a rough voice, he said, "You asked my name. I am Bertu Fenu. I own a warehouse on Sardinia. Nieddu worked for me. I gave the bastard a job, and he paid me back by assaulting my daughter. She was a lovely, innocent child, and now she's pregnant. Her life will never be the same. I tracked the wretched rapist from Sardinia to Florence. To claim vengeance for my daughter's honor, I'll follow the bastard, to Hades if I must, until I find him. Then he will pay." Fenu muttered something under his breath, then turned and stormed away.

21

Vanni rode into camp on a wagon piled high with wood. He wished that he could have gone with the seasoned mercenaries and recent recruits to raid the nearby village, but he and the other recruits had to take turns doing chores. His assignment today was to help with the cooking. He had already gathered an ample supply of wood for the cooking fire. Later, he would help the chief cook butcher and roast the animals taken in the raid. They all welcomed fresh meat, with lamb and pork being everyone's favorites.

Although Vanni missed the chance to go on that raid, he had gotten a swordsmanship lesson earlier in the day from one of the most experienced mercenaries. They practiced for an hour, his mentor pressuring him relentlessly, coming at him repeatedly and slashing fiercely. Only once was Vanni's sword knocked out of his hand. When the lesson ended, his teacher said, "I fought men in Urbino who didn't handle the blade as well as you."

Vanni recalled that praise over and over while he was gathering wood, and each time the memory made him smile. "How long before I am ready for battle?" he had asked.

"Don't worry, boy. Your time will come soon enough."

Vanni had nearly finished unloading wood from the wagon when he heard the sound of hooves hitting the ground. The raiders were returning. He had no doubts that the raid was successful. The only question was what booty had been taken.

Horses entered the camp single file on a narrow path cut through the dense forest. Captain Attendolo led the column, followed by riders whose horses carried animal carcasses and sacks of grain. Vanni counted at least four piglets already dressed and ready for butchering. The next four horses each carried two riders: a mercenary and behind him a boy taken from the village.

When the new boys dismounted, they huddled together like lost lambs with blank expressions too disoriented to show even fear. Vanni focused his attention on one boy with a baby face, curly hair, and puffy cheeks. The boy reminded Vanni of his younger brother. Would they have taken someone so young?

Attendolo's lieutenant led the boys toward a circle of benches in the middle of the camp. They sat while he paced behind them, instructing them in the rules they must follow, what they must do, what they must not do, and the punishment that awaited them if they disobeyed. His lecture brought the boys close to tears. This talk was known among the mercenaries as the vinegar talk. Next would come the honey talk delivered by a recent recruit to tell the boys how wonderful their lives will be as mercenaries. Vanni would never forget the time he had endured the vinegar and honey talks.

"Vanni," a forceful voice called from behind him. He turned to face Captain Attendolo. Vanni's hands trembled. Had he done something wrong? "Go tell your story to the new recruits."

"Sir, I'm supposed to help with the cooking."

"Another recruit will help the cook."

Vanni knew that he might be called upon one day to give the honey talk, but he expected that he would have had more time to prepare. He set down the last armful of wood unloaded from the wagon, ran to his tent, changed his clothes, brushed his hair, and then hurried to the indoctrination circle. He reached the circle just as the lieutenant finished delivering his rant and walked away, leaving the four boys on the verge of tears.

Vanni stepped into the circle. Unlike the lieutenant, Vanni sat on a bench facing the others. His purpose was to gain trust, not to intimidate. "Four weeks ago, I sat in your place as a new member of this family," he began. "Since then, I've had adventures beyond my dreams. I've seen a world that I couldn't have imagined."

Vanni spread his hands. "These men have become my brothers. They promised that I would learn skills that would make me the envy of any man, and they kept that promise. They taught me to fight hand-to-hand and with a blade." As he tapped the scabbard hanging from his belt, he scanned the group and found the boys' attention locked on his every word.

"Two weeks past, I accompanied two *compagni* to buy weapons from an armorer in Bologna. I could hardly believe it. Bologna is at least one hundred times larger than my father's village. Buildings there rise higher than the tallest trees in the forest." He withdrew his sword from its scabbard. "I was allowed to choose this sword as my own from all that the armorer had to offer.

"We ate at one of Bologna's fine restaurants. All the women wore fancy dresses, and the men wore stylish tunics. I felt foolish because I wore a peasant smock," Vanni gestured at the boys, "like yours. My *compagni* saw my worry and bought me this tunic." He ran a hand down the front of his tunic, fine fabric, light blue like the morning sky. "They said Attendolo's men must have style."

One boy found the courage to ask a question. "Do you miss your mother and father?"

"Sometimes I think of them and my brother, but I have come to realize that our lives were unusual. Only in small villages do boys grow into men in the homes of their fathers. In towns and cities, boys our age leave home to apprentice with craftsmen, to go to school, or to join the army. I sent a letter to my father to let him know that I am happy with my new life. Someday I may visit him, but I do not want to go back and live in his village."

One of the mercenaries stepped into the circle and faced the boys. "Now I will show you to your quarters." As he passed Vanni, he said quietly, "You did well." The boys rose and followed him toward a row of tents.

Vanni sat alone after the others departed. *Do I miss my parents? What a foolish question. Every night when I close my eyes, I see my mother's smile.*

22

Nico departed on the two-day journey to Bologna early the following morning. Thankfully, he had pleasant weather with a clear blue sky and a light, refreshing breeze. It had been barely eight months since he had last traveled the Via Flaminia Minor, the most direct road between Florence and Bologna. On that occasion he had been headed in the opposite direction, returning to Florence after his university graduation.

His mount had no difficulty flowing along with other travelers on the road, so Nico let his mind recall professors and fellow students. He hoped to find time to visit with Simone Pisani, a student from Venice who had become a close friend during Nico's time at the university. By Nico's reckoning, Simone should be in his final term and preparing for graduation in a few months. Nico wondered whether Simone would be joining a law firm or taking a position in the Venetian government upon graduation. Simone's father held an important position in the Venetian ruling council. That influence, coupled with Simone's accomplishments at the university, would surely open many opportunities for the soon-to-be lawyer.

A full day of riding took Nico to the Castrum Inn in the town of

Firenzuola, high up in the Futa Pass of the Apennine Mountains approximately midway between Florence and Bologna. The inn took its name from the town's signature building, a fortress built a century earlier to defend the northern territory of the Florentine Republic.

Nico left his horse with a girl at a nearby livery. Skeptical at first that the young girl knew how to care for the animal, he watched as she deftly removed the saddle and watered the horse. She must have been the owner's daughter, he decided, because despite her obvious abilities, no one else would hire such a young girl to work in a livery.

Nico rented one of the eight rooms for travelers on the Castrum Inn's upper level. His room had only enough space for a bed, a small table, and a place to hold his duffel. Nico tested the bed and found, as he expected, that its thin pad afforded little cushioning. "It will do for one night," he told himself.

The room had no facility for bathing, only a large wash basin. Nico filled the basin from a pail of water given to him by the innkeeper and proceeded to wash away the layer of road dust and grime he had accumulated on the journey from Florence. He shivered at the first splash of icy cold water drawn from the stream behind the inn. He donned a clean tunic and went to the dining area on the inn's lower level.

Three dining tables were occupied by men who wore blank expressions and moved slowly, as though drained of all energy from a long day in the saddle. At another table, an older man gave a courteous smile as Nico entered the room. He wore a clean tunic of fine silk, reflecting an elevated social status. Rather than dine by himself, Nico walked to the man's table and asked, "Do you prefer to dine alone, or may I join you?"

The man's eyes brightened. "Pleasant company is always welcome at my table, young man." He gestured to a chair across the table. "Are you traveling toward Bologna or Florence?"

"Bologna," Nico replied. Then, recalling the pretense for his journey, he added, "The magistrates' guild in Florence has asked me to assess one of the students in the law school at the university."

"Then you are a lawyer. A Florentine? Is this your first visit to Bologna?"

"You are correct on two points. I am a lawyer and a Florentine, but this is not my first time in Bologna. I graduated from the University of Bologna one year past. I never thought I would be back in Bologna so soon."

"Ah, it is good to meet another Florentine. I too am a Florentine although I've spent the past year here in Bologna as an agent of the Bardi bank. Bologna is a fine city, but I miss Florence. I'm eager to return home. Tell me, has it been a good year in Florence?"

"It's been uneventful," Nico replied, then he laughed inwardly as he thought about his own experiences: facing one assassin in Siena and another in Milan.

Their conversation was interrupted briefly by a server who brought Nico a glass of wine and a plate of pasta, the first course of the dinner of the day.

Nico said, "You seem in good spirits, so I trust the reason for your return to Florence is for a favorable purpose."

"Indeed it is. The Palazzo Communale, which houses the government offices in Bologna, is to be refurbished. It is a major project in the hands of a noted architect, and I have secured the financing arrangements for the project on behalf of the Bardi bank. I would ask you to share a bottle of fine wine with me in celebration." The man lifted his wine glass. "Unfortunately, the inn has nothing other than this barely passable house wine."

"I expect my mission to Bologna will be brief," Nico said. "We can celebrate your success when I return to Florence."

"I'll look forward to that," the banker said. Then he drained his glass, signaled the server for a refill, and shifted the conversation. "At the time of Cosimo de Medici's death, rumors circulated in Bologna that Florence was in turmoil. I am pleased to learn that those rumors proved false."

"Our republic is resilient. Cosimo's death was unsettling, but calling it turmoil would be an exaggeration. The sun still traverses the sky and the Signoria still governs." Nico took a sip of wine, tasted the pasta, then asked, "What am I likely to encounter in Bologna?"

The banker leaned back in his chair. "Ah, you will find Bologna to be a bit more complicated. The Province of Bologna is a Papal State, so in principle it is governed by a Papal Legate. But in some respects, the legate is little more than a figurehead. The legate has power outside the city, but within Bologna itself, there is a governing body called the *Reformatori*. Sixteen members of that body are loyal supporters of the Bentivoglio family. They constitute the true power in Bologna. Giovanni Bentivoglio, the family's patriarch, wields control in Bologna, just as the Medici family does in Florence. Giovanni is young and has been the family head for only a short time. He expends most of his energy establishing new monuments, so he rarely becomes involved in the matters of daily life. He ignores activities that do not threaten his power."

Although Nico knew how Bologna's government was organized from his time at the university, he found the other comments enlightening. He decided to take advantage of his companion's knowledge. "No rumors of difficulties in Bologna have reached Florence, so can I assume there are no threats of concern to the Bentivoglio family?"

The banker's brow furrowed in surprise at Nico's mention of threats. "Threats are not aired in public," he replied. Then he lowered his voice and continued, "Many years past, Giovanni Bentivoglio's father was assassinated. Those known to be involved in the assassination were killed or exiled, but some of the opponents escaped identification. Recently, I heard it whispered that there is new opposition to the Bentivoglios, being financed by a foreigner." He spread his hands and smiled thinly. "But who can say? We bankers hear many stories, and few of them are more than fabrications."

Nico could tell from the man's expression that the banker was uneasy, so he did not press further. The remainder of their conversation centered on Nico's experiences at the university.

23

Nico arrived at Bologna in mid-afternoon and left his mount at a stable outside the city. "I have business at the university and at the government offices. Can you recommend an inn convenient to both?" he asked the stable boy.

"I don't know. Wait here," the boy replied. He tethered Nico's horse and walked out of sight behind the stable.

Moments later, a broad-shouldered man wearing a heavy apron and carrying a pair of tongs came around the side of stable. "The boy said you need an inn."

Nico clarified his request. "Preferably one located between the university and the center of the city, if possible."

The man's eyes swept Nico from head to foot. Dust in Nico's hair and clinging to his tunic suggested that he had just completed a long ride, but beneath the dirt, his clothes showed him to be a person of respectable standing. "Many gentlemen choose the inn on Via San Donato. Go through the city gate, then straight. The inn is on the left. I don't recall its name, but it has a sign with a picture of a duck." The man turned away without waiting for a response.

∼

Unlike his austere room in Firenzuola the previous night, his spacious room at the Yellow Duck Inn had a wardrobe for his clothes, a desk and chair, and a lantern mounted on the wall next to the bed. The bed had a thick pad with a soft covering and a heavy blanket. A servant carrying a bucket of water followed Nico to the room and filled his washbasin. "Can I get you anything else?" the servant asked.

"Nothing now," Nico replied.

The helpful servant added, "The inn does not have a dining area, but there are many fine restaurants nearby. The trattoria across the road is popular with our guests."

Nico washed, changed into clean clothes, and walked to the university. The sight of familiar buildings revived fond memories of his years as a student. The clock in the central piazza told him that the afternoon law lectures would be ending shortly. Law students had a long-standing tradition of ending each day with a brief visit to a nearby tavern before starting their evening of study. Nico had the address where Gerhard Ritter, the student he was sent to interview, was rooming with other students. To save time, Nico opted to visit the tavern favored by law students in hopes that Gerhard would be there with his classmates.

Not surprisingly, the interior of the tavern had not changed since his last visit. It had probably remained unchanged for decades, except for the list tacked to the wall behind the bar. The list grew whenever the names were added of students who successfully met the challenge of downing a gladiator-sized mug of beer within a prescribed time. Nico recalled the time that one of his classmates accepted the challenge. Everyone in the tavern cheered and goaded him to finish. He took the last swig, but before he could swallow it, he dropped the giant mug and raced out into the street, where he regurgitated the entire contents of the mug onto the cobblestones.

Nico positioned himself against a wall near the door so he could listen to students as they entered. If Gerhard came with other

Austrian students, there was a chance that they might be conversing in a German dialect. Nico didn't speak German, but he felt that he could distinguish it from Italian or Latin.

When the door swung open, a steady stream of young men funneled in. The barkeep had anticipated the crowd and lined the bar with mugs filled with beer. Students filed past the bar, took a mug, and dropped a coin in its place. Although Nico had participated in that parade many times when he was a student, this was the first time he had witnessed it as an observer. He became so engrossed in the nearly theatrical display that he failed to notice if any of the entering students were speaking German.

Once the students were seated, Nico meandered past tables to hear whether German was being spoken at one of the tables, but he found all were speaking Italian, although not all spoke the language fluently. He was about to abandon the tactic when one student turned quickly. His elbow swiped against a book, sending it skidding across the table and onto the floor. "Scheisse!" the student exclaimed. Nico had heard that word often from two Austrian students when he was at the university.

Nico approached the table. "Scusa, might one of you be Gerhard Ritter?"

Heads turned toward one member of their group, who looked up at the questioner apprehensively. Realizing that he must be Gerhard Ritter, Nico declared, "You will be graduating soon. I would like to discuss an opportunity with you." Ritter sat wide-eyed and said nothing. "Can you meet me for dinner later?" Nico asked. Overwhelmed by the stranger's request, Ritter simply nodded slowly.

Nico named one of Bologna's finer restaurants only a short distance from the university. "Do you know it?" Again, Gerhard nodded. Although he was puzzled by the unusual request, Gerhard assumed that at the very least he would be treated to a good meal. Nico exited the tavern, leaving Gerhard and his friends to speculate on the nature of the opportunity.

During his time at the university, Nico and his roommates had cooked most of their own meals. On special occasions, such as the end of exam periods, they celebrated by treating themselves to dinner at a nearby restaurant. However, none of those restaurants compared to the one Nico had chosen for dinner with Gerhard. He was greeted at the door by a server who escorted him to a table covered with a white cloth and flanked by chairs with padded leather seats. Nico had heard that table coverings were favored by French nobles, but he had never seen them before in Italy.

The server announced, "The dinner specialty today is wild boar sausage with balsamic glazed onions. And we have a delicate Valpolicella wine from the Veneto, which is an excellent complement." Nico accepted the server's wine recommendation but waited to order food until Gerhard arrived. Several other patrons had arrived and were seated before the lanky Austrian student stepped hesitantly through the doorway. His eyes scanned the room, absorbing the elegant surroundings and searching for Nico. The server, cued by Nico's instructions, led Gerhard to Nico's table.

Nico introduced himself as he poured a glass of wine for his guest; then he explained, "The magistrates guild believes that Florence can benefit from the diverse perspectives of people from other nations, so they follow the academic achievements of students at Bologna law school. I am here at the guild's behest to invite you to Florence when you graduate from the university."

"Are you a guild officer?"

Nico held his tongue while the server brought plates of the wild boar specialty. The savory aroma sent both men reaching for their knives and spoons. Nico tasted the delicacy then replied, "No. I am a guild member, but not an officer. I graduated from the law school one year past, so the guild consuls thought it would be appropriate for me to speak with you."

"You traveled all the way from Florence to Bologna just to speak with me?"

"That is one reason for coming here. I have other business in Bologna as well." Rather than continue talking about himself, Nico shifted the conversation to the purpose of their meeting. "Earlier, I mentioned possible opportunities for you in Florence. We understand that you favor mercantile law. As you know, there is no larger center for trade and commerce than Florence. We have a mercantile court devoted exclusively to resolving trade disputes involving both Florentine and international merchants."

Gerhard listened as he ate, but his expression showed that Nico's words did not excite him. To probe for Gerhard's lack of enthusiasm, Nico said, "You are from Austria. Are you obligated to return to Austria upon graduation?"

"Not at all. The practice of law in Austria is..." Gerhard searched for a word. "Predictable. "All important decisions are made by the ruling House of Hapsburg. The only excitement comes from occasional rivalries between family members, such as the recent conflict between Frederick and his brother Albert. I would like to practice law in a more fluid environment.

"However, my preference isn't mercantile law. That seemed attractive when I enrolled in the university, but in the past six years, my eyes have been opened to other possibilities. I now appreciate the legal challenges presented by the complex relationships between Italian states. That is the area of legal practice I find most exciting." Gerhard cut into another sausage link, then asked, "What is the legal specialty of your firm?"

Nico ran a finger around the rim of his wine glass as he composed his answer. He found no reason to withhold the truth. "I am not employed by a private firm. In addition to private law firms, Florence has many government commissions. I am a member of the Florentine Security Commission."

Gerhard's eyes widened. "Here at the university, we've been told that Italian states have been at peace since the signing of the Treaty of Lodi. Is that not so? Why does Florence have a security commission?"

"The Italian states hold to the treaty, but other forces are not bound by the treaty."

Gerhard responded quickly, almost finishing Nico's thought. "Such as mercenaries." Then he asked, "Is it the mercenaries that bring you to Bologna?"

Nico stiffened. "What makes you ask about mercenaries?"

"I overheard one of my professors telling another about a mercenary band active in the Province of Bologna."

"Do you recall what was said?"

"I only heard a brief comment as I walked past. He called them renegades."

Nico felt he could no longer keep his true purpose a secret. "Another reason I am in Bologna is to understand the intent of those renegade mercenaries. If the professor has information about the mercenaries, I would like to speak with him."

"A discussion about renegade mercenaries spurred by someone sent from Florence sounds intriguing. I'd like to listen to that conversation, but if I give you the professor's name, you would speak to him alone and I wouldn't be included." Gerhard's expression evolved into a smirk. "I might get a better appreciation for the concerns of Florence if I were to join the meeting. I can introduce you to the professor tomorrow after the afternoon lecture classes."

"You're a clever fellow. I can understand why the magistrates' guild is eager to bring you to Florence."

24

Morning sunlight illuminated the shops along Via San Donato as Nico headed to the palazzo that held the offices of the government officials and the Papal Legate. He paused outside to admire the imposing building that extended the full width of Bologna's central square. Atop the two-hundred-year-old structure, workers were completing the construction of a new bell tower. "It's already more than twice the size of our Palazzo della Signoria and they're still adding to it," Nico said to himself.

Nico climbed wide stone steps to the building's second level. His footsteps echoed in the cavernous space that was eerily quiet for a building that held all the important government offices. Two corridors led away from the second level landing. A small sign and a crucifix indicated which corridor led to the papal offices. Nico stopped at the first office where a priest was writing in a ledger. When the priest saw Nico, he set down his pen, looked up, and asked, "How may I help you, my son?"

"I have a message for the Papal Legate from the Archbishop of Florence."

The priest's eyes narrowed as he considered Nico's statement.

Never in his memory had there been direct communication between the Archbishop of Florence and the Papal Legate in Bologna, but the priest's concern eased when he noticed that the envelope Nico carried bore the seal of the Florentine archbishop. "The legate has been called to Rome."

"Is there a delegate that I can speak with?" Nico asked.

"Yes, Cardinal Capranica was sent by Rome to act as Vice Legate. I can see that your message is delivered to him."

"It would be better if I were to deliver the message personally. I have knowledge of the matter, so I can elaborate should His Eminence have any questions."

The priest slid his chair back from the desk. He grimaced as he pushed himself up and took hold of an old wooden staff for support. "Come with me," he said and hobbled out of the office.

Nico followed him to the end of the corridor, where the priest tapped on a closed door. A voice inside the room bid them to enter. With effort, the priest pushed the door open and announced, "Eminence, this gentleman bears a message from the Archbishop of Florence."

Peering in from the hallway, Nico saw a man seated behind an oversize desk. He wore a scarlet mozzetta marking him as a cardinal of the church. His pale skin, unusual for a Roman, contrasted with the intense color of his clothing. A priest wearing a simple black cassock stood at the far side of the desk. He had a thin face, dark eyes, and a pointed Roman nose.

The cardinal looked up from the document he had been reading and motioned for his visitor to enter. Nico approached the desk, dipped his head respectfully, and held out the archbishop's message. "Your Eminence, my name is Nico Argenti. The archbishop of Florence requested that I deliver this message to you."

The cardinal gestured for Nico to be seated. The chair creaked as Nico lowered himself into it. "Fear not, my son. The chair creaks the same when it holds Father Giuseppe, whose weight is at least twice yours. But it also creaks when bearing Sister Caterina, who can't weigh more than a bundle of feathers."

The cardinal took the envelope from Nico's outstretched hand and read the letter. He inhaled deeply, air whistling through his teeth, when he reached the statement that mercenaries were conscripting young boys. He looked up at Nico. "You have knowledge of these mercenaries?" he asked.

"I have not seen them myself, Your Eminence. I visited the village of Case del Monte, where two boys were taken. I spoke with villagers who described the raid and the abductions."

"Case del Monte," the cardinal echoed; then he reflected for a moment. "I do not know that name, but I assume the archbishop is bringing this matter to my attention because the village is in the Province of Bologna."

Nico nodded. "Yes, the village is in Bologna. It was just by chance that a report of the attack reached Florence. A monk visiting a nearby abbey heard about the incident. When the monk returned to Florence, he reported it to the archbishop."

The cardinal's eyes narrowed. "It was not chance. the Lord leaves nothing to chance. The report came because the Lord willed it." Nico reddened slightly at the cardinal's rebuke. "What is your connection to the archbishop?" the cardinal asked.

Nico regained his composure and replied, "I am a member of the Florentine Security Commission. The archbishop informed the Florentine government of the attack, and members of the Signoria became concerned that a rogue mercenary band in the mountains might cross the border and prey on Florentine villages. We know of only one village being attacked, but conceivably others have been as well. If that is so, we thought reports of the attacks might have reached Bologna."

"I have not heard of rogue mercenaries operating in the Province of Bologna, but that is not surprising since contact with villages in the mountains is infrequent."

The cardinal gestured toward a priest, who had been working

quietly at a desk across the room and listening intently to the conversation. "Father Alfonso is the secretary to the Papal Legate. I have been in Bologna for less than one year, but Father Alfonso was born here. I've come to believe that he knows nearly everyone in the province, from the unfortunates who roam the alleys at night to members of the most respected families. He can make inquiries among his contacts to learn whether any other villages have been raided."

Upon hearing the reference to him, the priest looked up and assessed the visitor, but said nothing.

Cardinal Capranica glanced down again at the letter before continuing. Then he said, "Unprovoked attacks on villages and the abduction of innocent children are unholy acts; however, my ability to deal with them is limited. The only means at my disposal is the Papal Army, and the detachment normally assigned to Bologna is temporarily occupied in the south. I am certain that the army's Captain General, whom they are serving, will view this matter as minor compared to the hostilities he is facing."

Nico said, "But there is also the city's governing body, the Reformatori. Surely they must not want mercenaries operating within the province."

"Traditionally, the Reformatori concern themselves only with matters inside the city. If I were to ask them for assistance…" Seized by a lingering frustration, the cardinal stopped speaking abruptly and threw up his hands. "The Reformatori do not always give credence to findings and petitions from this office, even when our evidence is strong. In this instance, there is only a letter from a foreign bishop and hearsay from distant villagers. If I were to bring this matter to the Reformatori with only that meager evidence, they would not be persuaded to act."

With a hint of desperation in his voice, Nico asked, "Does Bologna have a defense force other than the Papal Army?"

"The patriarch of the city's leading family, Giovanni Bentivoglio, has his own mercenary band. He claims that it provides for the city's defense, although in truth its loyalty is to the Bentivoglio family."

Nico bit his lip as he digested the cardinal's statement. Seeing his reaction, the Cardinal said, "I sense you are wondering whether it might be Bentivoglio's mercenaries who are raiding the villages. I am confident that is not so. His mercenaries are generously supported by tax levies and there are men eagerly waiting to join his force. They have no reason to attack villages and abduct boys.

"I've been invited to attend a birthday celebration this evening for Giovanni's wife. If you wish, you can attend with me and form your own opinion of Giovanni Bentivoglio."

Nico's blank expression reflected his skepticism. "But I haven't been invited."

"That's not an impediment. Giovanni is a great admirer of Florence. He will consider it an honor to have a Florentine envoy attend the celebration."

Nico glanced down at his plain tunic and scuffed shoes. "I don't have clothing suitable for a formal event." He brushed a hand through his hair. "And I'll need to visit a barber."

Cardinal Capranica waved a hand to dismiss Nico's concerns. "Father Alfonso can help you with those matters." He managed to suppress a smile while adding, "Members of the Reformatori are sure to be in attendance. You will find their behavior enlightening."

The comment about the Reformatori's behavior piqued Nico's interest, but instead of asking for clarification, he returned to the discussion of the mercenaries and said, "You mentioned that Bentivoglio's men are funded by tax levies. The rogue mercenaries must also have a source of funds."

The cardinal said, "There are those in Bologna who do not admire the Bentivoglio. They are jealous of that family's power and influence, but I have seen no indication that they would entertain violence against the Bentivoglio family or papal authority." He rubbed his chin and added, "And I doubt there are any other families in Bologna wealthy enough to fund a mercenary army. Such wealth exists in Florence and Venice, but not here."

Capranica's mention of Venice triggered an idea in Nico's mind.

"Recently, the Florentine ambassador in Venice informed us that two Florentine exiles who had been living in Venice for many years have recently left that city. We don't know their reason for leaving or where they went."

The cardinal shrugged. "Florence has exiled many. I don't recall the names of all those it has cast aside."

"The ones who left Venice recently are two brothers, members of the Strozzi family," Nico explained. "They were prosperous bankers who were forced to leave Florence after a bitter feud with Cosimo de Medici. They left with their wealth intact, so they certainly have ample resources to finance a mercenary band. The family split, with some members going as far as Naples. The two brothers went to Venice. From their behavior in Venice, it is clear they are still seeking retribution against the Medici family."

Cardinal Capranica said, "I have not heard the name Strozzi mentioned. Do you have reason to believe the brothers are in Bologna?"

"We have no reports suggesting that the Strozzi brothers are here, but it's possible. You may not have heard of them because if they are indeed in Bologna, they might not want their presence known. They might have cohorts in Bologna who are protecting them."

Father Alfonso spoke for the first time. "There are those in Bologna who regard the Florentine Republic's influence here as interference. They would welcome opponents of the Medici."

The priest's comment surprised Nico. Momentarily, they locked eyes, but Nico broke contact when the cardinal said, "If the Strozzi brothers are in Bologna, they might try to remain hidden; however, little happens in Bologna that escapes Father Alfonso's sources. He should be able to discover whether the brothers are here. Give the good father time to approach his sources; then we can discuss this matter further.

Nico rose to leave, his head bent in disappointment. Although Cardinal Capranica was sympathetic to Nico's plea, the cardinal had little information to offer and limited ability to act. Nico descended the stone steps to the piazza. The cool morning air did little to restore his spirit. Must there be raids on more villages before action is taken? Will it take groups of villagers coming to the city and pleading for help before someone confronts the mercenaries?

∼

Several hours remained until afternoon lecture classes would end and Nico could meet with Gerhard Ritter, the student whose professor might have knowledge of mercenaries operating in Bologna. Nico chose to use the time to wander through the streets that comprised the Mercato di Mezzo, the city's bustling central market. Butcher shops and fishmonger shops lined the streets while wagons displayed produce from farms in the fertile Po River valley.

Nico took comfort in seeing that the market had not changed since he shopped there as a student looking for bargains in second grade produce. Even the pungent fish aromas and the earthy scents of fresh vegetables brought back pleasant memories. Nico's favorite was the yeasty scent at the lone shop that sold bread and other baked goods. Its items came from a bakery in the San Felice district, far from the city center. As a student, Nico discovered that the shop owner was willing to drop prices significantly at the end of the day. Taking that cue, Nico began bargaining with other shop owners at day's end. While women flocked to the market early in search of the freshest items, Nico had shopped late in the day to get the best prices.

Men who worked in the market were common folk. They dressed in loose smocks and had long, often uncombed hair. Nico's attention was drawn to a man who stood out from the others. He wore a clean, stylish tunic and had well-groomed hair. The man's profile resembled that of Patrizu Nieddu, the Florentine orphanage administrator who had fled the city to avoid prosecution for improper management.

Did the man catch a glimpse of Nico and quicken his pace, or was it merely Nico's imagination? Curious to know whether the man was indeed Patrizu Nieddu, Nico gave chase. He ran through the market, threading his way past a group of women at a fruit stand. As he got close enough to confirm that it was indeed Nieddu, he collided with a woman's basket, scattering vegetables onto the ground. Nico stopped to apologize and to retrieve the vegetables. By then, Nieddu had disappeared around a corner. Nico leaned against a wall to catch his breath.

Although Nico had no proof that Neiddu had found another position to exploit here in Bologna, he now had good reason to investigate that possibility. Unlike Florence, where the Signoria appointed orphanage overseers, Nico recalled that a group of laymen called the Company of Angels supervised Bologna's orphans. Nico felt certain he would have no difficulty finding one of the Angels.

Nico's enthusiasm cooled when he considered how many issues were already competing for his attention: rogue mercenaries, the Strozzi brothers, and the law student Gerhard Ritter. Yet he couldn't dismiss the fact that he had seen Patrizu Nieddu. Nieddu was a criminal who mistreated children in Florence. Nico knew his sister Alessa would never forgive him if he allowed Nieddu to do the same in Bologna. Back in his room at the inn, he penned a letter.

> Vittorio,
>
> Patrizu Nieddu is in Bologna. I spotted him in the central market, but before I could confront him, he escaped through the crowd. He fled from Florence before he could be prosecuted for his crimes. I intend to make sure he can't flee again if he is using the same scheme here in Bologna. But first I need to find him and that would be easier with the help of a talented investigator.
>
> Nico

Vesper bells from nearby San Martino church echoed through the streets when Nico and Cardinal Capranica arrived at Palazzo

Bentivoglio. A servant directed them to the courtyard, where the celebration was underway. The sound of a spirited tune filling the air drew Nico's attention to a young girl who was singing and dancing to the music. "The girl is Constanza," the cardinal explained. "She is Giovanni's wife's daughter by a previous marriage." He sighed. "It can be a struggle to remember their relationships. The young man at the far end of the courtyard surrounded by others, that is Giovanni."

"He's young," a surprised Nico observed.

"Yes, he's near your age. He became the first citizen of Bologna two years past when his cousin died."

"First citizen," Nico echoed. "I didn't think that title had been used since Roman Times."

"Here in Bologna, it's not an official title. It's a recognition of the Bentivoglio family's influence in the local government, much like the Medici have in your home city. The men crowded around Giovanni are members of the Reformatori. As you can tell from their solicitous behavior, they maintain their status by pleasing Giovanni."

"Like piglets suckling a sow," Nico said as he watched one man move closer to Giovanni by using an elbow to nudge another man aside. Nico's analogy brought forth a snicker from the cardinal.

Across the courtyard, another group of men clustered around a row of tables laden with an assortment of food items ranging from roast pheasant to creamy desserts. Following Nico's gaze, Capranica said, "Those are businessmen. Some already have dealings with the Bentivoglio family; others are hoping to secure arrangements in the future."

"Why aren't *they* crowded around Signor Bentivoglio?"

"They've learned that Giovanni never discusses business at his celebrations. They attend to show devotion... and to maintain their waistlines by partaking of his delicious fare."

Nico returned his gaze to Giovanni and his minions in time to see a man come out of the palazzo, force his way through the flock, and whisper something into the leader's ear. Even though Giovanni was across the courtyard, Nico noticed his frown as he jostled free from his followers and stomped into the palazzo.

With Giovanni gone, his disciples dispersed, some going to the food tables, some talking in small groups, and others wandering aimlessly. None paid attention to Giovanni's wife even though the celebration was being held in her honor.

"Come with me," the cardinal said, and with Nico following behind, he crossed the courtyard to where the woman stood alone, watching her daughter dancing happily.

She caught a glimpse of the cardinal as he approached. "Your Eminence, I am pleased that you are able to join us."

The cardinal offered his hand to the woman. "I wish to offer my blessing as you begin your twenty-fifth year. May the Lord grant that your future years are even more bountiful than those of your past."

She took the cardinal's hand, bowed her head, and replied simply, "Your Eminence is most kind."

When she looked up, the cardinal said, "May I present Messer Nico Argenti, an envoy of the Republic of Florence."

Her eyes brightened, and she began a lengthy conversation, asking Nico about news of Florence. Nico explained that he looked forward to visiting the city as soon as his official duties permitted. Strangely, at least in Nico's mind, she did not ask about Nico's mission in Bologna.

25

Nico waited for Gerhard Ritter outside the Palazzo dei Notai where law school lectures were held. Moments after the end of afternoon lecture sessions, students began streaming out of the building. Some moved slowly, drained by sitting through the long lectures. Nico understood their fatigue having himself sat through intense lectures day after day during his six years at the university. He watched the mass of students heading toward nearby taverns. Nico also recalled how, almost mystically, a mug of beer had restored his energy. At the time, he had never viewed the trek from lecture hall to tavern as a ritual; now, watching the parade of other students, he found it amusing.

From behind him, Gerhard Ritter called, "Messer Argenti."

Nico turned. The tall, slender Austrian student walked toward him so gracefully that he almost seemed to be floating. "Since we are not meeting to discuss a legal matter, it would be more fitting for you to call me Nico."

Nico expected that they would be meeting with the professor at the law school building; instead, Gerhard began walking in the opposite direction. Nico said, "I understood we were going to meet one of your professors."

"A professor, yes, but not one of mine. He is a professor of canon law. I heard him speaking with another professor in the library. That is when he mentioned mercenaries. He does research in the library every afternoon, so we can meet with him there."

Inside the library, Gerhard scanned the reading room; then he pointed to a man sitting alone at a table in an alcove. "There he is."

The professor was taking notes from books spread across the table. His dark hair and smooth skin showed him to be younger than most professors. Without considering that he was interrupting the professor, Gerhard approached the table and spoke in Latin. "Professor Allard, may I present Messer Nico Argenti? He is here from Florence on important business."

The professor looked up from his notes, both confused and intrigued why a student whom he did not know was introducing him to a Florentine lawyer.

Following Gerhard's lead, Nico also spoke in Latin. "I apologize for our intrusion, professor. Would you grant me a few moments of your time?"

The professor nodded and gestured for the two men to be seated. "Unless you are here to discuss ancient Romans, we can converse in Italian." The professor spoke Italian without difficulty, although his words had the nasal quality of a native French speaker.

As Nico looked down to pull out a chair, he noticed that the books on the table contained treatises on philosophy and humanism. Of all the required courses in the law school program, philosophy was Nico's least favorite. He found the subject to be nebulous and opinionated. One philosopher would propose a concept, another would put forth a contradictory theory, and philosophy professors happily accepted and taught both inconsistent ideas. Nico preferred law courses that dealt with facts and evidence.

Seeing Nico's apparent surprise, the professor asked, "Is something wrong?"

"I was told that you were a professor of canon law, and I haven't known any law professors to have such a great interest in philosophy."

"Your source is misinformed, but the error is understandable. Two of my close friends who come from the same region in France teach in the college of canon law. I enjoy their company, so we often spend time together, although I am often the source of their amusement. They scoff at my chosen path, saying that philosophy, the oeuvre of Socrates and Plato, is but a nebulous and opinionated art." Nico struggled to keep from laughing at hearing of his own thoughts echoed. "Now that you know my credentials, tell me, how can I be of service? If it is religious discourse that you seek, I can only refer you to one of my colleagues."

"I graduated from the law school one year past and I never chanced to have you as one of my philosophy lecturers."

"From your dress, I presume your course of study was civil law. Most of my lectures are purposed for students of canon law."

Nico observed the professor spinning his pen between his fingers, so he ended the banter, saying, "I was told that you have information about a rogue band of mercenaries operating in Bologna."

The professor set his pen down on the table and leaned back in his chair. "And why does a Florentine lawyer come to Bologna to inquire whether mercenaries are operating in the province?"

"Officials in Florence are worried that the rogues might move across the border into the Florentine Republic."

The professor picked up his pen, dipped it in ink, and drew a line across a page in his notebook. For a long moment, he studied the line while he considered how to respond. Nico wondered whether the professor somehow saw the line as relating to their conversation. Philosophers had their own way of connecting disjoint topics. At length, Allard said, "Your statement is perplexing. If Florentine officials believe Bologna is hosting mercenaries who could pose a threat to Florence, they would send an army, or at least an envoy, to meet with the Papal Governor, the legate. They wouldn't send a lawyer to question a philosopher."

Nico held out the letter that named him as a member of the Florentine Security Commission. "I did speak with the Vice Legate, Cardinal Capranica; however, he had no knowledge of the mercenaries, so I am exploring other sources for information."

The professor pointed at Gerhard. "And this student led you to me?"

"I overheard you mention mercenaries," Gerhard explained.

In a stiff voice, Professor Allard snapped, "Students are better served by studying than by eavesdropping on others."

Gerhard dropped his hands into his lap and leaned away from the table. Now it was Nico who grew impatient. "The mercenaries are abducting boys as recruits," he said forcefully.

That revelation startled both Gerhard and the professor, who asked, "Do you know this to be true?"

"I spoke with the parents of a boy who was taken."

"Slavery is a crime in the Papal States. The mercenaries can be prosecuted if they are holding the boys captive."

Nico thought back to his conversation with the boy whose friend had been taken. The boy said his friend often spoke about wanting to leave his village. Would a boy like that be willing to testify? Nico shook his head. "To prove a case of slavery, I need to find a boy willing to testify that he is being held against his will, and to do that, I first need to find the mercenaries and their sponsors." He leaned forward, rested his elbows on the table and repeated, "I was told you have information about the mercenaries. Do you?"

Allard leaned back in his chair. "Work being done recently in San Procolo church caused damage to the beautiful altarpiece that depicts the martyrdom of Saint Procolus. As a member of the church council, I was the one who arranged for repairs by the carpenter who had built the altarpiece. The carpenter is the one who mentioned mercenaries."

"Do you recall what he said?" Nico asked.

"At first, I thought he was speaking of Giovanni Bentivoglio's men, so I didn't give his words my attention. Bentivoglio has a group of mercenaries for a reason that I fail to comprehend. But then the carpenter mentioned raids on a village, and I know Bentivoglio's men would not do that. Still, I didn't listen carefully." Allard shrugged. "I was more interested in having him say when he could repair the altarpiece. What a pity. It fell when one of the altar boys moved it and one of the wood panels cracked completely in half. After the panel is replaced, we'll have to find an artist to repaint the scene because the original artist has died."

Hoping that he wouldn't be perceived as inconsiderate, Nico steered the conversation. "The carpenter, where is his shop?"

"When he built the altarpiece, he lived here in San Procolo parish, but he now lives in the town of Dozza. He is a true artist, the only person we would entrust to make the repair. After I contacted him, he came to Bologna to witness the extent of the damage. He explained that the altarpiece was made from fine-grained chestnut wood, and he would have to find a suitable chestnut tree to make a replacement. I expect him to return one week from now."

26

Three hours on horseback from Bologna, Nico got his first glimpse of the fortress called The Rocca by the citizens of Dozza. During his time at the university, Nico had heard stories about the battles waged at the fortress a century past, but this was the first time he had seen the venerable structure. Nico rode through the town, hoping he might spot the carpenter's shop. Many tradesmen had their shops along the town's main street, but not the carpenter. When Nico reached the far end of town, he reversed course and headed for the butcher shop.

In a grassy clearing next to the shop, he found the butcher's apprentice skinning and gutting rabbits. Nico had seen the chef at his cousin Donato's restaurant deftly prepare rabbits with a few swift cuts. The apprentice lacked that skill and pulled awkwardly at the animal's muscle. "Mi scusa, I am looking for the carpenter's shop."

The apprentice waved the bloody knife over his shoulder. "That way. Go past The Rocca. When you enter the woods, you will see his house on the left. His shop is behind the house."

Two young children scampered around the house. They were running together, or one was chasing the other. It was difficult to tell.

One child was a girl, the other may have been a boy. That also was difficult to tell. In the city, boys and girls wore distinctively different clothing, but in the country, children inherited the clothes of older siblings regardless of gender. Their mothers, the ones who cut their hair, found no reason for individual styling.

The carpentry shop was locked, its interior dark and quiet, when Nico peeked through a window. "He is away," a voice called from behind him. Nico turned to see a squat woman, her hands on her hips, standing in a doorway at the back of the house.

"Buon giorno. I've come to see the carpenter. He has done work for Professor Allard at the church of San Procolo in Bologna. The professor told me that the carpenter spoke with men whose village was raided by mercenaries."

"The carpenter is my husband. He is out looking for wood to fix the altarpiece at San Procolo."

"When do you expect him to return?"

"Maybe soon or maybe not until tomorrow. He said he might have to go as far as Imola to find the right tree. Chestnut trees are everywhere, but he needs one that can match the altarpiece."

Nico's shoulders slumped. "I came here all the way from Bologna, especially to talk with him, to ask him about the mercenaries. Did he say anything to you about mercenaries?"

"My husband passed through a village when he was out searching for new stands of wood. Men told him that the village had been raided by mercenaries. They were surprised that the mercenaries took a count of all the animals but didn't take any of them. They took only eggs from the farms that had chickens. What worried the villagers was that the mercenaries searched every house looking for boys. One man heard a mercenary say that his son was too young."

Nico reasoned that since no boys were abducted, the villagers couldn't be strong witnesses. Still, they might have useful information. "Did your husband say the name of the village?"

"He didn't tell me the name."

Nico opened his mouth to ask how many villages were in the area, realized it was a foolish question, but asked it anyway. The woman responded with a blank expression. "Is there anyone else who might have information about the mercenaries? Someone your husband might have told about them?"

Again, the blank expression until finally she said, "The butcher. He knows all the rumors."

"My name is Nico Argenti. I'm staying at the Yellow Duck Inn in Bologna. I may be able to return tomorrow, but if I cannot, please ask your husband to contact me when he next goes to Bologna." He wrote the names Nico Argenti and Yellow Duck Inn on a slip of paper and handed it to the woman before riding back into town to the butcher shop.

This time Nico bypassed the apprentice, who was still struggling with half-skinned rabbits, and went into the shop where a squat man with a broad face was carefully cutting thin slices from a cured pork belly. When the butcher saw Nico, he held a slice up for Nico to examine. "Any thinner and you could see through it," he said proudly. "One of my customers prefers these slices with bread for his midday meal."

As a courtesy, Nico came close and studied the slice. "You must have a sharp knife and a steady hand," then he quickly steered the conversation. "Have you spoken with the carpenter recently? Has he said anything to you about mercenaries in the villages?"

The curious butcher set down the meat and his knife. His expression changed from pride to suspicion as he appraised the stranger. "It's been days since I've spoken with the carpenter." He paused a beat then said, "You mentioned Mercenaries. Around here? I've heard nothing."

The sky filled with thickening clouds, mirroring Nico's frame of mind as he mounted his horse for the long ride back to Bologna. He told himself, "I've wasted the better part of a day for little gain. If I were to return tomorrow, there is no guarantee that the carpenter might not be away again searching for the ideal chestnut tree. It could be another wasted day." The first drops of rain fell as Nico passed The Rocca on his way out of town.

In his room at the Yellow Duck Inn, Nico sat on the bed and kicked off his boots. A quick change to fresh clothes and a beer at the local tavern might heal his spirit. A rap on the door interrupted his thoughts. "Signor Argenti, it is Gerhard."

The smiling student's outstretched hand held a folded sheet. "This note is from Professor Allard."

"What does it say?" Nico asked.

Gerhard's face reddened as he replied, "I haven't read it."

Nico took the paper and read, *I have additional information about the mercenaries. Come to the library.* Nico exhaled a long breath. Although he was eager to learn what new information Allard had uncovered, he was too tired to meet with the professor now. "I spent most of my day in a saddle. I'm in need of a refreshing drink. Join me for a mug of beer."

The first mug served only to whet their appetites for a second mug, this one accompanied by a platter of smoked meat. The third mug loosened Gerhard's tongue. "Today, my civil law class was about inheritances. The lecturer spent the entire morning talking about a situation where one brother is present before the magistrate, and the other brother is absent when the case is adjudicated. He began with a case from the Digest of Justinian a thousand years past. He followed with similar cases, one after another, from Justinian's time to the present. I struggled to stay awake, and I wasn't the only one. How likely will we ever have a case like that—one brother present and one absent? Why spend an entire class discussing it? Where did he even find enough of those cases to fill the entire lecture?"

Nico noticed the beer's effect on Gerhard, so before responding to Gerhard's questions, he ordered a plate of roast vegetables and another of cheese as a counterbalance to the alcohol. "I sat through a few lectures like that. Even the best lecturers sometimes disappoint. When that happened, I closed my ears, reviewed my notes from the previous day's lecture and told myself that the following day would be better."

Gerhard set his mug down hard, sloshing beer onto the table. He laughed at his own clumsiness. In a wobbly voice, he said, "One thing I'm looking forward to is the Founders' Fay celebration. Imagine, it's been three hundred seventy-five years since the university was founded."

"Three hundred seventy-seven," Nico corrected.

Gerhard continued, "There's a rumor that His Holiness Pope Paul will be at the celebration. He'll be passing through Bologna on his way from Rome to Venice." Gerhard took another swig of beer. "The celebration will be next week, and alumni are invited. You're an alumnus. You should attend."

"I enjoyed Founders' Day when I was a student. If I'm still in Bologna next week and I'm not otherwise engaged, I'll be there." Nico slid the plate of cheese across the table—closer to Gerhard than his beer mug. "Try the Parmigiano. It is excellent."

27

Nico found Professor Allard in the library at the same table when they had first met. As before, the tabletop was covered with an assortment of philosophy texts. Allard looked up when he saw Nico approach. "Ah, you received my note. Were you able to speak with the carpenter?"

"I went to his shop and spoke with his wife. Unfortunately, he was away searching for wood to repair the altarpiece. His wife didn't know when he might return, and she knew nothing about mercenaries, not even the name of the village that had been raided. I left word for him to contact me at the Yellow Duck Inn when he comes to Bologna. Your note said that you have additional information about the mercenaries."

"At yesterday's meeting of the San Procolo church council, I told the other council members what you had said about the mercenaries. One of the other members said that his neighbor, a man named Bellini, is an armorer with a very successful business. He sells weapons not only to Bentivoglio's men but also to soldiers in Ferrara and Venice. Recently, he boasted at a tavern that a new client had begun purchasing arms from him. He bought drinks for everyone at the tavern to celebrate his good fortune. He said the client's men claimed their numbers are growing, so they would be making additional purchases in the future."

Nico asked, "Did Bellini say the name of his new customers? Are they mercenaries?"

"No, he only referred to them as new customers. But who else would be buying a large quantity of weapons?"

"I can pay a visit to the armorer's shop. At least it's in Bologna," Nico joked, "It will be less painful than spending six hours on horseback."

Allard's mouth curved into a smile. "Bellini's shop is not far. You can walk there. It's on Via delle Lame. Take any road north and Via delle Lame will cross it shortly after you pass over the Reno Canal."

～

From the bridge over the Reno Canal, Nico peered down into the murky water, trying to recall whether the professor had said that he would reach the armorer's shop before the canal. If so, he had missed it, but he decided to continue a bit farther before turning around. In this district, away from the center of the city, buildings were spread apart. Most were small houses with only a few rooms, surrounded by gardens or patches of weeds.

Beyond the bridge, Nico passed several houses and a bakery when he heard the rhythmic clanging of a hammer against metal. He followed the sound to a storefront. Inside, an assortment of swords hung on one wall. One had a long grip, which Nico identified as a hand-and-a-half sword, the same kind his father had worn as a member of the Florentine army.

The shopkeeper had been working outdoors behind the shop. He saw Nico arrive and came inside to greet a potential customer. "That's a fine blade you're looking at. It's a favorite of soldiers because it can be wielded with either one or two hands. I made one just like it for Lord Este of Ferrara. He's never used it in combat because he has others to fight his battles now," the shopkeeper chuckled, "but he wears it proudly on ceremonial occasions."

Bellini quickly decided that Nico was not a fighter. A fighter would have taken hold of the sword to feel its weight in his hand. "Perhaps a blade designed for defense might better suit your purpose." The shopkeeper removed an item from the wall and held it out for Nico to examine. "This *cinqueda* is the preferred blade of gentlemen. It is shorter than a sword, so it is ideal for use in close quarters."

"Perhaps another time. Today, I am here for a different purpose. Are you Signor Bellini?"

Bellini stepped back. He stiffened and his smile vanished. "I am."

"I understand you made a large sale recently to a new customer."

Bellini had shared that information freely at the tavern, so he said without reluctance, "I was fortunate to find new business." As soon as the words left his mouth, he had doubts. This man was neither a friend nor a local. How could he know about the sale?

Nico said, "Your new customer could be a band of rogue mercenaries."

Bellini barked, "Who are you?"

"Mercenaries are raiding villages."

Bellini took a step forward and waved the *cinqueda* close to Nico's face. "Get out of my shop! Get out!"

He watched briefly as Nico crossed the street and headed toward the university district. Then he locked his shop and ran to a nearby trattoria where two of Attendolo's men who had visited his shop earlier were enjoying a meal. "A man came to my shop asking about you. He said something about villages being raided."

"What man?"

"I don't know his name. I've never seen him before. He just left my shop."

∼

Back in his room at the inn, Nico penned a letter.

Massimo,

I have located an armorer who I believe is selling weapons to the mercenaries. He may know how to find them, but he refuses to talk to me. By refusing to talk, I mean he threatened me with a dagger. It will take more than lawyerly skills to get information from him. If you can pull yourself away from the arms of your latest woman, I could use your help.

Nico

28

For the second time in as many days, Nico entered the Palazzo Comunale that held Bologna's administrative offices. It would take at least a few days for Massimo to arrive in Bologna in response to Nico's plea for help, so Nico decided to use that time to search for Patrizu Nieddu. He followed a dimly lit corridor to the chancery office at the rear of the building. Stacks of papers across the chancery clerk's desk kept the clerk from noticing Nico. When Nico announced his presence, the thin, sandy-haired clerk said, without looking up, "The chancellor has been called away. The meeting is postponed until tomorrow."

Nico smiled inwardly at the clerk's erroneous assumption. "I'm not here to meet with the chancellor. I need information."

The clerk raised himself enough to peer over a pile of documents. "I'm sorry. I thought you were here for the meeting. How may I help you?"

"I want to contact the Company of Angels. Can you tell me how to find them? Do they have an office in this building?"

"Here at the chancery we keep only official government records.

The Company of Angels that cares for orphans is a group of laymen, not a government agency."

Nico gazed out a window that faced the narrow street behind the palazzo as he considered other options for contacting the Company of Angels. He could go to one of the foundling homes. Surely, people caring for orphans must know how to contact the angels. While Nico pondered his options, the clerk stood and walked around his desk to face Nico. "I can tell you how to find one member of the company. He owns a flour mill on the Moline Canal. I don't remember his name, but his mill has a sign over the door, a picture of a sailing ship."

∽

Nico had passed near the Moline Canal only once before. Fulling mills, spinning mills, and grain mills lined both sides of the waterway. With so many waterwheels drawing power from the canal, it seemed remarkable that the water could flow at all. Nico found himself mesmerized by the slowly turning wheels lifting water higher than his head, then freeing it to cascade back down into the canal. He easily spotted the mill with a ship insignia above its door, although the image of an ocean-going sailing ship under full sail appeared out of place in an inland city such as Bologna.

A fine cloud of flour hung in the air inside the mill. In contrast to the placid sounds of the waterwheels outside, wooden gears rubbing against each other and shafts laboring against centering blocks created a deafening sound inside the mill. A lone worker up on a catwalk poured grain into a hopper above the grinding stone. After he finished filling the hopper, he climbed down and approached Nico, who leaned close to the worker's ear and asked in a loud voice if he were the mill owner. The worker's cap pulled down over his ears as protection against the machinery noise prevented him from hearing Nico, but he understood the question by watching Nico's lips move. He pointed to a door on the far side of the millstone.

Nico wound his way past bins of grain to reach the door. He

raised his hand to knock but realized that with all the noise, a knock would not be heard by anyone in the room, so he pushed the door open and entered the mill owner's office. Machinery noise came into the room along with Nico, woke the mill owner, and alerted him that someone had entered. He lifted his head, opened his eyes, sat up straight, and managed a guilty smile. "I've been here since before daybreak," he offered to explain his nap. Nico introduced himself as a Florentine commissioner, then asked, "Are you a member of the Company of Angels?"

"Yes. Yes, I am," the man replied, puzzled that a Florentine lawyer had come to his place of business to ask about the Company of Angels.

Nico explained, "A man named Patrizu Nieddu misrepresented himself to get appointed as administrator of the orphanage in Florence. In that capacity, he delivered boys to a buyer who was possibly an agent for a band of mercenaries. Nieddu fled Florence to avoid prosecution; he is now in Bologna."

The mill owner looked at Nico with wide eyes as he absorbed the flood of information. "You think he is somehow involved with orphans here?" Nico nodded. The mill owner shook his head. "No one named Patrizu Nieddu is working with orphans in Bologna. I am certain of that."

"It's possible that he's using a different name. Have any newcomers approached the company recently?"

"Yes, there are some newcomers. We thank the Lord that there are always new people willing to help the poor children of our city. It's a blessing because there are so many orphaned and abandoned children who need our help. But we have had problems with strangers in the past, so now we are careful in approving new volunteers. Everyone we accept must bring a reference from his or her parish priest. We never accept people who are unknown to us."

Nico said, "I wish we had done that in Florence." He thought for a moment, wondering whether Nieddu had found another way of accessing children without contacting the Company of Angels. He asked, "Have you heard of any children going missing mysteriously?"

The question surprised the mill owner. "No. No children in the care of the Company have gone missing, and I would certainly know if they had."

Nico thanked the mill owner and turned to leave. As he reached the door, the mill owner called to him. "Wait, I just thought of something. Another member of the Company owns a bakery near the central market. At the end of each day, he gives away bread that hasn't been sold to beggar children. This city has even more beggars than orphans. When I last saw him, he mentioned that some children who had been coming to his shop regularly suddenly stopped coming. He asked the other children about them, and they said those children had just disappeared."

"The missing children... were they boys about age fourteen?"

"He didn't mention ages, but he did mention some names. I don't remember the names, but I do recall that at least one of the beggars was a girl."

Nico thanked the mill owner and headed back toward the center of the city to visit the baker. As he crossed the bridge over the Moline Canal, Nico considered whether Neiddu might have taken the missing children or whether they had simply drifted to another part of the city where begging was better rewarded.

Nico opted to stop at the Yellow Duck Inn en route to the bakery. He climbed to the second level of the inn. As soon as he opened the door to his room, a powerful arm grabbed him from behind and pushed him into the room. He struggled to free himself, but the man held him firm with the strength of a bear. A punch in his ribs from a second person made Nico's entire body shudder; another punch drove the air from his chest and made him double over. A fist rammed down on the back of his neck like a crushing weight. He grunted in pain and went limp. His vision blurred, and he nearly lost consciousness.

The first assailant wrenched Nico's arms outward, forcing him to his knees. He growled, "What happens in Bologna is not your business. Go back to Florence."

Nico could manage only a dull moan. The second assailant drove his knee upward, striking Nico's chin. He bent low until his menacing sneer filled Nico's vision. Then he began striking Nico's cheeks again and again with his heavy leather glove until Nico's vision went black, and he collapsed onto the floor. One final kick and a warning: "This is not a place for Florentine troublemakers. Leave Bologna while you still have breath."

As the two assailants left the room, one said with satisfaction, "That should teach the bastard a lesson."

29

Three days later

Nico lifted himself slowly from the bed to answer the knock on his door. Fearful that his assailants might have returned, he asked, "What?"

Massimo replied, "Are you having such a good time here in Bologna that you can't remember inviting me?"

As soon as Nico opened the door, Massimo scanned the red and blue bruises on Nico's face, the welts on his neck, and his puffy eyes. "Holy Saint Joseph, what happened to you?"

To protect his injured ribs, Nico stepped back to avoid any contact with his colleague. With a croaking voice, he replied, "Two thugs attacked me when I came to my room."

"When?"

"I'm not sure. Maybe three days past." Nico sat on the edge of the bed. "I'm better now. You should have seen me then."

"You still look like you've been whipped by the devil. Have you seen a physician?"

"I haven't seen a physician, but I did go to the *farmacia*. The *farmacista* took one look at me and said he knew exactly what I needed."

Nico gestured toward three jars on a side table. "He gave me these bottles of salve. He told me how to apply them, but I can't remember his instructions."

Massimo opened the three jars and sniffed them, then held one up. "This one is for the bruises. I've used this concoction so many times that it's like an old friend. Hold still." Massimo spread a layer of the brown ointment over the bruises on Nico's face and neck.

Nico gasped. "I hope it cures the bruises before the smell kills me."

"I know that it smells like shit, but you'll get used to it. Do you have any other bruises?"

"No bruises, but my ribs complain every time a take a breath."

"This stuff won't help with injured ribs." Massimo sniffed the remaining two jars again. "Maybe one of these is for your ribs, but if so, I don't know which one. I can take the bottles back to the farmacista and ask him for instructions. Do you want to rest now? I can come back later."

"All I've been doing lately is resting. I want to get back to work."

Massimo pulled over a chair and sat facing Nico. "You're not in any condition to work. Did you recognize the men who attacked you?"

"It happened so quickly; I barely got to see one of them. The one I did see had a scar, possibly a burn mark, on the right side of his face. He wore heavy leather boots. I saw the boots because he kicked me repeatedly. The other one was behind me, so I didn't see him. He's the one who grabbed me as soon as I opened the door to my room."

"They must have had a reason for attacking you. Did they take anything?"

"No, they weren't robbers. They took nothing. They kept telling me to go back to Florence and stop asking questions about mercenaries."

"Did you report the beating to the local authorities?"

"No. Other than going to the farmacia, I haven't left this room."

"You must have been asking the right questions for someone to have sent the thugs. Most likely they were Attendolo's men, unless there are other mercenaries in Bologna, or troublemakers who roam the city just to take pleasure in beating people."

"I don't know about troublemakers, but there are other mercenaries in the province. Cardinal Capranica, he's the Vatican's Vice Legate, told me that the Bentivoglio family sponsors a group of mercenaries, but the cardinal assured me that they are not raiding villages. And Bentivoglio's men would have no reason to attack me. None of my questions were targeted at them."

Massimo raised an eyebrow. "Who are the Bentivoglio family and why do they need a band of mercenaries? The Papacy should be providing protection for the Province of Bologna."

"The Bentivoglio family has been a powerful force in Bologna for generations. Giovanni is the current head of the family. When he was a child, his father was assassinated by a member of a rival family. Perhaps he keeps a band of loyal mercenaries, so he doesn't meet the same fate as his father.

"The city is governed by a council known as the Reformatori. The Bentivoglio family influences the Reformatori in the same way that the Medici family influences our Signoria. Cardinal Capranica gave me the impression that the Papacy and the Reformatori aren't always in agreement. The cardinal's ability to govern is hampered by the lack of support from Rome because the Papal Army is busy in the south, so he can't call upon them. He can only pressure the city government with words."

"Your letter mentioned an armorer who refused to talk with you about mercenaries. Could he be the one who told the thugs about you?"

"I believe so, since he's the only person I spoke with who objected to my questions. I'm sure he's selling weapons to Attendolo, and he wants to protect that business."

"Tomorrow," Massimo said. "Tomorrow, if you're feeling better, we can pay another visit to the armorer. For now, let the salve heal your bruises."

"I have other news," Nico said. "I saw Patrizu Nieddu. He's here in Bologna."

"Vittorio told me that he received your letter. He intends to come to Bologna as soon as he finishes the project his is doing for Chancellor Scala. If anyone can find Nieddu, it will be Vittorio, but can Nieddu be prosecuted in Bologna for crimes in Florence?"

"No, he can't. The only way to prosecute him here is if Vittorio can find that Nieddu is violating a Bolognese law. I spoke with an overseer of the orphans who told me that Nieddu isn't involved with the orphanage or foundling homes, but he also said that some street urchins have disappeared. It's not clear, though, whether Nieddu is involved with their disappearance."

As Massimo rose to leave, he remembered the message he carried. He pulled an envelope from his duffel and handed it to Nico. "This letter from your sister Alessa might keep you from thinking about your injuries."

Nico waited until Massimo left, then opened the envelope and read the note.

Dearest Nico,

Bianca came to Florence yesterday to deliver a dress to one of her clients. I saw the dress, and it is beautiful, burgundy with silver trim on the collar and cuffs. Bianca had hoped to see you while she was in Florence. She did not know you had gone to Bologna. Don't you write to tell her when you are leaving the country? You need to be more considerate if you want your relationship with her to flourish. Since you weren't available, she had dinner with Joanna, Donato, and me. We told her about all of your flaws–well, not all of them.

Since you write so rarely, it is good that Chancellor Scala keeps your family informed of your activities. He told Donato that you spotted Signor Nieddu in Bologna. He knew I was concerned about the children missing from the orphanage, so he sent a chancery clerk to tell me that Vittorio will be joining you in Bologna to help with the search. No other children have disappeared in Florence since Signor Nieddu fled the city.

Keep yourself safe. It seems that you are injured every time you travel to a foreign country. I hope that does not happen again in Bologna.

With love from your sister, Alessa

30

On the terrace of a country villa overlooking the Navile Canal, Ercole Strozzi admired the panorama before him. He could see almost as far as Bologna, ten miles to the south. "What a wonderful sight. Just look at the prosperous mills alongside the canal and the fertile farms stretching all the way to the horizon," he said to a disinterested house servant. He ran a hand through his graying hair, then said, "I missed these views when I was in Venice. Of course, this view doesn't compare to Tuscany. There is something special about late afternoon light in Tuscany." In a softer voice to himself, he added, "Someday...."

The villa belonged to the last surviving relative of the family that had murdered Giovanni Bentivoglio's father. Giovanni was only two years old when his father was killed in a clash between two families vying for control of the city government. The villa owner, merely a boy at the time of the feud, bore his family's outcast status. He and Ercole Strozzi, who had been exiled from Florence for opposing the Medici clan, had somehow found each other. He was pleased to let Strozzi use his villa.

The scenery was breathtaking, but ambitious men need more than visual pleasures. In Florence, Ercole Strozzi had headed a banking empire where he constantly pitted his prowess and cunning against the Medici, the Bardi, and the Peruzzi families. When he fled from Florence, he brought his vast wealth with him; yet the Venetian council had refused him permission to operate a bank in their republic. Instead, he used his business skills and resources to buy struggling companies. First he acquired a small glass maker, next a shipping company. With a few management changes, he made the companies profitable. It took surprisingly little time or effort to achieve sizable rewards.

Ercole devoted most of his energy to seeking other discontents who wanted to end the Medici dominance in Florence. He dreamed of spurring war between the two powerful republics, Florence and Venice. Unfortunately for Ercole, the Venetians were busy fending off the Ottoman Empire's attacks on their foreign territories. They had no desire to stoke another rivalry. After failing to find support for his ideas in Venice, Strozzi sought other options. A discredited noble, the son of an accused assassin, invited Strozzi to Bologna and offered him the use of a countryside villa. The two men had different goals: the villa owner had a vendetta against the Bentivoglio family while Ercole wanted to unseat the Medici, but both agreed that building a powerful mercenary force would serve their interests.

Strozzi turned his chair to face the road coming north from the city, to watch for the intermediary bringing word of Attendolo's progress. Soon he saw a column of dust rising in the distance. Moments later, the approaching rider came into view.

"Refill this pitcher," Ercole called to the house servant. "No, wait. He won't have eaten, so bring something for him to eat. And bring a bottle of wine, and two glasses."

Strozzi's uncharacteristically thoughtful behavior surprised the servant. He took the pitcher and retreated quickly, trying to get out of sight before Strozzi's normally bitter demeanor returned.

The rider left his horse with the stable boy, brushed a coating of dust from his shirt, and climbed to the terrace. "Ah, I need this," he said as he filled one of the wine glasses.

Strozzi dispensed with any pleasantries and said, "Tell me, is Luigi finally ready to do something other than terrorize villagers?"

"Captain Attendolo sends you his greetings." Nieddu downed half the wine in his glass, refilled it, and leaned back in his chair before continuing. "Training of the recruits is proceeding faster than expected and this week the captain's men added four new boys."

Patrizu Nieddu had reestablished contact with Attendolo's mercenaries when he arrived in Bologna. His initial plan had been to insinuate himself with the Bolognese foundling homes and then use his position to obtain boys for the mercenaries as he had done in Florence. Since Attendolo's men were having good success getting able-bodied boys from small villages, Captain Attendolo didn't want to risk attracting attention by taking boys from the city. He proposed, instead, that Nieddu take on the role of intermediary between himself and the man funding his operation, Ercole Strozzi.

Eyeing Nieddu, Strozzi thought, *the pompous assworm. He speaks as though the accomplishments are his.* "My objective is not to fund a camp for boys. When will Luigi's men be ready to engage meaningful targets?"

"That depends on the targets. Giovanni Bentivoglio's men are a formidable force. It will take time to build enough strength to go against them."

"Bentivoglio? I don't give a shit about Giovanni Bentivoglio. My quarrel is with Florence and the Medici. The Florentine army is pathetic because the Signoria is unwilling to spend florins to maintain a capable force. Whenever Florence is pressured, it counts on its friends in Milan to come to its aid. But moving an army from Milan to Florence takes time. That means Florence is vulnerable to a swift strike."

"But you're here at this villa. I thought…"

Strozzi interrupted before Nieddu could finish. "The one who owns this villa might care about the Bentivoglio, but I'm the one funding Luigi… and you. And all I care about is the Medici."

"If you're right about the Florentine army being weak..." Nieddu began.

Strozzi slammed his fist down onto the table and bellowed, "If I'm right? Of course, I'm right. I'm always right."

"Captain Attendolo could be ready to move soon. The men he brought with him to Bologna have fought with the papal forces in Le Marche. They are experienced men, eager to use their skills."

"Then tell him this," Strozzi instructed. "There are two targets in Florence, the Signoria and the villa of that weakling Piero de Medici. They must be struck simultaneously. I have a contact in Florence who will know when the Signoria meets. I'll get that information and you can pass it to Luigi."

As Ercole rose and headed into the villa, Nieddu poured himself another glass of wine. The now empty bottle had no tag or label. Most likely, it came from a local vineyard. Nieddu called to the house servant, "Bring me another bottle. This isn't bad, but it doesn't compare to Cannonau wine from Sardinia. When I go back to Sardinia, maybe I'll send Ercole a bottle."

Unburdened by the wine, Nieddu's thoughts drifted to his past and his future. *Damn, I miss Sardinia. But I had to leave or that crazy warehouse owner would have cut me for defiling his daughter. I should have been more careful, but ah, she was a lovely prize. Then, just when I was getting comfortable in Florence, that lawyer Argenti started asking questions. And now the bastard shows up here in Bologna, my personal demon.*

31

"The salve must have worked. You look better this morning, Nico. Not good enough for any woman to give you a second look, but better than yesterday. How are your ribs?"

Nico pressed gently on his ribcage, first on the left, then the right. Each time, he winced. Seeing Nico's reaction, Massimo said, "Ribs don't heal quickly. They'll take a week or more. Any problems other than the bruises and the ribs?"

"Only that I'm bored doing nothing. I can't just sit here waiting to recover. Let's get something to eat. There's a trattoria nearby that offers breakfast."

Massimo laughed. "You're sounding like a soldier if eating is one of your remedies for boredom."

Nico tilted his head and looked at Massimo with a sideways glance. "One of the remedies? Are there others?"

"I thought you would have known by now: gambling and women."

For breakfast, the trattoria served only onion tarts and a hot, steaming liquid that the server called breakfast tonic. "Breakfast tonic?" Massimo repeated. He lifted the cup to his nose and inhaled the earthy aroma. "A physician once gave me a tonic that smelled like this."

Nico took a sip. "It's made from herbs. My adopted sister Alessa makes brews like these from various herbs. She said everyone drank it in her village in Morocco. She calls it Atay."

Mollified by Nico's explanation, Massimo tasted the liquid. "I admit that it does taste better than the physician's brew." After beckoning for the server to bring another onion tart, he said, "You were limping when we walked here from the inn."

"There isn't a part of me that those two thugs didn't kick, so I'm fortunate that I can even limp."

"I'm going to pay a visit to the armorer. Can you limp from here to his shop?"

"Certainly. I've been wanting to return there for the past three days."

Nico walked slower than normal and paused at the bridge over the Reno Canal to regain his strength. He looked forward to questioning Bellini using verbal pressure and veiled threats, but he didn't get the chance.

Upon seeing Massimo enter his shop, Bellini approached him and opened his mouth to offer a pleasant greeting. Before he could utter a word, Massimo grabbed him by the throat and shoved him backward against a wall. Massimo pulled a *cinqueda* from the display wall, the same dagger that Bellini had used to threaten Nico.

Massimo pressed the blade's tip against Bellini's cheek, just hard enough to pierce the skin. He drew the blade forward, tracing a thin red line across the cheek. "You have done well with your craft. This blade has a fine edge."

Massimo's grip on Bellini's throat prevented the armorer from answering or even gasping for air. Massimo waited a few seconds for panic to swell in Bellini's eyes, then he removed his hand and held the *cinqueda* at the armorer's throat.

Bellini glanced over Massimo's shoulder. He noticed Nico and his bruises. Massimo called, "Come closer, Nico. Let him see what his friends did to you." Then to Bellini, Massimo said, "Three days ago they beat him so badly that he couldn't stand. His ribs may be broken. They will take weeks to heal."

Bellini said feebly, "I didn't send anyone to beat him. I just told…" He stopped before mentioning a name. "I didn't know that would happen."

"You didn't know," Massimo mocked. "What did you think would happen? The men you are dealing with are outlaws. They kill for money. Messer Argenti is fortunate to be alive. And you are to blame for the pain they caused him."

Massimo repositioned the dagger with its point pressing against Bellini's face between his nose and his upper lip. "Now tell me how to find those men."

Before Bellini could answer, they heard a sound above their heads, like an animal running across the ceiling. "What is that?" Massimo asked.

"My son."

"Your son?"

"We live in the apartment above the shop, my son, my wife and me."

"The mercenaries. How can I find them?" Massimo repeated.

"I don't know where they are. I swear to the Blessed Mother, I do not know."

"What do they look like?"

"They're big men, like you. They wear leather."

Massimo turned to face Nico, winked, and said, "He is not being helpful. Maybe his wife can be more helpful. Let's go ask her."

"Wait," Bellini pleaded. "I have more weapons ready for them. They will be coming to get them."

Massimo leaned close to Bellini. "When are they coming back?"

"Today. Later, today," Bellini stammered.

"What weapons?" Nico asked.

"Swords. They wanted eight, but I told them I could have only four ready today."

Nico stepped forward and said to Bellini, "When they come today, tell them you will have the remaining swords ready in two days." Then to Massimo he explained, "It might be useful to make them return again in the future."

"I can't do that. I can't have more ready in two days. I don't have the material," Bellini protested.

Massimo rubbed his chin as he pondered Nico's proposal. "It matters not what you can do, armorer. Tell them to return again in two days."

Massimo lowered the *cinqueda*. "Nico, find a stable and rent horses for us. When the mercenaries leave here with the weapons, we'll follow them." He turned back to Bellini. "We will be in the apartment with your wife and son, so when the men get here, you will tell them nothing about us."

Bellini shivered. "No, please, not my wife."

Massimo returned the *cinqueda* to the display wall. He withdrew a rapier and waved it in the air. "We are not savages. If you don't divulge our presence, no harm will come to you or your family. Now go back to your work." Bellini went outside to the forge behind his shop. He moved around idly, unable to concentrate.

"Horses will be ready for us whenever we need them," Nico reported upon his return to the armorer's shop.

Massimo pointed to the stairway. "Now it's time for us to meet Bellini's wife." The two men climbed to the second level and pushed open the apartment door. The wife and the young boy froze in place at seeing two strangers enter the room. Her face turned ashen. She grabbed her son and pulled him to the far corner of the room. "Who?" was the only word she could manage.

Nico said, "We are going to wait here while your husband does business with others. Don't be afraid."

The boy looked up at his mother and whined in protest at being restrained. When she saw that the two strangers were remaining by the door, the woman released her son's hand. Slowly, color returned to her face, but she trembled when the boy's play brought him close to the unwanted visitors. As she took his hand to lead him away, Massimo said, "My friend and I will be leaving Bologna on horseback. He has bruised ribs that need to be protected during the journey. Do you have any cloth?"

Without a word, she turned, walked into another room, and returned with a length of rough linen. Massimo cut the cloth into wide strips and wrapped it tightly around Nico's chest. "That should hold your ribs in place."

"Any tighter, and I won't be able to breathe."

"You'll be thankful when you're bouncing on the back of a horse."

Nico placed a coin on the table. The woman looked at it, confused, but did not touch it. "For the cloth," Nico explained.

Later, when the woman began preparing the boy's midday meal at the end of the longest morning in her memory, voices from below filtered up through the floor. Massimo moved quietly out of the apartment and descended part way down the stairs to overhear Bellini's conversation.

The armorer's words reached him. "As promised, here are the four blades." Massimo cupped his ears, but he could not hear the mercenary's reply. Other exchanges between Bellini and the mercenary were indistinguishable, then Massimo heard the men moving and Bellini said, "In two days' time, I will have four more blades ready."

The shop door closed and a few seconds later Bellini rushed to the stairway, where he nearly impaled himself on the point of the rapier in Massimo's grip. "My wife?" Bellini uttered feebly.

"You did well. She and the boy are unharmed."

Bellini slid past Massimo and sprang up the stairs to his apartment. Massimo and Nico left the shop and followed the mercenary. Nico said, "He's heading toward the same stable where I rented the horses." They waited out of sight in an alley until the mercenary mounted his horse and rode away; then they followed at a discreet distance.

32

Nico and Massimo followed the mercenary out of the city through the Porta San Mamolo gate, then onto a road heading south parallel to a narrow river. They rode for several miles through a valley dotted with farms. They still had a long way to travel, and already Nico's head throbbed. Gently, he rubbed the bump above his ear where one of the thugs had kicked him. *I should have gotten more salve from the farmacista*, he thought.

At a hamlet that a local identified as Zena, they turned onto a trail that climbed into the Apennine foothills. On one craggy stretch, Massimo noticed Nico grimace and asked, "How are your ribs?"

"They complain every time the road is rough, but I'm trying to ignore them. I wouldn't be able to do this if you hadn't wrapped them."

The forest grew denser as they rose from the valley floor, causing them to lose sight of the mercenary. At one fork in the trail, Massimo dismounted to examine hoofprints in the dirt. "They went right," he announced.

The smell of a cooking fire was their first clue that they were nearing Attendolo's camp. They secured their horses to a stand of trees and moved ahead cautiously on foot. Using the cover of shrubs to keep them from being seen, they circled the camp. "That's him. That's Attendolo," Massimo whispered and pointed toward the mercenary captain.

"The camp is bigger than I expected," Nico said. "There must be at least forty men here."

"Yes, at least," Massimo agreed. "Whatever their purpose, it is certainly more than just raiding villages. Look there!" He pointed. "Those must be the boys they abducted. There are at least ten of them."

Nico spotted a footpath that led down a slope away from the camp. "I saw movement. There's someone down there."

The two men moved carefully down the path to avoid making any sound. At the end of the path, they found a boy sitting on a rock beside a small stream. They watched him drawing figures in the dirt with a stick. Next to him, a fishing pole sat propped against the rock, with its line trailing off into the stream. Nico approached the boy and asked casually, "What's your name?"

The boy looked up, startled to see men standing on each side of him. The one questioning him didn't look like one of the mercenaries. The other one wore leather like a mercenary, but his was different. "Gasparo," the boy replied. Then, without being asked, he added, "I was told to catch fish."

"You're not having much success," Massimo observed. "Are you with them?" Massimo asked and gestured toward Attendolo's camp.

Gasparo hesitated, not sure how to respond. "Were you taken from your village?" Nico asked. Again, the boy hesitated. "Is your village near here?"

"I don't know. We rode at night."

"When were you taken?"

"Two days ago."

"Are you happy here or would you like to return to your home?" Nico asked.

Gasparo's eyes widened, but he said nothing. Were these men

mercenaries sent to test his commitment, or could he trust them? He was still undecided when Massimo said, "If you want to leave here, come with us." Massimo and Nico turned to leave. They took only a few steps before Gasparo rose and followed them. He paid no notice to the tug on the fishing line.

Gasparo climbed onto the horse behind Massimo and the three wound their way down the hillside to the valley floor. At Zena, Gasparo grew excited. "I know this village. I've been here before." He pointed to a church at the top of a nearby hill. "That's Santa Maria di Zena. My village is on the far side of that hill."

"The mercenaries do not camp in any place for long. They move around. Until they move, it would not be safe for you to return to your village. When they discover that you are missing, they might go there looking for you, and if they were to find you, they would punish you. They might even punish your family." Nico's words dampened the boy's enthusiasm.

"Where can I go?"

"We can take you to Bologna. You can stay there for a few days. Then, when the mercenaries have moved away, you can return to your village."

Gasparo slumped. First he was taken to a mercenary camp, and now he was going to Bologna. Would he ever see his family again?

33

Nico, Massimo, and Gasparo were already seated at a table in a trattoria across the road from the Yellow Duck Inn when Vittorio arrived. Massimo poured a glass of the house red wine for the newcomer. As soon as Vittorio reached the table, Nico raised his glass in a welcoming gesture. "It is good to have you here, Vittorio."

Vittorio sat, took a drink, then said, "Your letter implied that you could use my help."

"Indeed, we can. But before we discuss the situation here in Bologna, was there a serious problem that held you in Florence?"

"The issue ended as more of an embarrassment than a serious problem. The Signoria became concerned because one of its members suddenly went missing. There were rumors that Signor Jacobi, the missing man, had a heated exchange with a merchant from Siena. Some in the Signoria feared that the disagreement might have turned violent. They wanted the matter resolved before the merchant returned to Siena, so Chancellor Scala asked me to investigate."

"I know Signor Jacobi," Massimo injected. "He's a timid little man. Did you find him hiding under a bush?"

"Not at all. I found him at a villa in the country, with a woman."

Massimo guffawed at the news. "Jacobi, with a mistress? He must have a quality that I never noticed."

"She wasn't a mistress. She's a woman who Jacobi employs at his mill."

Massimo clenched his jaw. "Then he's worse than I thought. Weasels like him are always finding ways to take advantage of vulnerable women and they never suffer any consequences."

"Oh, he is suffering," Vittorio replied. "Members of the Signoria told their wives about the tryst, and the gossip eventually reached Jacobi's wife. Her father had lent Jacobi money to buy the mill and now he's forcing Jacobi to pay back the loan or forfeit the mill.

"Except for Jacobi's personal pain, that matter is settled. Now, tell me what is happening in Bologna."

"We are facing three challenges: the mercenaries, the Strozzi brothers, and Patrizu Nieddu." Nico paused a moment, then added, "We're like the travelers in Dante's Commedia who faced the three-headed dog Cerberus at the entrance to Hades."

Massimo turned toward Vittorio and winked. "Indulge him, Vittorio. The beating he received from the two thugs must have him recalling memories from his literature classes at the university." Then to Nico, he said, "At least there are four of us here to battle our three adversaries."

Vittorio looked across the table at the boy, who was slathering soft goat cheese onto a piece of flat bread, and asked, "And who is this young man?"

Nico replied, "His name is Gasparo. Attendolo's mercenaries had abducted him from his home." Hearing his name, the boy looked up. Clearly, he was listening to the conversation.

"You rescued him?"

"We didn't rescue him. He chose to come with us when we left the mercenary camp. We're keeping him in Bologna until it's safe for him to return home."

Vittorio raised an eyebrow. "You were at the mercenaries' camp?"

"Massimo and I followed one of the mercenaries from the armory where they got their weapons to their camp in the hills. That is where we found Gasparo. Attendolo's force is larger than we expected. He has at least forty in total, counting the new recruits. They're building their force and acquiring weapons, so they must be planning to act soon. Unfortunately, we don't know their intention."

"Your letter asked for my help in locating Signor Nieddu. I can pursue Nieddu. That will leave you and Massimo to deal with the mercenaries and the Strozzi brothers. The letter said that you had seen Nieddu in the central market."

"Yes, I saw him. I tried to approach him, but he disappeared into the crowd before I could reach him."

Vittorio asked, "Have you been able to find out what Nieddu is doing in Bologna? Is he involved with the orphanage?"

Since I wrote to you, I've learned some things that may prove useful," Nico said. "I spoke with an overseer of the orphanage, who assured me that Nieddu is not involved with the orphanage. However, he also told me that the owner of a bakery shop near the central market has noticed beggar children have been going missing recently." Seeing Vittorio raise an eyebrow, Nico added, "I realize the baker's observation is vague and might not be related to Nieddu's activities."

"It's a place to start. I've begun investigations with less," Vittorio replied. He took another drink of wine and then said, "Chancellor Scala is eager to learn the whereabouts of the Strozzi brothers. Have you made any progress in finding them?"

"I met with the acting Papal Legate, Cardinal Capranica. He's not aware of the Strozzi brothers being in Bologna, so he believes that if they are here, they must be well hidden. But he feels confident that his sources can find them if they are indeed in Bologna."

"Chancellor Scala's interest in the Strozzi brothers was heightened when chancery informants found that Ercole Strozzi has been corresponding with a cohort in Florence."

"To what end?" Massimo asked.

"The Chancellor has been asking that same question, and he has tasked his informants with learning the name of the Strozzis' Florentine contact."

Gasparo held his spoon at the ready as a server brought bowls of lentil soup to the table. Conversation paused while the three men joined Gasparo in devouring the soup. After emptying his bowl, Gasparo said, "My mother makes lentil soup, but hers doesn't taste as good as this one."

"You must never tell that to your mother," Nico advised.

"If I ever get to see her again," the boy lamented.

Nico caught the boy's eyes and said, "You will see her soon. I promise."

After the server removed the empty bowls from the table, Vittorio asked, "Now that you know the location of the mercenaries' camp, what are you going to do with that information?"

Nico answered, "Cardinal Capranica said that the Bolognese city council would not act on reports of mercenary activity even if the reports were made by Florentine envoys and the Florentine archbishop. He said the Reformatori would dismiss those reports as vague hearsay. Now we have substantial evidence, enough that the Reformatori should be swayed and moved to act. Gasparo can tell them about his abduction, and we can tell them the location of the mercenaries' camp."

"Who or what are the Reformatori?" Vittorio asked.

"Bologna has a city council," Nico explained, "similar to our Signoria. Within that council are sixteen elite members who call themselves the Reformatori. They are the real power behind the local government, and they have the resources to deal with Attendolo's mercenaries. The Reformatori are meeting this afternoon, so as soon as we leave here, I intend to petition them."

34

A clerk at the government offices directed Nico, Massimo, and Gasparo to the chamber where the Reformatori were meeting. A heavy wooden door sealed the chamber, and a guard posted at the door stopped them from entering. "The Reformatori are in session. Their meetings are private. You cannot enter."

Nico announced, "We have important information that needs to be brought to their attention." The guard's expression did not soften. Nico added, "It concerns the security of the province." Still, the guard was unmoved.

Nico pulled out the document that introduced him as an envoy of the Florentine Republic. The guard read the paper, looked up at Nico, then read the paper a second time. He was unsure how to respond, but he did not wish to offend the envoy of a powerful republic. "Sometimes the Reformatori accept petitions from the public at the conclusion of their meeting." He pointed toward chairs lined against the opposite wall. "You can wait there. You must be silent until they have finished their business."

At the end of the first hour, Gasparo began fidgeting. By the end of the second hour, even Nico became impatient. He approached the guard again and asked, "How many hours are their meetings?" The guard shrugged.

Only Massimo sat quietly, his eyes closed, and his arms folded across his chest. In the army, waiting was a skill that was well practiced by Massimo. Eventually, the chamber door opened, and a man dressed in a black robe stepped out. His smooth unmarked skin showed him to be too young to be one of the Reformatori. An aide, thought Nico. The guard spoke briefly with the man, then gestured toward the three visitors sitting across the room. The man whispered something to the guard and disappeared back into the meeting chamber. Several minutes passed before the man re-emerged from the meeting room. He approached the visitors, said, "The Reformatori will hear your petition," and escorted the three to the meeting room.

A large table filled the center of the room, but none of the Reformatori were seated. They stood in small groups throughout the room. Some were engaged in conversation while others were enjoying refreshments. Clearly, their formal meeting had ended. The aide spoke with one member of the group, a large man with a pronounced chin and ruddy complexion. He glanced at the newcomers, then announced to his colleagues, "An envoy from the Florentine Republic wishes to address us."

Conversations hushed as the sixteen members of the Reformatori turned to face Nico. All were stylishly dressed and well-groomed except for one short fellow whose cheeks held a beard stubble. His tunic was marked with a dull red smear on the cuff, possibly a wine stain. The men remained standing, and those who had been drinking continued holding their glasses. Either they didn't expect the interruption to last long or they didn't deem it to be a serious matter. Nico took their attention as the cue for him to speak.

"I am Messer Nico Argenti. My colleague Signor Massimo Leoni and I are envoys from the Republic of Florence. We came to Bologna after receiving reports of villages being attacked by mercenaries who are roaming the mountainous region of the Province of Bologna. Our government is concerned that renegade mercenaries are operating close to Florentine border. We have spoken with villagers whose children were abducted by the mercenaries, and recently we discovered the location of the mercenary camp."

Nico gestured toward Gasparo. "This young man is one of those who was abducted from his home. He can tell you of his experience."

The short man with the stubble crossed the room and stood facing Gasparo. "You were taken from your home by mercenaries?" he asked.

"Yes," Gasparo answered in a confident voice as Nico had coached him.

"How were you restrained when you left the village?"

Gasparo, unfamiliar with the word 'restrained' or unsure of how to answer, looked for guidance to Nico, who said, "Tell him how you were taken."

"I was tending sheep in a field when the men came. One of them grabbed my arm and pulled me up onto his horse. He said they would hurt my family if I didn't go with them. They took one other boy too. It was night when we left my village. We rode through the darkness to their camp."

"Did they threaten you? Did they hit you or tell you they would harm you if you didn't go with them?"

"No, they didn't hit me, but they had swords. I was worried that they would hurt my family."

"When you reached the mercenaries' camp, were you tied or beaten by guards?"

"No, nothing like that, but they said we would be punished if we didn't obey the rules."

"They didn't hurt you. They didn't beat you," the man repeated.

Gasparo turned to Nico again, upset by the questioner's aggressive tone. Nico place a reassuring hand on the boy's shoulder.

The man continued. "That's all? They said you must obey the rules?" He turned his head to face his colleagues and raised a hand, palm up, in a gesture of resignation. "All they said was follow the rules or suffer the consequences. That's no more intimidation than school teachers who demand the same of their students." Then back to Gasparo. "How did you escape?"

Waving his hand to indicate Nico and Massimo, Gasparo said, "These men found me."

"They found you? What does that mean? What were you doing when they found you?"

"I was at a creek fishing. All the newcomers were given chores. I was told to fish."

"Were there guards to keep you from running away?"

Gasparo cast his eyes down as he realized how weak his position sounded. "No, there were no guards."

The man threw up his hands and walked back to stand with the other Reformatori. He sighed in exasperation. "One month past, we heard testimony from a victim who had welts across his back from beatings. One of his eyes was swollen shut. He was beaten in his home by bandits. That matter called for our attention, but this…." He let the thought hang.

Another Reformtore addressed Nico. "Do you have evidence that these mercenaries represent a threat to the city of Bologna?"

"The mercenaries are increasing their numbers by abducting children as recruits, and they are acquiring weapons. There must be a reason for their actions."

"Can you testify as to their intent?"

"I do not know their purpose, but at the very least, they are violating the law by abducting children."

A third man stepped forward. He spread his arms wide and said, "We are all caring men. We realize this boy has been through a painful experience and we agree it is unacceptable for mercenaries to abduct children. However, the authority of this council is limited the city. The enforcement of civil laws outside the city proper is the responsibility of the papal authorities. If you want action, you should bring the matter to the Papal Prosecutors."

"What about Signor Bentivoglio's mercenaries?" Nico asked.

"Signor Bentivoglio would call upon his forces if there were a clear threat to the security of the city of Bologna, but you have given us no evidence of such a threat. Your concerns should be addressed to the papal authorities."

Before Nico could say anything further, some the Reformatori resumed their conversations. They had lost interest in Nico's argument. His plea had failed. Dejected, Nico leaned down toward Gasparo, said, "The brute shouldn't have pressured you," then turned and they left the room.

Outside, Gasparo questioned, "Are they going to do nothing?"

Massimo responded, "They're a bunch of asses. They won't act unless the mercenaries occupy the central piazza."

Nico wandered to a stone bench in the piazza, sat, and stared off into the distance, dejected. Massimo turned to Gasparo. "There is a *pasticceria* on the next street. Let's get a pastry while Nico considers his options."

35

Nico watched Massimo and Gasparo until they turned a corner and were out of sight. His gaze drifted across the piazza until it settled on the government office building. Suddenly, he rose from the bench, strode across the piazza to the building, and raced up the steps to the offices of the Papal Magistrates on the second level. He swept into the anteroom and announced, "I wish to speak with a Papal Prosecutor."

The notary, taken aback by Nico's brusque manner, didn't ask Nico's name or purpose. He simply pointed to a hallway and said, "Second office on the left."

There, a lone man with dark eyes and an angular jaw sat behind a large desk. He held a single sheet of paper in one hand and a knife in his other hand. His brow furrowed as he looked back and forth between the two items. Nico rapped on the office door and as soon as the prosecutor looked up, Nico stepped into the room and announced in a firm voice, "Crimes are being committed that need your attention. Children are being abducted."

Nico's outburst perplexed the prosecutor momentarily. He set the paper down but continued holding the knife as possible protection against the intruder. Realizing that he needed to calm himself lest he sound like a fool, Nico inhaled deeply before continuing. "I am Messer Nico Argenti." He reached into a pocket to retrieve his letter of introduction from the Florentine Signoria and held it out to the prosecutor, who read it and indicated that Nico should be seated.

"I am Papal Prosecutor Matteo Fontana. You said that children are being abducted. As a civil crime, abduction falls under the jurisdiction of the city security force. You should bring the matter to a Bologna city council prosecutor."

Nico, still incensed from his previous meeting, grumbled, "The crimes are occurring in villages outside the city. I met with the Reformatori. They said the papal authorities have jurisdiction for crimes outside the city." Unable to contain his disdain for the Reformatori, he added, "They seemed too preoccupied with drinking and gossiping to care about justice."

Fontana smiled. "Some members of the Reformatori are honest, caring men but, as you have discovered, they have a share of pigheaded louts. However, they are correct in saying that crimes outside the city fall to the papal authorities." He leaned back, appraising his visitor. "I am puzzled why you have made the long journey from Florence to tell authorities here in Bologna about crimes in our own territory."

"A band of mercenaries has been raiding mountain villages. Thus far, the raids have been in the Province of Bologna, but the villages are close to the Florentine border. Our Signoria worries that if the renegade mercenaries are unchecked, their crimes will spill across the border."

"How did you learn about the raids?" Fontana asked. "Surely Florence isn't routinely sending investigators into Bologna."

"A monk who had been administering to villagers in the mountains told of the raids upon his return to Florence. He was unsure whether the villages he had visited were within Florentine territory, so a colleague and I were sent to investigate. We spoke with some of the villagers. They told us that during the raids, the mercenaries were abducting boys to add to their numbers. The villagers told us that they are Bolognese."

"Were they able to identify their attackers?"

"From their description, we've determined that their leader is Luigi Attendolo."

The prosecutor cocked his head. "Captain Attendolo. I've heard of him. What could have brought him to Bologna?" Fontana asked rhetorically.

"We were able to locate the mercenaries' camp where we found one of the abductees by himself, away from the camp. He chose to come away with us rather than stay with them. We promised that he will be returned to his home."

"You have one of the boys who was abducted? How did you manage that? I would like to speak with him."

"We are keeping him here in Bologna until it is safe for him to return home. He is at a pasticceria in the piazza. I can bring him here."

"If he is nearby, we can go to him." Fontana picked up the knife which he had previously set on the desk. "I've been trying to determine whether the markings on this knife match a witness's description. It's a tedious process and a change of place might help clear my thinking."

As Nico rose to leave, Fontana held up a hand. "Unlike the Reformatori whom you encountered, I do care about justice, but you must know my situation. It is true that we, the Papal Prosecutors and Magistrates, are responsible for charging those who break provincial laws, but our means to enforce the laws is the Papal Army. In normal times, an army detachment is stationed here in Bologna. Now, however, that detachment is deployed elsewhere. Their deployment is said to be temporary, but I have heard no word on when they might return. Not having them available to enforce the decisions of our magistrates is a problem."

Nico nodded. "I received the same caution from Cardinal Capranica."

Fontana raised an eyebrow. "You spoke with His Eminence?"

"Yes, when I first arrived from Florence. That was before we visited the mercenaries' camp and before we found the boy. The Florentine Signoria sent me to inform the Papal Legate that a mercenary band was operating in the Province of Bologna."

"I'm surprised that I hadn't heard of your visit to His Eminence. We in the Papal Office are close, so news and rumors usually move quickly through our number."

As Nico led Matteo Fontana across the piazza to the pasticceria, he explained how they came upon the abducted boy and how his search for the mercenaries had landed him a beating. When he reached the table where Massimo and Gasparo were seated, Massimo waved a hand toward Gasparo. "This boy must have gone his entire fourteen years without eating, just waiting for this day. That's his third torta and his second glass of cherry ale." Made self-conscious by Massimo's comment, Gasparo wiped crumbs from his face with the back of his hand.

"This is Messer Fontana, a Papal Prosecutor," Nico announced.

Fontana dipped his head and said, "Formality can be reserved for the courtroom. Here I am Matteo."

Massimo introduced himself to which Nico added, "Massimo is also a member of the Florentine Security Commission."

Fontana turned to Gasparo. "You must be the boy who was taken from his home by the mercenaries. What's your name?"

Recalling his harsh questioning by the Reformatori, Gasparo shrank back in his chair and answered softly, "Gasparo."

"I was sorry to learn of your abduction." Gasparo said nothing, but his gaze held on the prosecutor. "Where is your home?" Fontana asked.

"Ceresa Basso."

"It's a hamlet within six miles of *il Passo della Futa*, the mountain pass that connects Bologna with Florence," Nico explained. "The mercenaries are only a short distance from the Florentine border; that is why Florentine officials are troubled."

Fontana said, "I know of Ceresa Basso. There are other villages nearby. The mercenaries were taking a risk attacking Ceresa Basso because those villages band together for their mutual defense against bandits. It's possible that someone from the village could have escaped to alert the others."

The prosecutor asked the boy, "You have family and friends in Ceresa Basso?"

"Yes, my mother, my father, and my sister, Lucia."

"They must be worried, not knowing what's happened to you. I'll arrange for one of my aides to inform your family that you will be returned to them when it is safe to do so. But first you will need to testify...." Fontana hesitated, then reformed his statement. "You will need to tell a magistrate about the raid on your village and how you were taken by the mercenaries. Can you do that?"

Gasparo looked at Nico, who said, "Your story could help prevent other boys from being taken from their families."

Massimo nodded in agreement. Encouraged by his new friends, Gasparo replied, "I can do it."

Fontana turned to Nico. "Gasparo's testimony and your account of discussions with the villagers will be enough for a magistrate to open a case against the mercenaries."

Nico seemed pleased, but Massimo asked, "What will follow from the filing?"

Nico replied, "A notary assigned by the magistrate will advise the defendant, Captain Attendolo, of the charges against him and a date when he must appear before a tribunal."

Fontana added, "Once charges are levied, the accused can either appear before the tribunal to defend himself or he can flee."

"Into self-imposed exile?" Massimo posited.

"Exactly."

Massimo shook his head. "From what I know of Attendolo, I don't believe that charges by a tribunal will cause him to flee, but neither do I believe that he will honor a summons."

"That is my belief as well," Fontana agreed. "It's more likely that

Captain Attendolo would simply ignore a court summons. He knows the Bolognese detachment of the Papal Army has been sent to Le Marche, so our tribunals have no strong military at their disposal to enforce their rulings."

Massimo frowned slightly. "The criminals of Bologna must be delighted to have the entire army detachment away from the province. They can be active night and day."

"The situation isn't that grim. A few soldiers stayed in Bologna," Fontana replied. "They're able to apprehend lone criminals, but they wouldn't be effective against Attendolo's number. Without a strong military force for leverage, words are our only weapons, so I'll ask the magistrate to let me present the charges to Attendolo rather than having a notary do it. I can be more eloquent than a notary."

Nico, who had been silent during the exchanges between the other men, finally spoke. "There is another powerful military force closer to Bologna than the Papal Army. Milan has perhaps the most powerful army on the Italian Peninsula."

Fontana's brow creased. "That may be, but there is no agreement between Milan and the Papal States that would let the Milanese army enter Bologna. Without a treaty, the Papacy would object to any intrusion by the Milanese army. And the Bentivolgio family would see it as an invasion."

"True," Nico agreed. "But Milan is a close ally of Florence. If we could convince Attendolo that Florence is upset with his behavior, he might believe that Bologna would look away while Milan stepped in to support Florence." Nico chuckled. "Although convincing Attendolo of that scam will be a real test of your eloquence."

Fontana said, "With your statements and that of the boy, I can file charges with a magistrate. Then we can visit Attendolo and see if your ruse is effective."

Massimo grinned. "Deception. Did they teach that in your law classes?"

Nico responded with a thin smile. To Fontana, he said, "Massimo and I are envoys of the Florentine Republic. We should accompany you to meet with Attendolo because our presence can help convince him that his behavior is unacceptable to Florence."

Massimo slapped a hand down on the table. "Are you thinking clearly? It would be risky for you to confront the mercenaries. You've already been beaten by two of their thugs. Facing them directly could invite another beating... or worse. I can go with Matteo to represent Florence. They wouldn't dare attack a Papal Prosecutor, and they'd certainly regret any hostility aimed at me."

"We don't know that the thugs were Attendolo's men," Nico argued.

"Who else would they be?" Massimo persisted.

Nico shrugged. "I was alone then. Now I have you to protect me. I can't simply cower in the face of opposition."

"Are all lawyers this stubborn?" Massimo groaned; then, seeing Gasparo picking crumbs from his plate, he rose and said, "I'd better take Gasparo back to the inn. If he eats one more torta, he might burst."

As he watched Massimo leave, Fontana said, "You and Massimo have an interesting relationship. The way you jest with each other... like friends who've known each other for many years."

Nico smiled. "It does feel like I've known Massimo for years, but in truth, we only met when we were appointed to the Florentine Security Commission less than one year past. My father was a soldier. He died when I was young, so my memory of him has gaps, but one thing that stands out was his buoyant spirit. He could always find a positive side in any situation. Massimo has the same optimistic nature. Maybe it comes from being a soldier."

"Many boys follow their fathers. Were you ever on a path to becoming a soldier?"

"Not that I remember. My father was a legate who often traveled with emissaries as part of Florentine delegations. I saw the respect he had for our envoys, many of whom were lawyers. He never openly urged me to become a lawyer. I was only nine years old when he died, but maybe somehow I sensed his view of the profession."

36

Vittorio turned right after passing the church of San Donato. He continued walking for a distance, but he saw no sign of the central market. This was his first time in Bologna, and its angled streets challenged his sense of direction. He wished he had gotten better directions from Nico before setting out in search of Patrizu Nieddu. A woman carrying bags in each hand came toward him. As she drew near, he detected the aroma of fresh bread coming from one of her satchels and said, "Scusa, signora. I am new to the city. I am looking for the bakery in the central market."

Reflexively, she attempted to raise an arm to point, but the heavy bag prevented her from doing so. Instead, she jerked her head sideways, attempting to point with her nose. "That way. The market is that way."

Vittorio thanked her and turned onto the street she had indicated. In a short distance, he came to a street angling to his left that held several vendor carts surrounded by shoppers. Vittorio wandered through the warren of streets comprising the central market until he found the bakery. Inside the shop, a short, heavyset man was wrapping an assortment of rolls for a customer. Vittorio waited until the baker finished serving the customer, then he approached the counter. "I understand you are a member of the Company of Angels."

The baker replied suspiciously. "Yes, I am."

"Another member of the Company of Angels mentioned that you noticed some beggar children had disappeared recently."

Taken aback by Vittorio's statement, the baker stood silent, waiting for him to explain his purpose.

"I am a member of the Florentine Security Commission. Recently, children have gone missing from the orphanage in Florence. We learned that the person responsible for their disappearance is now in Bologna and we're concerned that he may be preying upon children in this city."

Vittorio's explanation let the baker relax. "Beggar children come here for scraps. Some have been coming for a long time, so I've gotten to know them. As you said, a few of them have stopped coming recently, but I can't say their absence has an unholy cause. Children, especially these poor beggar children, are unpredictable." The baker rubbed his chin, leaving a trail of white from his flour covered hands. "Until now, I gave no thought to their absence."

Vittorio said, "I'd like to ask the children, the ones who still come here, if they know what has happened to the others."

"Beggar children survive by asking strangers for handouts, but at the same time they are wary. I doubt that they would answer your questions. It would be better if I question them. They trust me. You can listen and gauge their answers. "

Vittorio nodded his agreement to the baker's suggestion.

The baker continued, "The children come to the central market when the shops are preparing to close. Most of the shopkeepers and vendors take pity and give them scraps and leavings. Come back then and we'll see if the children know anything."

Vittorio roamed the city until late afternoon. In his travels, he found two other markets. Both were smaller than the central market, but he realized that the children might appear to be missing from the central market because they are frequenting one of the other markets.

Vittorio returned to the bakery at closing time. Soon, two young boys appeared at the shop's rear door. The baker handed them crusts of bread but did not question them. After the boys left, the baker explained, "I didn't question those boys because children keep together in small groups. These two boys are always together, so they wouldn't know whether children of other groups are missing."

A thin girl with stringy hair accompanied by a small-boned boy entered through the rear doorway. They looked like brother and sister. The baker winced and mouthed "Poor souls" at seeing them. He took two rolls, spread them with a layer of pork fat, handed them to the two children, and said, "There used to be three of you. What happened to the other one? Where did he go?"

The boy, busy licking the pork fat, did not respond. The girl waved a hand in a dismissive gesture. "I don't know. He's gone." She thanked the baker for the food, turned, and walked out. The boy followed. Vittorio gritted his teeth, wishing that the baker had pressed the girl harder for information.

Next to enter the shop were two boys, and they too offered no useful information. Vittorio paced across the shop, ready to conclude that this approach would not be successful. Moments later, a lone boy stepped through the doorway. He looked older than the others. He was not underweight, his face was clean, and, unlike the other children, this one moved with confidence. Vittorio's patience had ended. He moved out from behind a counter and faced the boy. "I'm seeking information about the children who have disappeared recently. Might you know what happened to them?"

The baker opened his mouth to object to Vittorio's intervention, but he held his tongue when Vittorio flashed him a stern look.

The boy's neck muscles tensed, and he stepped away from the questioner. But as the baker held out some pieces of bread and smiled encouragingly, the boy's fear faded enough for him to reply. "Taddeo, Dofo, and a girl. I've not seen them lately."

"Do you know where they've gone?" Vittorio asked.

"No," the boy said hesitantly, fearing that he might be accused of being responsible for their disappearance.

"Have you seen a man, a stranger, approach any of the children?"

Somewhat confused by the question, the boy said, "Strangers don't approach us. They try to stay away from us. We are the ones who approach them to ask for money."

"The man I am looking for is different from others. He may be trying to snatch children, so he will be seeking strong boys like you."

Startled, the boy asked, "Why does he want children?"

"He lied about his motive when he was asked that question in Florence; then he fled to Bologna, and he's been seen here recently in the central market. When I find him, I'll learn his true purpose. Since you know this area, perhaps you can help me find him." Vittorio pulled a denaro from his coin purse and held it aloft.

The boy stared at the silver coin and said, "I can look, but how will I know him?"

Nieddu had no distinct physical features, so Vittorio cited Nieddu's only identifying characteristic. "He is a Sardinian." As soon as the words left his mouth, Vittorio realized they would have no meaning to the boy. He thought for a moment, then said, "Sardinians use different words from us, words like *Ajò* instead of *andiamo*, *Eja* instead of *si*, and *Ite* instead of *come*."

The boy cocked his head. "Say those words again."

Vittorio repeated slowly, "*Ajò*, Eja, and Ite." The boy echoed the words. His pronunciation was not perfect, but passable. Vittorio nodded, then asked, "And what is your name?"

"I am called Perso."

"Perso, tell the other children I am offering a reward for anyone who can lead me to the Sardinian."

The boy nodded. "*Ajò*, Eja, and Ite," he repeated as he turned. He repeated the words once more and left the shop.

37

A rhythmic thumping pulled Nico from a sound sleep. He rubbed the night from his eyes and stood to gaze out his room's small window to the street below. The Yellow Duck Inn fronted on Via San Donato, one of Bologna's busiest roads where a procession of carts jostled over the cobblestones. In the pale early morning light, vendor carts piled high with produce were making their way from farms and mills to the central market. A whiff from the heavily leaden fish monger's cart passing below caused Nico to pull his head back into the room and shutter the window.

Nico washed, dressed, and was about to comb his hair when a knock on the door announced Massimo's arrival. "I thought we were going to confront Captain Attendolo this morning. You look ready to attend a masquerade as a farmer," Massimo jested.

Nico deflected the jibe by waving his comb in the air and saying, "I received a message from Matteo Fontana. A magistrate summoned him to participate in a court proceeding this morning, so he'll be delayed."

"A lengthy delay?"

"The note didn't say. I intend to join Matteo after breakfast to get a sense of when he might be free. Do you know whether Gasparo will be with us for breakfast?"

"When I left the room, he was sleeping soundly, curled up on a pallet on the floor. I thought it best not to wake him."

"I trust he'll find a way to spend the day while we're occupied with the mercenaries."

Massimo laughed. "Do you recall Gasparo saying that he's seen wonderful things in Bologna?" Nico nodded. "Last night, he confided in me that in his mind, one of the wonderful things in Bologna is the innkeeper's daughter. I'm certain Gasparo will welcome the chance to spend time with her."

"That could be a problem. The innkeeper is a crusty sort who won't want Gasparo paying attention to his daughter. The boy could get himself in trouble with the old man."

"That's unlikely. Gasparo is a farm boy. He might know his way around pigs and chickens, but he has no idea of how to approach a woman. He'll probably spend his time just gawking and trying to find the courage to speak to her." Nico rolled his eyes when Massimo added, "Maybe I should give him a lesson."

~

After a leisurely breakfast, Nico walked to the Palazzo Comunale, which housed the criminal courts. Inside the only occupied tribunal chamber, two men whom Nico did not recognize sat at one table. Across the room, Matteo Fontana sat at another table and alongside stood a young man, whom Nico assumed to be a notary. The magistrate's bench was empty, leading him to assume that the proceeding had not yet begun. Fontana's hands waved in the air, his head bobbed side-to-side, and he shifted constantly in his chair. Seeing the prosecutor obviously agitated, Nico hesitated to approach him. He waited until the prosecutor finished speaking with the notary, then asked, "Is something wrong?"

"We have a lawyer in the Papal Legate's office who normally

handles these kinds of cases, but he is sick, so the magistrate called upon me to take his place. The magistrate was here earlier to read the charge. Then, since this matter is entirely new to me, he declared a brief recess to give me time to prepare. An hour. How can anyone create an effective position in one hour? This magistrate is usually fair, but in this instance...." Fontana squeezed his hands into fists. "As a prosecutor, I'm familiar with all routine criminal statutes, but this case puts me in the position of a defense lawyer. I've always said that prosecutors depend on the law while defense lawyers rely on loopholes and tricks. And I don't have experience as a trickster."

"Nor do I, but perhaps I can help. What is the charge?"

Fontana settled in his chair and leaned toward Nico. "An envoy from Ferrara was passing through Bologna on his way to Ravenna. The city security force detained him because a Bolognese merchant claims that the envoy violated a contract by refusing to pay a debt. The Ferrarese ambassador here in Bologna is furious. He maintains that diplomats must be given free passage; therefore, the envoy should be released. The magistrate expects me to represent the Ferrarese position. If I had more time, I could research the archives, but with only one hour, I can't possibly search the entire archive."

"I seem to recall studying a similar case when I was at the university." Nico rubbed his chin and stared at the ceiling for a few moments. "Salvetti... no... it was Castro. Yes, I remember now. It was the jurist Paolo di Castro who rendered an opinion that resolved a similar case in Lucca."

With an uneasy voice, Fontana asked, "Was the diplomat freed?"

"Yes, but not without consequence. His embassy had to guarantee that they would stand as proxy for the diplomat in the charges being brought against him."

"That seems like a reasonable compromise, one that might be acceptable to our magistrate."

Fontana dispatched the notary to fetch details of the Paolo di Castro declaration from the university library. Then, after many minutes of waiting, he rose and began pacing across the chamber impatiently. At every turn, he glanced at the closed door, willing it to open and the notary to emerge. The panting notary finally returned and presented his handwritten notes to Fontana just as the magistrate entered the tribunal chamber. Fontana barely had time to read the notes before the magistrate called on him to present his argument.

By the time Massimo arrived in the chamber, the two lawyers had finished presenting their positions. The magistrate had accepted Fontana's argument and was in the process of relating his findings to a city security officer and a representative of the Ferrarese embassy. Massimo took a seat in the gallery at the rear of the chamber and gave a quizzical glance at Nico.

Nico responded by joining Massimo in the gallery. "The magistrate is issuing his orders. He should be finished soon, so we should be able to leave shortly. Did you see Gasparo? Did you give him your expert advice on how to speak to the innkeeper's daughter?"

"No, he was still sleeping when I left the inn. I spent the past hour with Vittorio walking through markets, searching for Nieddu. Vittorio found two markets other than the central market. He's been dividing his time between the three. We didn't see Nieddu, but, in addition, Vittorio has recruited street urchins as spotters. Vittorio is confident that with enough eyes looking for Nieddu, he will be found eventually."

By the time the three men left the courthouse, it was late morning. On their way to the stable, they bought smoked fish at a fishmonger's cart and bread from a bakery to take with them. They took the same road south along the river that they had followed on their previous visit to the mercenaries' camp. They passed through the Idice Valley and paused for lunch alongside the ruin of an ancient fort on a hillside overlooking the hamlet of Zena.

After swallowing his last morsel of fish and licking his fingers, Nico said, "I should have taken your advice, Massimo. I should have gotten two pieces of fish. One wasn't enough."

Massimo, who was busily applying a greasy spread to a chunk of bread, chuckled. "I was just thinking that two pieces of fish weren't enough, and I should have bought three." He scanned the farms dotting the broad valley in the distance. "We can stop at one of those farms later when we return to the city. Farms always have good food that they're willing to sell to travelers."

Fontana, who was looking toward the hamlet, pointed and said, "Two riders are approaching. They're coming this way on the road from Zena."

When the riders got closer, Massimo observed, "They're wearing leather and long swords. Most likely, they are two of Attendolo's men. At least we know he hasn't moved his camp."

After they finished eating, the men continued south until they came to the narrow trail that headed up the hillside toward the mercenaries' camp. They moved in single file along the trail, with Massimo in the lead. The trail, narrow and steep at first, widened and flattened as it neared a large clearing cut into the forest. Thick tree stumps told that loggers had recently been at work in the area. As soon as they came within view of the camp, the riders paused and studied the setting. Nico said, "They're packing up their equipment and preparing to leave. If we had come much later, they would have been gone."

Fontana took in the scene; then he sat up tall in his saddle and eased his mount forward into the camp. He said, "It's time to meet the devil." Nico and Massimo positioned themselves on either side of the prosecutor. Initially, a few of the mercenaries working near the camp's periphery noticed the arriving strangers. They stopped working and watched as the three riders rode onward toward the center of the camp. Gradually, others noticed the interlopers, and they too stopped working. Fontana rode close to one of the gawking men and said, "I wish to speak with Captain Attendolo."

The man said nothing and merely pointed to one of the tents that had not yet been disassembled. The three riders dismounted, secured their horses to a stump, and walked toward the tent. Attendolo, alerted by one of his men, emerged from the tent and stood with his arms folded across his chest, waiting for the intruders to reach him. Three of his lieutenants moved in and stood behind him.

Fontana came to within an arm's length and stood eye-to-eye with the mercenary captain. "I am Papal Prosecutor Matteo Fontana." Gesturing first to Nico, he added, "This is Messer Nico Argenti," then to Massimo, "and this is Signor Massimo Leoni. These gentlemen are emissaries of the Florentine Republic."

Attendolo raised an eyebrow upon hearing mention of the Florentine Republic. "I am honored to be in the presence of such esteemed dignitaries. I regret that I cannot offer you any hospitality, but as you can see, our camp is being dismantled."

"We have not come here for social niceties. Our purpose is to inform you of a legal matter. Charges have been filed against you and your men for looting villages and abducting young boys. You are ordered to appear in two days' time before a magistrate in Bologna to answer these charges."

"Charges? Who is making charges against me?"

"I am not at liberty to say at this time, but details of the charges will be made known to you when you appear before the tribunal."

"Those charges are absurd," Attendolo sneered. "Passing armies have always called upon on towns and villages for food. Surely you learned men know that Emperor Frederick, the one called Barbarossa, burned towns and conquered Milan when townspeople refused to supply his troops with food. My men have destroyed no towns and conquered no one. We have taken only what we need.

"And as to the charge of abducting boys, look around. Do you see any boys being held as prisoners? When we pass through villages, we give boys the choice of continuing their dull lives in squalid homes or joining us and experiencing an exciting world they had never even imagined. Here they learn to become men… men with dignity."

Attendolo swept his arm in a broad gesture. "Go talk to my young recruits. Ask if any are being kept against their will. You will find none who want to leave." Again, he folded his arms and stood defiantly.

Unfazed by Attendolo's tirade, Fontana replied calmly, "You will be given the opportunity to defend your actions when you appear before the magistrate."

Attendolo spit on the ground, stiffened, and in a harsh voice, said, "Tell your magistrate that I have other business. I have no time for legal nonsense."

As Attendolo turned to walk away, Fontana said, "There will be consequences if you fail to appear."

Attendolo spun back to face the prosecutor. "Consequences? What consequences? Do you take me for a fool? I know the Papal Army is in the south and since I am no threat to Bentivoglio, he has no cause to send his army into these hills. What recourse is open to your magistrate?" Attendolo snorted, then laughed. "Will he dispatch a team of lawyers to detain me?"

Nico stepped forward. "The Florentine government is troubled by your mercenaries committing lawless acts close to its border."

"So they sent you here to tell me they are troubled? My men are better trained and outnumber the puny Florentine Army. Go back and tell the members of your Signoria to say a rosary and pray for God to preserve them. God would be their only defense if my men were to cross into Florentine territory."

Massimo clenched his fists at Attendolo's labeling of the Florentine Army as puny, but he held his tongue. Nico responded to the captain's threat in a steady voice. "As a peaceful nation, Florence has no need for a large aggressive military, but we have valued alliances with other states. Milan has the most powerful military on the Italian peninsula. It is a loyal ally that has fought alongside Florentines in the past and is committed to do so again, should Florence be threatened. As you know, as members of the Italic League, both Milan and Florence are bound to support the Papal States against any aggressors. We believe that pledge encompasses aggression by renegade mercenaries. You fought bravely alongside the Papal Army in Le Marche. What can be the purpose now that has you pillaging villages in Bologna?"

Attendolo's cheeks reddened. He gritted his teeth and barked, "You will soon learn my purpose." He spun around and bellowed at his lieutenants, "Remove these men from my camp!"

The three brawny subordinates advanced toward Nico, Massimo, and Fontana. Other soldiers moved closer in support of their comrades. Fontana turned and began walking to where the horses were tied. Nico followed. Massimo remained fixed and glowered at the approaching soldiers. When they were close enough for him to smell their foul breaths, he said, "You were once honorable soldiers. Now you serve a Judas." Two of the lieutenants moved their hands to grasp the hilts of their swords. Greatly outnumbered, Massimo turned and followed his colleagues.

The men rode silently in single file along the narrow trail leading down the hillside, each man thinking what he might have said differently and wondering whether their appearance at the camp would have any effect on Attendolo. They passed through the hamlet of Zena and continued riding through the valley until Massimo spotted a farm off to their right and pointed. "Sheep. I can already taste the mutton and cheese."

Massimo led the others along the dirt path that led to a cluster of farm buildings. Near the barn, a farmer and a young boy stood looking at a wagon that was tipped over on one side and missing a wheel. The wheel lay on the ground nearby. Massimo dismounted, walked to where the farmer was standing, and said, "We are travelers who would like to buy some food if you have some to spare."

The farmer assessed the three men, and his eyes brightened. "There is a pot of chicken soup in the kitchen, and we have fresh pecorino cheese, but it is not for sale. However, you can earn your portions by helping me fit the wheel back onto this wagon." He gestured toward his son. "Someday he will be strong enough, but not today."

Massimo and Fontana lifted the wagon and held it while Nico helped the farmer re-mount the wheel. With the repair complete, he escorted the men to the farmhouse where his wife served them bowls of soup and slices of cheese and crusty bread. As they sat eating, Fontana said, "We delivered our message, but I don't believe it will cause Attendolo to change his behavior, and he certainly has no intention of appearing at the tribunal in Bologna to answer the charges against him."

Nico nodded. "I found it disturbing when he said that we will soon learn his purpose. It sounded ominous."

Massimo said, "We can watch the main road from this farm. If Attendolo's men are moving north, they will pass this way. If not, it will mean they are moving south, closer to Florence."

They spent the afternoon helping the farmer with other chores. The sun had dipped low in the sky when they left the farm to return to Bologna. They had seen no sign of the mercenaries. "They must be moving closer to the border," Nico opined.

38

Vittorio was already out searching for Nieddu when Nico, Massimo, and Gasparo met for breakfast. Massimo watched Gasparo's slow, almost plodding gait and downcast gaze as the boy approached the table. "You seem discouraged. Didn't you spend yesterday with Maria?" he asked.

"Maria?" Nico questioned.

"The innkeeper's daughter," Massimo explained.

"I spent all morning in my room trying to decide what to say to her. When I finally went out, she was in the hall carrying a bucket of water and things for cleaning the rooms. The bucket looked heavy, so I offered to carry it."

Massimo patted Gasparo on the back. "You seized the opportunity. I'm proud of you."

"We talked, but only for a few minutes before her father saw us and sent Maria away. He sent an old woman to finish the cleaning."

"Maybe Fortuna will smile upon you today," Nico said. "Earlier, I saw the girl leaving the inn and going to the market. Her father would have no way of knowing if you were to meet her by chance at the market."

Gasparo's face brightened. "I'm not hungry," he declared, jumping up from the table and scampering out of the trattoria.

"He may never want to return to his home in the mountains," Nico jested. The two men watched the boy leave; then Nico said, "Cardinal Capranica requested that I meet with him this morning at the cathedral. He may have information about the Strozzi brothers. It would be good for you and Matteo Fontana to attend the meeting as well, so we can tell the cardinal about our encounter with Attendolo. But right now, Gasparo might benefit from your advice before he charges after the girl and does something foolish."

"I can share one or two of my secrets with the amorous lad." Massimo winked and rose from the table.

Nico was about to leave when the server refilled his mug with watered wine and placed a plate containing another torta in front of him. Nico opened his mouth to say that he hadn't asked for another torta when the server said, "This torta is from the chef. It's a new recipe, and the chef is trying to decide whether to add it to his menu."

Nico took a bite of the pastry and immediately recognized the spice that had been used for flavoring. "Nutmeg," he said loudly.

The chef, who had been watching to see the reaction to his latest creation, heard Nico's outburst and rushed over to the table. "Yes, yes, it is nutmeg," the chef said, both surprised that the spice had been identified and pleased that the person enjoying the pastry had such a finely tuned palate. "How did you know?"

"My cousin Donato owns a restaurant in Florence." Grinning, Nico said, "I can say without hubris that it is the finest in that city."

The chef interrupted, guessing, "The Uccello?" Seeing Nico's startled reaction, he continued, "I had dinner there the last time I was in Florence—excellent roast grouse with chestnut stuffing. My experience leads me to agree with your assessment that the Uccello is the finest restaurant in Florence."

The chef's comment made Nico smile. "Donato once served a cake made with Sicilian mulberries and flavored with nutmeg at a party for an Austrian prince. He is always searching for new recipes to enhance the reputation of his restaurant. He travels throughout the Italian peninsula looking for unusual foods. On one of those travels, he obtained nutmeg from a merchant in Genoa who trades in the Levant. The Austrian prince and his attendants loved the cake. Donato would like to serve that cake again, but nutmeg is too expensive for any but the most lavish occasions."

The chef nodded vigorously. "Yes, yes, that's correct. Until now, nutmeg has been very expensive, too expensive for any eatery in Bologna. But recently, I was in Venice, and I came upon a merchant who discovered an inexpensive source of nutmeg in Anatolia. I intend to keep the knowledge of that nutmeg merchant a secret here in Bologna, but you can tell your cousin the merchant has an office across from the church of Santa Marta in the port of Venice."

"That will be welcome news to Donato, and the next time you go to the Uccello, I'm sure Donato will have a confection that includes nutmeg on his menu."

∼

After breakfast, Nico and Massimo collected the prosecutor at Palazzo Comunale en route to the cathedral. Morning mass was nearly finished when the three men arrived, so they waited in the sacristy for the cardinal. As he removed his vestments, the cardinal said, "His Holiness has elevated me to be a cardinal of the church, but I am still a priest and I remind myself of that by saying mass at least once each week." He ushered the men to a small table where Nico introduced Massimo; then Cardinal Capranica began the meeting, saying, "Two days past, a carpenter came to repair the desk in my office. Since he does business in towns outside the city, I asked whether he might have heard the name Strozzi and he replied that a person representing Signor Ercole Strozzi had come to him looking to have work done at a villa."

Nico asked, "Did he say where the villa is located?"

"He didn't recall the location, but said it was written on a note in his shop. He promised to get the information and bring it to me."

"A bit of good fortune," Fontana remarked.

Nico recalled the rebuke he had received from the cardinal when he had mentioned an event occurring due to good fortune. This time, though, the cardinal did not react similarly to Fontana's statement. Instead, the cardinal cast his eyes downward and said, "The apprentice never came. I sent a clerk to the carpenter's shop to get the information, but when the clerk returned, he reported that the carpenter has gone missing. For the past two days, no one has seen him."

In a bleak voice, Nico said, "It can't be a coincidence that shortly after reporting that he had seen Ercole Strozzi, the carpenter went missing. The carpenter was the only link to the Strozzi brothers, and now he is lost."

"I don't believe in coincidences," Massimo asserted.

"Nor do I," the cardinal agreed. "But would anyone know that the carpenter had seen Strozzi? Who else might he have told other than me?" Capranica asked rhetorically. He rubbed his forehead while thinking, then said, "It surprises me that Father Alfonso's contacts haven't reported any information about the Strozzi brothers. Little has escaped his sources in the past, so I can only assume that the Strozzis are well hidden."

For several moments, the men considered the situation before Nico broke the silence. "We also have information for you, Your Eminence. Messer Fontana filed charges against the mercenaries for their atrocities."

Before Nico could continue, Cardinal Capranica swung his head in Fontana's direction and interrupted Nico's account. "You filed charges against the mercenaries? Do you have evidence or witnesses ready to testify?"

"We have a boy whom Signori Argenti and Leoni rescued from the mercenaries' camp. The boy is willing to testify, and I believe we may also be able to convince some of the villagers to come forward."

When the cardinal leaned back to consider the situation, Fontana said, "Yesterday we went to the mercenaries' camp to inform Captain Attendolo of the charges against him and his men."

The cardinal's eyes widened. He gasped, and echoed, "You went to the mercenaries' camp. That was a bold and dangerous move. I wouldn't expect Captain Attendolo to entertain that challenge to his authority."

Fontana responded, "The law requires that an accused person be informed of the charges against him, but you are correct, he did not react well. After we stated our case, he became livid and had us ejected from his camp. He stated firmly that he will not appear before a magistrate to answer the allegations. He was emboldened by the knowledge that the Papal Army is in the south. We told him there would be consequences if he fails to appear before a magistrate. Messer Argenti even suggested that treaties among Milan, Florence, and the Papal States would allow the Milanese Army to become involved if Attendolo does not cease his aggressive behavior."

Cardinal Capranica looked askance at Nico, who added, "It was a veiled threat, and one that only angered Attendolo further."

"People only become angered by things that disturb them, so your threat must have troubled him," the cardinal declared. "However, when he reflects on your words, he'll conclude that no one here would welcome or permit the Milanese Army to roam throughout the Province of Bologna. He'll realize that he faces no real opposition."

"We are of the same opinion," Fontana agreed. "Captain Attendolo said he is preparing to act on behalf of a patron and that he may be ready to act soon."

"What action is he planning?" Capranica asked.

"He didn't say," Nico replied. "But Massimo and I are apprehensive because Attendolo moved his camp to a location closer to the Florentine border. I retained a courier to deliver a message with that information to the chancellor in Florence."

Massimo said, "I've known many mercenaries, and none act

without being well paid. If we are to stop Attendolo, we need to find his patron and end his source of funds."

Nico nodded his agreement. "The Strozzi brothers have both the funds and motivation to retain Captain Attendolo and his men. Now that we know Ercole Strozzi is in the Province of Bologna, and both he and Attendolo came here at nearly the same time, it is a reasonable conjecture that Ercole Strozzi is Attendolo's patron."

Fontana held up his hands in resignation. "But we know neither Strozzi's location nor his purpose."

As the men's frustration grew, Massimo asked sharply, "Is anyone searching for the carpenter?"

Fontana replied, "Surely his family and his employees are looking for him, but unless it can be shown that a crime has been committed, the Bolognese Security Force will not expend effort searching for him."

Nico and Massimo said nearly simultaneously, "We need to speak with the carpenter's family."

39

The carpentry shop was a low stone building set beside a canal just outside the city wall. Two small windows flanked a door leading to an office area at one end of the building. At the other end was a door wide enough to accommodate large wagons. Openings in the roof let light into the building's work area.

A black dog curled up on the floor greeted Nico and Massimo when they entered the office. He raised his head, gave a single yip, and then returned to his nap. The office was vacant except for the dog, but two men could be seen through the opening into the work area. One man was sweeping the floor while the other was stacking lumber. Nico approached the nearest man and asked, "Is this the shop of Signor Borso Gritti?"

The man finished stacking the wood he had been carrying, then said, "Yes, this is his shop, but he is not here. I am one of his apprentices. May I help you?"

"I am Messer Nico Argenti and this is Signor Massimo Leoni. Cardinal Capranica told us that Signor Gritti is missing. We are hoping you might have information that could help us find him."

The apprentice took in a deep breath at hearing Nico mention the cardinal. "His Eminence sent you?" he asked in a shaky voice.

To avoid a lengthy explanation, Nico replied simply, "Yes, His Eminence prays that Signor Gritti is safe." Then he added, "What can you tell us about his disappearance?"

"Two days past, Signor Gritti went to the Palazzo Comunale to repair a piece of furniture in the office of the Papal Legate. When he returned to the shop, a customer was waiting for him to discuss changes to a kitchen to please the customer's new wife. Signor Gritti went away with the customer to see the kitchen. That was the last time I saw him."

"Do you know the customer's name or where he lives?" Massimo asked.

"I don't recall his name, but we did work for him in the past, so his name will be in a folio in the office."

The second apprentice, the one who had been sweeping the floor, overheard the conversation and came to join the others. His childlike face made him appear no older than thirteen years. "This may mean nothing, but after Signor Gritti left, two men came to the shop and asked for him. They wouldn't say why they wanted to see him; they said I couldn't help them. They asked if he would return to the shop later, and I told them that I wasn't certain, but that he would probably return. They left without saying another word, but later, maybe an hour later, I saw them again. They were standing at the side of the shop, intently watching the street. If they were waiting for Signor Gritti, they could have waited inside the shop. I thought it strange that they preferred to wait outside."

"Did you invite them to come inside?" Nico asked.

The apprentice grimaced. "They were not the most genial of men. They were talking to each other, and I felt no urge to intrude if they wanted to remain outside."

Massimo asked, "Can you describe the two men?"

"They were big and..." he hesitated, reluctant to disparage the men, "ugly looking. They wore leather, like soldiers going into battle, but they weren't soldiers. At least they weren't members of the Papal Army. Their leather was different. One of them had a scar."

"The scar, was it on the right side of his face? Did it look like a burn mark?" Nico asked.

The apprentice's jaw dropped. "How did you know?"

Nico and Massimo looked at each other. "It must be the same thugs who came for you," Massimo said. Then, turning to the apprentices, he asked, "Does Signor Gritti have family?"

One of the apprentices replied, "A wife."

The apprentice cringed when Nico told him, "Tell her priest to prepare the woman. Signor Gritti may have met a vile fate."

Nico turned to the other apprentice and explained, "Cardinal Capranica is eager to find a man named Ercole Strozzi. Signor Gritti had been approached to do work at Strozzi's villa and he promised to tell His Eminence the villa's location. Is there a record of the location here in the shop?"

"If there is a record, it would be in the office." Nico and Massimo followed the apprentice into the office. He spread a file across the desk. "These are the most recent orders.

"Strozzi, Strozzi," he repeated as he scanned through the papers. Finally, he looked up and said, "There is no mention of Strozzi in this file."

Nico said, "Is there mention of a villa in a town north of the city?"

Once again, the apprentice sifted through the papers, then looked up and said, "The only listing outside the city is the town of Bazzano. Bazzano is not north of Bologna, and that paper mentions work in the town at the church of Santo Stephano. There is no mention of a villa."

Nico exhaled a long breath. "Damn," he muttered. "Signor Gritti must have taken the information about Strozzi's villa with him, and if he did, it is lost."

"Are you going to find Signor Gritti?" the apprentice asked.

Massimo replied, "We're going to continue searching for Ercole Strozzi. When we find him, he may lead us to Signor Gritti."

40

Vittorio divided the city into sections, and each day he explored a different one. In the mornings, when shoppers were out buying goods for their evening meals, he spent time surveilling the local markets, hoping for a glimpse of Patrizu Nieddu. Later each day, he visited the local establishments to ask whether anyone remembered a stranger with a peculiar accent. Knowing Nieddu's penchant for beer, Vittorio's first targets were the taverns. Next priority was the restaurants and trattorias. Then came warehouses and factories where goods were stored and moved because they demanded the same abilities that Nieddu had developed as a dock worker. Finally, he traveled each road in the section asking about Nieddu at each business along the way. Vittorio's experience as an investigator had given him patience and kept him from becoming discouraged.

On the third day, while exploring the Poggiale district, Vittorio inquired at a stable. "Yes, two weeks past, I rented a horse to a Sardinian," the stable master replied to Vittorio's question. "I have a cousin who is married to a woman from Sardinia, so I recognized his accent. It was a surprise because there aren't too many Sardinians in Bologna."

"Did he say his name?"

"No."

"Did he say why he wanted to hire a horse? Or where he was going?"

"No, but he did say that his patron — that was the word he used, patron—liked wine and he wanted to bring his patron a bottle of fine Sardinian wine. He asked if I knew an enoteca that sold Sardinian wine. I think he called it Canou."

"Cannonou," Vittorio corrected.

"I had to laugh. We Bolognese pride ourselves on our fine local wines. Many enotecas won't even sell wines from neighboring Tuscany. They certainly wouldn't sell wine from Sardinia. And other than him, who would want to buy it?"

"He came here only the one time?" Vittorio asked.

"No, he came once before." His nose wrinkled as he thought. "He may have also come at other times. If he came when I was not here, the stableboy could have rented a horse to him."

Although Nieddu had no distinguishing physical characteristics, Vittorio described Nieddu's appearance to the extent possible. The stable master nodded enthusiastically. "Yes, that's him. That's the Sardinian."

Vittorio reasoned that Nieddu hired horses at that stable, either because he lived in the area or because the stable was closest to the Porta Lame city gate. If the latter reason were correct, then Nieddu's patron would be to the north.

"For how many days did he need the horses?"

"The first time, he took a horse one day and returned it the following day, but the second time, he took a horse in the morning and returned the same afternoon.

"So, his destination is not far from the city," Vittorio said to himself. He resolved to spend more time searching in the Poggiale district.

Every afternoon, Vittorio returned to the bakery in the central market to connect with the children he had recruited as informants.

Buoyed by the possible lead to Nieddu at the stable, Vittorio stopped at a butcher shop on his way to the bakery. There he bought a *libbra* of smoked meat and had the butcher cut it into small slices. These would encourage the beggar children to continue searching for the Sardinian.

Half of the smoked meat slices had been distributed when the boy named Perso swept into the shop. "I found him. I found the Sardinian," he bubbled.

The corners of Vittorio's mouth turned up in a smile, as much in response to Perso's enthusiasm as to his words. "Did you get a close look at him? Describe him."

"He's as tall as you. He has dark hair and thick arms."

That was not much of a description, but it was as much as anyone could say about Nieddu. "Where did you see him; here in the central market?"

"No, it was in Piazza del Mercato, the old market."

The old market wasn't close to the stable, but at least both were in the northern part of the city, so that could narrow the future search. Before Vittorio could ask anything further, Perso said, "I followed him from the market to his apartment."

Vittorio's eyes widened. "You followed him," Vittorio mirrored, then pulled a denaro from his coin purse and handed it to Perso. "Another of these if you lead me to the apartment and he is indeed the Sardinian I am seeking."

Perso quickly pocketed the coin and exclaimed, "Follow me!" as he scampered out into the street.

Vittorio left the remaining smoked meat slices for the baker to distribute, then ran out the door after Perso. Rather than taking a direct route, Perso led the investigator on a circuitous route through alleys and narrow streets, many of which had no names. Perso stopped near the two-hundred-year-old Chiesa di San Benedetto, the church of Saint Benedict. He pointed to a building across the street. "I saw him enter there; the doorway next to the cobbler's shop."

Through the doorway was a stairway that led to an apartment on the second level. Vittorio stared at the small windows of the apartment, trying to detect any movement within, but saw not even a wavering shadow. Perso shifted his focus back and forth between Vittorio and the apartment. After several minutes, he said, "Are you going to the apartment to see if he is the Sardinian you are seeking?"

Without taking his eyes from the building, Vittorio replied, "There is no one in the apartment now. I will wait to see who enters it."

Perso's shoulders sagged in disappointment that his reward would be delayed. He stepped to the front of the church, leaned back against a pillar, and slid down until he was sitting on the plinth.

"You need not stay. If the man I am seeking appears, I will deliver the second denaro coin to the bakery tomorrow. The baker will give it to you."

Perso sighed, "I have nowhere to go." After a time that seemed like hours to the boy, he jumped up and pointed to two men still a block away but coming toward them. "That's him!" Perso announced.

Vittorio studied the two approaching figures. One was indeed the Sardinian Patrizu Nieddu, and accompanying him was a priest. When they reached the corner, Nieddu continued straight ahead toward the apartment, but the priest turned onto a side street heading toward the city center. Nieddu passed by on the opposite side of the street from Vittorio and entered the apartment. Vittorio placed a silver denaro in Perso's outstretched hand. "You did well. He's the one I've been seeking."

"What are you going to do now?"

"I'm going to return tomorrow with my friends and have a discussion with him."

"He is there now. He may not be there in the morning. If we go now, I can help you."

Vittorio placed a hand on the boy's shoulder. "I appreciate all that you have done. You've been a help already, and maybe I will need your help again in the future, but not now. I am certain that Signor

Nieddu will be in his apartment when my colleagues and I return in the morning."

41

The sun had not yet graced the sky when Vittorio, Nico, and Massimo gathered outside the church of Saint Benedict. The street was quiet except for the whimpering of a distant dog. Nico shivered in the cool morning air and pulled his cloak tight around his shoulders. Vittorio pointed to the dark windows of the building across the street. "That's Nieddu's apartment."

They crossed the street, pushed open the outside door, and climbed to the building's second level. They weren't concerned that footfalls on the stone steps might reveal their presence because the building had no other exit. This time, Nieddu could not escape.

Vittorio tried the apartment door and, as he expected, it was locked. He stepped aside to let Massimo move forward. The strapping soldier accelerated as he reached the door and hammered his shoulder into the sturdy wood. Splinters flew from the jam, the lock ripped free, the door swung open, and the three men charged into the dimly lit sitting room. "Damn!" Massimo exclaimed as he rubbed his shoulder. "Doors must be getting harder."

Nico chuckled. "Either that or you're getting softer."

After a quick scan showed the space to be empty, Vittorio rushed ahead into an adjoining room. "He's here," Vittorio called to the others.

Nico and Massimo followed Vittorio into the bedroom, where Nieddu, half awakened by the noise, struggled to decide whether the three invaders were real or part of a dream. His indecision ended when Vittorio threw off his thin coverlet and demanded, "Get up!"

Slowly, Nieddu sat up and swung his feet down to the floor. In the faint light, he could not identify the intruders, and assumed them to be men sent by Luigi Attendolo. "You impudent bastards have no right to burst in here," he snapped.

Vittorio grabbed Nieddu by the arm, dragged him into the sitting room, and dropped him onto a chair. In the pale morning light coming through the windows, Nieddu recognized that the men standing before him were not Attendolo's mercenaries. "Who are you? What are you doing?"

Vittorio stood directly in front of Nieddu and bent low, their faces less than a *palmo* apart. "Don't you remember me, Signor Orphanage Administrator?"

Nieddu looked from one man to another. "Florentines," he said in disbelief. "This is Bologna. What are you doing here? What do you want with me?"

Nico stepped forward and stood next to Vittorio so they could question Nieddu using a technique that had proven effective in the past. Nico would ask the initial questions, and if an answer was not forthcoming, Vittorio would intimidate the subject until he gave an acceptable response. Nico called the method *uomo facile uomo duro,* easy man hard man. Massimo stood behind Nico, massaging his bruised shoulder and watching his colleagues perform their practiced routine.

Nico leaned toward Nieddu. "You lied to the Officials Over Orphans when you applied for the job as administrator of the orphanage. You told them that you were a manager in Sardinia, but you weren't. We have a sworn statement saying that you were never other than a dockworker."

Nieddu wasn't sure whether lying to the Officials was a criminal act. He was about to protest his innocence when Nico continued, "You failed to keep records of where the children were placed." Failing to keep records might indeed be a crime, so Nieddu remained silent. Finally Nico said, "And you took payments that rightfully belonged to the orphanage." Even Nieddu knew that was a crime.

Nieddu considered his situation for a moment, then snarled, "We are in the Papal States, not Florence. You have no jurisdiction here."

Massimo looked at Nico, expecting him to cite a provision that would give them legal authority. Instead, Vittorio grasped Nieddu by the collar and pushed him backward, suspending the chair on its two rear legs. "You are correct. We have no authority here, so we'll have to bring you back to Florence."

"You can't do that," Nieddu barked.

Vittorio grabbed Nieddu's arm and jerked him up from the chair. "Get dressed. We're going for a long ride, and for you, it will be a long ride to a cold prison cell."

"Wait, wait," Nieddu pleaded. "I admit that I might have neglected a few rules, but they were just minor things. I hurt no one. Perhaps you can overlook them in exchange for some valuable information."

Vittorio asked, "What possible information of value could scum like you have?"

"What if I could tell you about a threat to your republic?"

Nico cocked his head. "What threat?"

Vittorio swung around to face Nico. His muscles tensed and his hands balled into fists. "He's talking shit. How could he possibly know of a threat against Florence? Don't listen to him. He'd say anything to avoid prison."

Nieddu stepped back, away from the irate investigator. Directing his words to Nico, he said, "You are an honorable man. I trust that when you hear what I have to say, we can have an understanding... an agreement."

Nico thought about the charges. Nieddu's misrepresentation of his past to an official government body was a criminal offense, but only a minor infraction. Failing to create reports was a procedural matter, not a crime. Nieddu's only serious crime was stealing payments meant for the orphanage.

However, Nieddu's crimes weren't Nico's only concern. How could he explain to his sister Alessa if he did not make Nieddu pay for selling orphans to the mercenaries? Would she understand that sometimes justice demands compromise? Nico weighed all the issues in his mind, then said, "If your information is substantial, and if it can be verified, then we could have an arrangement."

Nieddu shook himself loose from Vittorio's grip and walked across the room, thinking of possible repercussions if he were to tell the Florentines about Attendolo's plot. Whether the Florentines could save their republic or not was of no consequence to Nieddu. All that mattered to him was that Attendolo not discover who had divulged the plan to the Florentines. "What I tell you must be held in confidence."

Vittorio and Massimo waited for Nico, who replied, "That is unacceptable. If there is a viable threat against the Florentine Republic, we must tell the Signoria so they can deal with it."

Nieddu shook his head. "You can tell them, but I can't have it known that the information came from me, or my life would be at risk."

"Your life will be at greater risk if there is a real threat, and you don't tell us about it. If a single Florentine suffers, there would be no place you could hide from us."

Vittorio interjected, "Our patience is waning. Tell us now, what is the threat?"

Nieddu wiped a bead of sweat from his forehead. "A band of mercenaries is planning to take Piero de Medici hostage and overpower the government of Florence."

Nico's entire body stiffened. "Piero," he murmured. As patriarch of the Medici dynasty, Piero de Medici symbolized the wealth, prosperity, and greatness of the entire country. If anything were to happen to him, it could destroy Florentines' belief in their republic's destiny.

Vittorio raised a hand to strike Nieddu, but held himself. "This lowlife will say anything to save his ass. Why should we believe him?"

Nieddu shrugged. "I can only tell you what I know. If you choose not to believe me...."

"When does he plan to move against Florence?" Nico demanded.

"I don't know exactly, but soon. He's been adding new recruits, and he now has enough men to do it."

As a reflex, Massimo blurted, "Attendolo." Nieddu registered surprise at the mention of the mercenary captain's name.

The three Florentines moved close to each other and spoke in hushed tones. "Now I understand why they're recruiting children," Massimo explained. "Piero de Medici resides in a villa outside the city. It may take battle-hardened men to take the villa, but once it is captured, the inexperienced recruits can hold Piero and secure the site. Attendolo can then take his experienced men into the city to gain control of the Signoria."

Massimo continued, "It would be risky for Attendolo to attack Florence. Our army is not as 'puny' as he believes. Also, his men would face citizens who would rise up to repel the invaders. His force would be outnumbered."

Vittorio said, "It may be true that the army could defeat Attendolo, but as you know very well, if an attack were to take place, innocent people would suffer. Remember what happened in all the battles at Lucca."

Nico spoke slowly as he formed a strategy in his mind. "Attendolo would take such a risk only if he were being well paid. When we were at his camp, he mentioned that he has a patron."

Nico turned to face Nieddu. "Someone is paying Attendolo and his men. What is the name of his sponsor?"

Since Ercole Strozzi had no way of taking revenge on Nieddu, the Sardinian had no reservation in divulging Attendolo's patron. "If I tell you his name, I can go free?"

Vittorio ignored the question and echoed Nico's request, growling, "Who is the sponsor?"

Nieddu threw up his hands. "I'm telling you much and getting nothing in return," he grumbled.

"First, make us happy, then maybe you will get something," Vittorio snapped.

Nieddu banged his fist against the wall and spat out, "Ercole Strozzi."

Nico took a step forward and stared directly into Nieddu's eyes. "How do you know about Strozzi and the mercenaries?"

Nieddu, finally resigned to his situation, replied, "Signor Strozzi hired me to deliver instructions to Captain Attendolo. He also had me bring money from his bank to pay Attendolo's men."

With disbelief in his voice, Nico asked, "You have access to Ercole Strozzi's funds?"

"Not all of his funds. He instructed the Bardi bank to release a set amount of money to me each week from his account. I deliver that money to the mercenaries."

"When is the next payment?"

"In two days' time."

Vittorio glanced at Massimo, who perceived Vittorio's plan and nodded his agreement. Vittorio looked at Nieddu and said, "Massimo and I will escort you to the bank."

"I have one last question," Nico said. "Where is Ercole Strozzi?"

"At a villa owned by Signor Mello Canneschi, near the Navile Canal, about ten miles north of the city." Nieddu observed Nico's reaction, saw that the lawyer was pleased by the information, then asked sarcastically, "Are you 'happy' now? Can you let me go?"

Nico replied, "First, we must see whether you are telling the truth. I'll be happy only when Strozzi is convicted by a tribunal. And to make that happen, you will need to testify."

Nieddu was about to object, but held his tongue when he saw Vittorio scowling at him. Nico scanned his two colleagues to see if they had any further questions. When neither man spoke, Nico jabbed a finger at Nieddu and warned, "We'll come here to get you when the tribunal is scheduled. Don't even think of leaving before then."

Nieddu spread his hands wide but said nothing. Then, as the Florentines turned to leave, Nieddu said, "You were trying to find one of the boys from the orphanage."

Nico nodded. "Armando."

"He's with the mercenaries. The other boys from the orphanage, them too. They're all with the mercenaries." Nico glared at Nieddu but said nothing. "Did you follow me all the way to Bologna just to find that boy?" Again, Nico held his gaze and remained silent. "How did you find me?" Nieddu asked.

Vittorio laughed and said, "We didn't find you. A young boy—a street urchin—found you. You can't blend in with the Bolognese by speaking like a Sardinian. With your Sardu dialect, you'll never be able to hide."

Outside, Vittorio said, "He won't stay here in Bologna. He'll flee as soon as he can to avoid having to testify."

Nico said, "I'll ask Matteo Fontana to post watchers to keep that from happening."

Massimo said, "I'll stay here until the watchers arrive to make sure he doesn't leave."

That evening, Nico sat in his room at the Yellow Duck Inn and began composing a letter in his head. *Should he tell Alessa that the orphan Armando had joined a band of mercenaries? Was Nieddu's information about the boy credible?* Nico picked up his pen.

Dearest sister Alessa,

Forgive me for not writing to you when I first spotted the runaway orphanage administrator, Patrizu Nieddu. I caught a glimpse of him in the central market, but I was not able to confront him. Recently, Vittorio came to Bologna to help in the hunt for Nieddu. I marvel at the way Vittorio finds ingenious means to get results. He paid one of the street boys to search for a man speaking the Sardinian dialect, and that clever idea proved successful. You will not be surprised to learn that Nieddu is involved in another nefarious scheme here in Bologna, one that is too complicated to explain in a letter. I'll give you the details when I return.

Give my regards to Donato and Joanna. I hope you are all in the Lord's good grace, and I look forward to coming home soon.

Your loving brother, Nico

42

A pleasant recollection of the previous evening's dinner with friends filled Papal Prosecutor Matteo Fontana's thoughts. He had barely arrived at his office and removed his cloak when a knock at his door dashed that memory. He turned, found Nico standing in the doorway, and motioned for him to enter. "Nico, come in, come in. What brings you to my office at this hour?" His lips curled into a smile. "I've always been told that Florentines never rise this early."

Breathless from his quick trek across the city and eager to deliver his news, Nico let Fontana's jibe pass unchallenged. Nico spit out words like a torrent cascading from a waterfall. "We found where Ercole Strozzi is staying- he's the one funding Attendolo's mercenaries- they're planning to attack Florence."

Fontana froze momentarily while he absorbed the implication of Nico's statements; then he raised a hand. "Wait, hold the details. Cardinal Capranica will want to hear them."

"Will he be in his office at this hour?"

"Yes, I'm sure. He is one of those who awakens the roosters."

Capranica heard footsteps echoing through the hallway of the quiet building. He looked up, watched the two men approach, and waved them to enter. Nico removed his cloak and was about to be seated when Father Alfonso passed the doorway. The cardinal beckoned for him to enter as well.

Fontana said, "Your Eminence, Messer Argenti has news that I think you will want to hear." The cardinal rested his hands on his desk and indicated that Nico should begin.

"One of my colleagues has been tracking a fugitive named Nieddu who fled from Florence to Bologna. Yesterday we intercepted Nieddu at his apartment. He claims to be an agent of Ercole Strozzi and says that Strozzi is funding Attendolo's men to mount an attack against the government of Florence. They also plan to take Piero de Medici hostage."

The cardinal leaned back in his chair and stared at the far wall of the room for several moments. Then he looked at Nico. "Those are serious allegations. Do you believe them?"

"Thus far, we have only Nieddu's word, but he did provide details that could help us confirm his story. He told us where to find Ercole Strozzi, and he told us that Strozzi is funding the mercenaries from an account at the Bardi bank here in Bologna."

Fontana said, "You've had time to think about this, Nico. How do you propose that we respond to Nieddu's accusation?"

"Nieddu makes a practice of fleeing to avoid culpability. He fled from Sardinia to Florence to avoid one problem; then he fled to Bologna to avoid prosecution in Florence. I worry that he'll try to flee from Bologna to avoid retribution from Attendolo or Strozzi. Can you provide watchers to prevent him from fleeing again?"

"Yes, I can do that," Fontana replied.

"If Nieddu is correct that Ercole Strozzi is funding the mercenaries for an attack against Florence, then I want to see charges brought against Ercole Strozzi. Nieddu has agreed to testify against Strozzi."

Fontana nodded. "I've already filed charges against Captain

Attendolo for raiding villages and abducting children. If Strozzi is funding the mercenaries, then he is complicit in those crimes. I can amend my filing to name both Attendolo and Strozzi as the accused."

Fontana raised his hands in a gesture of exasperation. "But no magistrate would accept an accusation that Strozzi and Attendolo are planning an attack against Florence. It may be different elsewhere, but here in the Papal States, plans are merely thoughts and words, not criminal activity."

"I understand," said Nico. "As a precaution, we will be sending a message to the Florentine chancery to warn them of the potential threat. However, we may yet find that Strozzi has acted in violation of your laws."

Cardinal Capranica looked from Nico to Fontana. "You can file charges against Signor Strozzi, but will you be able to gain a conviction if all you have are statements made by Signor Nieddu?"

Nico responded, "We will also have testimony from Gasparo, a boy who was taken from his village." Nico's statement elicited a frown from the cardinal, so Nico elaborated. "True, the words of a co-conspirator and a youngster aren't the basis for a strong case, but my colleagues and I are determined to uncover other evidence before a tribunal convenes."

Nico and Fontana returned to the prosecutor's office. As Fontana wrote an amendment to his initial filing, Nico told him of Vittorio's plan to accompany Nieddu to the Bardi bank. "Tomorrow, Nieddu is scheduled to withdraw the next installment payment from Strozzi's account and deliver it to the mercenaries. We will make Nieddu withdraw funds from the bank but delay their delivery to Attendolo. It could undermine Attendolo's commitment to Strozzi's scheme if he is not paid, and if he were to learn that charges had been filed against Strozzi."

Fontana suspended his pen in mid-air and looked up at Nico. "But how would he learn that Strozzi had been accused?"

"Attendolo buys weapons from an armorer in Bologna. They are in frequent contact. If word of Strozzi's situation were to reach the armorer, it would soon find its way to Attendolo."

Fontana grinned. "A clever idea. I can have one of my clerks visit the armorer under the pretext of buying a blade. While in the shop, he can casually mention Strozzi's plight."

43

"The Papal Prosecutor intends to file charges against you."

"Against me?" Strozzi retorted. "What charges? I've broken no laws. I hardly ever leave this villa."

"The filing claims that you are funding Attendolo's mercenaries."

Ercole Strozzi bolted up, nearly upsetting the table. He stomped across the room, then whirled around and barked, "Funding mercenaries is not a crime. No one objects to Bentivoglio having his own army. The prosecutor isn't charging him."

"Signor Bentivoglio isn't being charged because his men are not raiding villages and abducting children. Those are crimes, crimes being committed by Attendolo's men. Since you are supporting Attendolo's activities, the prosecutor maintains that you share in the responsibility for those crimes."

Strozzi bellowed, "What kind of laws do you have here in Bologna? I'm not the one raiding villages." Strozzi paused a moment, exhaled a deep breath, then in a calmer voice asked, "I don't tell Captain Attendolo how to conduct his affairs, so how can I be held responsible when he does something improper?"

"That I cannot say. I am not a lawyer."

Once again, Strozzi's face reddened. His entire body stiffened, and he pounded a fist against the wall. "How does the prosecutor know that I'm supporting the mercenaries? Who told him?"

Strozzi's outburst made Father Alfonso, the secretary to the Papal Legate, question whether he was wise to travel from the city to warn Strozzi of the impending charges. The priest said, "The prosecutor has apprehended one of your hirelings."

"My hireling?" Strozzi growled. He froze for a moment, then spat out a name. "Nieddu."

Father Alfonso nodded. "Yes, Signor Nieddu."

Through clenched teeth, Strozzi bristled, "Damn him. I never should have trusted that Sardinian bastard."

Alfonso recoiled at Strozzi's slur against Sardinia. Bologna's first citizen, Giovanni Bentivoglio, was said to be a descendent of a king of Sardinia, so Alfonso felt favorably disposed toward Sardinians. But Florentines respect none other than themselves, he thought.

Again, Strozzi gained control. He returned to the table, looked down at the priest, and said, "Nieddu is just one voice, and he cannot prove his accusation. Will a magistrate accept his word?"

Alfonso shrugged. "Perhaps not, but the accusation alone will prompt a trial where the motive for your association with Captain Attendolo will be questioned. And they might also produce other evidence."

Strozzi snatched a glass of wine from the table and flung it at the far wall. A crimson stain spread down the wall and glass shards scattered onto the floor. Drawn by the sound, a house servant poked his head into the room. Upon seeing Strozzi fuming and the wall splattered with vintage Barbera wine, he turned and exited without a word.

"I cannot accept the risk. Nieddu must not be allowed to testify. He must disappear." Strozzi pointed a finger at Alfonso. "The two thieves, the ones you found to beat up the meddling lawyer, have them dispose of Nieddu. Make sure they do the job right this time.

They weren't forceful enough with that damned lawyer. He's still in Bologna."

Strozzi's words made Alfonso's stomach roil. At the outset, Alfonso saw Attendolo's strike against Florence as payback for Bologna's subjugation by Florentine banks and merchants. Alfonso convinced himself that Attendolo could disrupt the Florentine government without harming anyone, and he appreciated the irony that a Florentine, albeit an exile, would be financing the move against Florence.

However, Strozzi's demand to have thugs assault Messer Argenti had given Alfonso pause. He tried rationalizing the act by telling himself that Argenti was a Florentine, but that failed. He had instructed the thugs to intimidate Argenti, not beat him. He should have known that men like that never listen. They seize every opportunity to inflict pain on others. Alfonso became sickened when he heard the extent of Argenti's injuries. Now Strozzi wanted to dispose of Nieddu. Alfonso knew what Strozzi meant by "dispose," but perhaps there was another way.

Alfonso's concentration was interrupted by Strozzi asking, "Will your men know how to find Nieddu?"

"The Papal Prosecutor appointed watchers to ensure that Nieddu does not flee. I learned the location of Nieddu's apartment because I overhead the prosecutor instructing his men."

"Will those men, the watchers, present a problem?"

"No, they won't be an obstacle. The men will be able to deal with the watchers."

Strozzi rubbed his hands together. "Good. Good. Tomorrow; it must happen no later than tomorrow."

Strozzi filled a fresh glass, downed a gulp of dark red Barbera, and bellowed to the house servant, "Get in here and clean this mess!"

∼

The following morning, Massimo and Vittorio set out for Nieddu's apartment in the Porta Galleria district. When they reached the Bardi Bank, Vittorio said, "This is where we will be taking Nieddu so he can make the withdrawal from Strozzi's account."

Massimo scanned the building's façade and the understated sign above the door. A group of men clustered outside, waiting for the bank to open. "They're all well-dressed. Probably businessmen," Massimo observed. "The bank must be selective in deciding whom it serves."

Vittorio said, "They're very selective. My father dealt with the Bardi bank in Florence when he was a consul of the Armorer's Guild. The bankers always told my father that there was little profit to be made by having workers as clients, so the bank dealt only with merchants and professional men."

As Vittorio and Massimo came within sight of Nieddu's apartment, a wagon passed them and stopped directly in front of the building. They surmised that the men in the wagon had business at the cobbler's shop on the street level, so they were surprised when two men climbed down from the wagon and entered the door that led to Nieddu's apartment on the second level. "Can they be from the prosecutor's office? Men that Signor Fontana appointed as watchers?" Massimo wondered aloud.

Vittorio replied, "No, they're not watchers. I heard Fontana instruct his men. He assigned three men to take turns watching the apartment, so there would be only one watcher here at a time." He added, "And the watchers wouldn't use a wagon."

Massimo looked at his companion with a puzzled expression and said, "If the men who entered the apartment are not watchers, we need to find out who they are and what they want with Nieddu."

As the two Florentines neared the building, they heard scuffling noises and then shouts coming from Nieddu's apartment. Something banged hard against a wall, then an object crashed to the floor. Massimo pushed the door open and nearly tripped over the hapless watcher who was moaning and lying limp in the stairwell. Massimo raced up the stairs with Vittorio at his heels. The door to Nieddu's apartment was open wide. Massimo vaulted over an upturned chair blocking the doorway.

A tall man had Nieddu pinned against a wall. One of his arms was wrapped around Nieddu's throat. Nieddu gasped for air and twisted side-to-side, struggling to free himself. A short, ugly man bent low, trying to ensnare Nieddu's legs with a coil of rope.

Massimo grabbed the tall man's arm and wrenched it away from Nieddu. Startled, the man threw Nieddu to the floor and spun around to face his attacker. Vittorio drove his foot into the side of the ugly man's head, knocking him to the floor. He yelped in pain and rolled away to avoid another kick.

The first man pulled a blade from a scabbard at his hip and waved it menacingly at Massimo, slashing it through the air side-to-side. Even in the low light, its sharp edge glistened. Massimo scanned the room, searching for something to use as a shield, but there was nothing within reach. The man and his blade advanced toward Massimo until he detected movement behind him—Nieddu. The man veered to the side, away from Nieddu and away from Massimo.

Massimo used the opening to grab a candlestick from a sideboard table. It was no match for a knife, but in Massimo's hand, it could be lethal. The man had a blade, but he counted the odds, three to two, against him. He backed away from Massimo and toward the door.

The second man pulled himself up to standing and hurled the rope at Vittorio. The coil unwound like a snake as it flew through the air. Vittorio sidestepped, but lost his balance and dropped to one knee. The man took the advantage and slithered around Vittorio to join his companion. One man shouted an epithet in a language understood by neither Massimo nor Vittorio as the two men turned and retreated down the stairs.

Vittorio moved to follow the men until Massimo held out a hand to stop him. "One of them has a knife, and he looks like he knows how to use it. The other one may have a knife as well," Massimo said.

Vittorio went to the window and watched the two men climb into the wagon and drive away. Massimo said, "One of them had a scar on the right side of his face. They're probably the same thugs who attacked Nico." He turned to Nieddu. "Do you know them?"

Nieddu, still rattled by the event, merely shook his head.

Massimo faced Nieddu. "They could return, so you can't stay here. We'll find a safe place for you after you make the withdrawal from the bank."

Vittorio mused, "I wonder how they knew where to find you."

44

Watching the three Florentines crowd into his office made Fontana laugh. "My office has never seemed so small before. Shall we move to a larger room?"

Massimo squeezed past Vittorio to a chair on the far side of Fontana's desk. "I've spent many hours in tight quarters; by comparison, this room is spacious."

Fontana waited until the others were seated; then he began, "The charges against Ercole Strozzi were delivered to him yesterday."

"Did you deliver them personally?" Nico asked.

"No, they were delivered by one of my clerks and, as a precaution, a Papal Army Sergeant accompanied him. The clerk reported that Signor Strozzi wasn't surprised that he had been accused. The clerk said that Strozzi seemed to be expecting the charges."

Vittorio said, "That means he's getting information from someone."

"Not from anyone in my office," Fontana said defensively.

Vittorio pressed his hands together. "But from somewhere."

No one spoke while they registered the implication of Vittorio's statement. Fontana continued, "Signor Strozzi has already retained a lawyer to represent him." Fontana's voice took on a deliberate cadence. "Baldo de'Rossi is the most unprincipled lawyer in Bologna. He'll do anything to win a case. He's been disciplined by the guild several times for deceitful practices. In one recent case, he paid people to testify favorably about his client's character."

"Is that permitted?" Massimo asked.

"All that matters to the magistrates is that witnesses tell the truth. The problem, as you can guess, is that payments can encourage witnesses to bend the truth. In de'Rossi's latest case, no one could prove that the witnesses were untruthful, but the prosecuting lawyer did show that the witnesses had only a tenuous connection to the defendant. That called into question the value of their testimony."

Nico asked, "Who is representing Captain Attendolo?"

"I've heard nothing about Attendolo. Remember, when we met with him at his camp, he derided the charges. He said he would ignore them, and he seems to be doing just that." Fontana set his palms flat on his desk. "Unfortunately, the cases against Attendolo and Strozzi rest solely on the testimony of single individuals: Gasparo, who can speak against Attendolo, and Nieddu, who can implicate Strozzi."

Nico said, "And they aren't the best witnesses. The magistrate will view Gasparo as a child, and Strozzi's lawyer will paint Nieddu as a co-conspirator. We may have no way to strengthen the case against Ercole Strozzi because Nieddu is the only one who can link Strozzi to the mercenaries, but we should be able to find other people who can testify against Attendolo." Nico paused for a moment then turned to face Massimo. "We can help the case against Attendolo by getting people from a raided village to testify."

"I can do that," Massimo said confidently. "I'll get someone from Gasparo's village to testify."

It was raining lightly when Massimo and Gasparo set out for Ceresa Basso, Gasparo's village. Both riders wore oilskin cloaks that kept them dry, but the dampness and gray sky weighed on their spirits. Massimo held the lead on the road from Bologna through the valley to the town of Zena. They spoke little on that portion of the journey.

At Zena, they left the main road and followed a track that would take them to the village at the base of Mount Cesera. As the countryside became familiar, Gasparo took the lead and grew talkative. He pointed out landmarks: a large boulder, a chasm, an old cellar hole, and other things of interest to the locals.

"Are you eager to see your home and family?" Massimo asked, smiling.

It took a while before Gasparo responded. "It will be good to see my mother and father, but life in Bologna is exciting and in Cesera Basso everything is so... plain."

No one was in sight when they reached the village. "That's my house," Gasparo pointed out. He dismounted, pushed open the door, entered, and strode to the kitchen, where his mother was at the fireplace tending a pot. His footsteps caused her to turn, and upon seeing her son, she dropped the spoon she had been holding. Her eyes went wide and filled with tears. Barely able to speak, she uttered his name, then ran to him, wrapped her arms around him, and stood rocking side-to-side. Gasparo the boy cherished her embrace. Gasparo the man flushed at her attention. Gasparo had barely begun telling of his adventure when his father came into the house. He, too, greeted his son with tear-filled eyes.

In time, Gasparo introduced Massimo as one of the men who had freed him from the mercenaries. Gasparo's mother raised her eyes toward heaven, crossed herself, and said, "Praise be to the Lord. He sent a saint to return our son."

Gasparo's father clasped Massimo's hand. "There is nothing we could do that would be enough to repay you for delivering Gasparo to us."

While the four sat for a midday meal of vegetable soup, Massimo described the need for Gasparo to testify at the tribunal in Bologna. "You have my word that I will return him to you after he testifies," Massimo promised.

The woman shuddered upon hearing that her son must go away again, but then said softly, "I understand."

Massimo explained that to strengthen the case, they also needed another person from the village who had suffered a loss to testify. "I would go with you myself, but one of our cows is ready to calf, so I need to stay with her," Gasparo's father declared. "But I'm certain my neighbor Marso will agree to testify. His son was also taken by the mercenaries."

When they finished eating, they walked to a nearby field where Marso was repairing a fence. Massimo explained the need for a witness from the village. Marso trembled upon learning that Gasparo had been rescued and gained hope that his son might be freed as well. "Have you seen my son? Is he well? Where is he?"

Massimo explained that testifying against the mercenaries might help to bring his son home. An hour later, three riders set out in the rain headed for Bologna.

∽

Nico led Gasparo and Marso into the courtroom. They walked up the center aisle to the prosecution table. Nico explained, "This is the chamber where the trial will be held. Tomorrow, when the trial begins, I will be sitting here with Papal Prosecutor Matteo Fontana.

"While you are waiting to be called upon, you will be in a small antechamber. I will ask Massimo to be there with you." Nico pointed to a side door near the front of the chamber. "When it is time for you to testify, a court clerk will come to get you. He will escort you to the witness stand." Nico pointed. "You will stand there when you are speaking."

"Will we both come in together?" Marso asked.

"No, you will be brought into the room one at a time." Nico

pointed to the bench atop a raised platform at the front of the chamber. "That is where the magistrate will be seated."

Marso glanced at the other table in the room, and asked, "Who will be there, at that table?"

"No one. That is the defense table, but the defendant will not be in the room when you are testifying. The only ones in the room with you will be the magistrate, the court clerk, Messer Fontana, and me. Messer Fontana will ask you to tell what happened when the mercenaries entered your village. Tell the facts as you remember them. You are testifying to the magistrate, so face him and speak so he can hear you.

"The magistrate may interrupt you with a question. If he does, answer his question; then continue telling your story. If you forget your place, look to Messer Fontana for guidance."

Nico led the two witnesses to the witness stand so they could get familiar with the courtroom from that position. Then he led them out the side door to the antechamber where they would be waiting until they were called to testify.

45

Trial day 1 – Part 1

In the courtroom at Palazzo D'Accursio, Nico and Matteo Fontana chatted while they waited for the magistrate to enter the chamber. On the raised platform at the front of the room, the court clerk plumped the cushion on the magistrate's chair and carefully arranged items on the bench. Messer Taddeo Pozzo, the longest tenured senior magistrate, was known among the clerks as "The Honorable Perfectionist." Clerks dreaded being assigned to tribunals where Pozzo served as the presiding magistrate, fearing his excoriation if they made even a tiny mistake in procedure.

Except for the two lawyers and the clerk, the chamber was empty. The witnesses were waiting in a nearby antechamber until they were summoned one at a time to give their testimony. The process was designed to protect the secrecy of accusers. Neither the defendant, his lawyer, nor onlookers were allowed in the room during this portion of the trial. After all the prosecution witnesses finished testifying, the defense lawyer would be given a transcript of the session absent the names of the accusers.

A single tap on the door connecting to the judicial offices signified that the magistrate was ready to enter. The clerk rushed to open the door, then quickly moved aside. Taddeo Pozzo swept into the room, his robe fluttering in his wake. With narrowed eyes, he scanned the bench that held a glass of water, ink and paper for him to take notes, and a Holy Bible. Finding nothing amiss, he grunted, took his seat, and motioned for the clerk to begin the proceeding.

The clerk stepped forward and delivered the same preamble he had recounted countless times before. "This honorable tribunal of the Province of Bologna sanctioned by the Holy Roman Church and His Holiness Pope Paul the Second is called to order. Magistrate Taddeo Pozzo acting with the blessing of the Holy Roman Church and His Holiness Pope Paul the Second is prepared to receive and examine witnesses, take and evaluate evidence, render judgments, and perform any other measures he deems necessary to discharge the matters brought before this tribunal."

Papal Prosecutor Matteo Fontana had appeared in tribunals before Taddeo Pozzo many times; however, Pozzo did not recognize the person sitting at the prosecution table next to Fontana. The magistrate scrutinized Nico, trying to decide whether he should recognize Fontana's associate. Finally, he concluded that he did not, but his pride prevented him from asking Nico to identify himself. Glancing at Fontana, he said sharply, "Begin."

Fontana rose. "Honorable magistrate. On behalf of the people of the Province of Bologna, I enter accusations against Signori Luigi Attendolo and Ercole Strozzi. Witnesses will testify that Signor Luigi Attendolo, acting as captain of a mercenary army, directed his vassals to maraud through the Province of Bologna, pillaging and plundering defenseless villages. Furthermore, Signor Attendolo has directed his men to abduct children from their homes for the purpose of enlisting them in his rebel army.

"You will hear from a different witness that Signor Ercole Strozzi, an exile from the Republic of Florence, has come to Bologna to fund Signor Attendolo's mercenaries for the purpose of mounting an attack against the government of the Republic of Florence."

As Fontana spoke, Pozzo's eyes lit. He leaned forward, folded his hands, and rested them on the bench. Clearly, this case would be more interesting than the string of unfaithful husband cases that had filled his docket recently.

Fontana concluded his introduction, saying, "With your permission, I will introduce the first witness." Pozzo's nod of approval to Fontana was followed by Fontana's nod of approval to the clerk, signifying that the clerk should escort the first witness into the chamber.

Gasparo came slowly into the room. He walked as though his feet were heavy weights that demanded great effort to move. His face had little color, and he wheezed with every rapid breath. Gasparo locked his gaze on Nico, whose smile helped to ease the boy's trepidation.

"Gasparo is one of the boys who was taken from his home by Luigi Attendolo's mercenaries," Fontana began.

Before Fontana could say anything further, Pozzo addressed Gasparo. "How old are you, boy?"

With quivering words, Gasparo uttered, "Fourteen, your excellency."

Counter to his well-established blustery character, Pozzo produced a thin smile and said, "If I were a bishop or an ambassador, the title of excellency would be fitting, but in this tribunal, you can dispense with titles. I understand you were taken from your home. Take your time and tell me how it happened." Nico and Fontana exchanged glances, registering their surprise at Pozzo's compassionate behavior.

Gasparo gave the account of his abduction as he had been coached by prosecutor Fontana. "I was outside my house feeding the chickens when I heard pounding noises. It sounded like distant thunder. When I turned around, I saw men on horseback, maybe twenty of them, riding into the village. They broke into small groups and began going from house to house. Three of them came to our house.

"My mother heard the noise and came to the see what was happening. She was standing in the doorway when one man pushed her aside and went into the house. When he came back out, he said, 'There's no one inside.' Then they spotted me. Two of them came and grabbed my arms. They said, 'You're coming with us.' The third man waved a knife in the air in the direction of my mother. The ones holding me said, 'If you don't want trouble, you'll come with us.' I was afraid they would hurt my mother, so I went with them. They put me on a horse behind one of the men, and we rode a long way from the village to their camp."

Pozzo said nothing as he absorbed Gasparo's account, so Fontana asked, "Were you the only boy taken in that raid?"

"No, three of my friends were also taken."

"Tell us what else the bandits took," Fontana prompted.

"Sacks of flour and pigs. They dressed the pigs before taking them. One of the men wanted to take chickens, but their leader told them to leave the chickens."

Fontana continued, cueing the boy. "Where did they take you?"

"We rode for hours to get to their camp on roads I had never been on before. When we got to the camp, all the boys were huddled together and one of the men told us to forget our past because we were now part of their family, we were mercenaries. He said we would be trained to fight."

"Were you afraid?" Fontana asked.

Fontana hadn't prepared Gasparo for this question, so the boy paused to reflect before answering, then said, "Yes. I didn't know what would happen to me. Some of the men were... crude. They swore and spit and smelled bad."

Pozzo asked, "Were you mistreated?"

"No, I wasn't beaten or anything like that. They made us do chores, that's all."

"How were you able to escape?" Pozzo asked.

"Catching fish was one of my chores. I was at a stream fishing when Signor Argenti and Signor Leoni found me. They asked if I wanted to leave, and when I said yes, they took me to Bologna."

Pozzo leaned back in his chair, indicating that he had nothing further to say, so Fontana asked his final question, "Did you learn the name of the man who is their leader?"

"Yes, he calls himself Captain Attendolo."

Fontana signaled the clerk to escort Gasparo from the courtroom and bring in the next witness. When the man reached the witness stand, Fontana faced the magistrate and said, "This witness is Signor Marso Potuesi, who lives in Cesara Basso, the same village as the previous witness. Signor Potuesi's son was also taken when Luigi Attendolo's men raided that village."

Fontana turned to Potuesi and nodded, indicating that he should tell his story. "My son was helping me clean the barn when the raiders came. One of the raiders pressed a sword to my chest while they dragged my son away. I could do nothing to stop them. They laughed as they held me, helpless to rescue my boy.

"My wife was inside the house when the raiders came. She didn't know anything until they were gone. She collapsed when she heard what had happened. She cried that night, all night, and even now she wakes up every night in tears."

"Have you heard any news about your son?" Fontana asked.

Signor Potuesi pulled out a paper, unfolded it, and held it up. "I received this note."

"Read it," Pozzo declared.

Potuesi turned toward Fontana, who looked at magistrate Pozzo and asked, "May I be permitted to read it?" Pozzo nodded. Fontana took the note and read, "Do not worry about me. I am well. These men have taken me into their family." Fontana studied the note, squinting, then said, "There is a signature, but it is illegible."

Fontana returned the note to Potuesi, whose eyes filled with tears as he took the paper. He looked up at the magistrate and said, "This was not written by my son. Like me, he cannot read or write."

The magistrate shifted in his seat. He waited until Potuesi had refolded the note, then asked, "How did you receive the note from your son?"

"A rider came to the village and delivered this note to me and similar notes to the other men whose sons were taken by the bandits."

"Did you see what else was happening during the raid? Did you see the other boys being taken?"

"I didn't see anything else while it was happening, but afterward I heard from others that the bandits slaughtered pigs and they took horses and grain." He paused, rubbed his forehead while trying to recall anything else he had been told, then said, "One of the men tried to take a girl. He pulled the girl onto his horse and was preparing to ride away when the bandit leader made him release the girl. The leader… the men called him Captain Attendolo, said that his men must not assault girls or women."

The magistrate had no further questions for Potuesi, so Fontana directed the clerk to fetch the next witness. Fontana waited until Nieddu had taken his position at the witness stand before addressing the magistrate. "The previous witnesses testified in support of the accusation against Luigi Attendolo and his band of mercenaries. Signor Patrizu Nieddu will testify in support of the accusation against Ercole Strozzi, the man who is funding Luigi Attendolo's activities.

"Signor Nieddu, tell this court how you became involved with Luigi Attendolo."

Nieddu embellished and twisted the story he had rehearsed with Nico and the prosecutor. "I encountered one of Captain Attendolo's men while I was briefly living in Florence. He told me there was an opportunity in Bologna that would be rewarding for a man of my talents. When I arrived, he introduced me to Signor Ercole Strozzi, who had recently come to Bologna from Venice. Signor Strozzi is a man of considerable wealth who needed someone to act as an intermediary to carry messages between him and Captain Attendolo. Signor Strozzi also arranged for his bank to disperse funds for me to deliver to Captain Attendolo."

Fontana said, "Tell us about the relationship between Strozzi and Attendolo. Why was Ercole Strozzi funding Attendolo's mercenaries?"

Nieddu placed a hand over his heart. "I never would have taken the job had I known at the outset, but after several meetings with him, Signor Strozzi revealed his true purpose. His goals are for Captain Attendolo to take Signor Piero de' Medici hostage and to overthrow the Florentine government. Captain Attendolo is recruiting young boys to increase the strength of his army so he can mount a successful attack against Florence."

Pozzo asked, "I assume you were paid by Signor Strozzi?"

Nieddu bowed his head slightly. "A modest sum."

Magistrate Pozzo narrowed his eyes. "Even when you learned Signor Strozzi's true purpose, you continued to work for him?"

"I feared that I would incur the wrath of Signor Strozzi and Captain Attendolo if I did not continue."

With scorn in his voice, Pozzo said, "You fear their wrath; yet you came here to testify?"

"Despite the risk, I decided it was the honorable thing to do."

Magistrate Pozzo shook his head. He looked toward the prosecution table and saw that Nieddu's answer made both Nico and Fontana wince.

46

Trial Day 1 – Part 2

Nico leaned close to Fontana and whispered, "The magistrate is not accepting Nieddu as a credible witness. We need to strengthen the case against Strozzi."

"I agree, but how? We have no one else who can testify against Strozzi."

Pozzo gave the two lawyers a moment to confer, then declared, "Messer Fontana, call your next witness."

Nico said, "I have an idea. Tell the magistrate that the next witness is missing. Ask him to recess the proceedings until a clerk can locate the witness."

Fontana took in a deep breath. "What...."

Before Fontana could finish asking Nico for an explanation, Pozzo bellowed, "Messer Fontana!"

Fontana closed his open mouth, turned to face the magistrate, and said, "Honorable Magistrate, I beg your indulgence, but the next witness is absent. I request a recess so he can be brought here."

Pozzo slapped his hands down onto the bench with such force that the Bible skittered off the bench and onto the floor. The startled clerk jumped out of his chair and raced forward to return the Holy Book to its proper position. Pozzo boomed, "Messer Fontana, you know better than to waste the time of this tribunal. You have a staff whose purpose is to ensure that all witnesses are present at the beginning of trials."

Fontana stood with a sheepish expression and his hands spread wide, hoping his career wasn't about to be tarnished by Nico's ploy.

Pozzo exhaled through gritted teeth, then announced, "This tribunal is recessed until the nones hour." He rose and strode from the chamber.

Fontana rested a hand on Nico's shoulder. "I hope you have a plan, my friend."

"There is a way to corroborate Nieddu's testimony," Nico explained. "Nieddu said that Strozzi arranged for funds to be withdrawn from his account to pay the mercenaries. If we can get an official from the bank to confirm Nieddu's claim, it will add credence to Nieddu's assertion."

All the clerks were helping customers when Nico and Fontana entered the Bardi Bank. Fontana strode past the chairs where customers were supposed to wait for an available clerk and marched directly to the office at the rear of the building. He announced himself with a rap on the office door, then burst in without waiting for the bank manager to respond. Fontana announced, "I am Papal Prosecutor Matteo Fontana, and this is Envoy Nico Argenti of the Florentine Republic."

The flustered manager stared up at the two intruders, puzzled by why these two men were in his office. "How may I be of service, bravi signori?"

"Signor Ercole Strozzi has an account at this bank," Fontana declared.

Although the bank manager knew Ercole Strozzi as a source of great aggravation, he recognized his duty to protect the privacy of the bank's clients, so he said, "We pride ourselves in giving personal service to all of our valued customers, but I must confess, I cannot recall the names of our many account holders."

Fontana pressed. "Signor Strozzi authorized the bank to dispense periodic payments to Signor Patrizu Nieddu."

"We provide a variety of services to accommodate our customers, but again, I cannot recall every detail."

Fontana's patience dissipated. He leaned over the desk, his face close enough that the manager could smell his breath. "Funds distributed by your bank are being used to fund a criminal activity. If you do not want the bank to become involved as a co-conspirator, you will refresh your memory, then come with us and testify to a magistrate about Strozzi's financial arrangement."

In a calm voice, the manager uttered a well-rehearsed policy. "Our customers expect us to protect their privacy, and we take pride in doing so. We cannot give out private information without permission from the account holder."

This time it was Nico who leaned down across the desk to look directly at the manager. "When the Florentine government sanctioned the Bardi bank to operate in Bologna, it believed the bank's behavior would reflect the high standards and integrity of the Republic of Florence. If the bank refuses to honor requests from the Papal Prosecutor resulting in its indictment as a co-conspirator in a criminal activity, I would be forced to report those facts to the Signoria, and I am certain the bank's continued operations in Bologna would be jeopardized."

The manager stood, said, "Let me check our account records," and left his office. A few minutes later, he returned holding a folio. He pulled a paper from the folio. "These are Signor Strozzi's instructions for maintaining his account. They authorize the bank to distribute twelve ducats every two weeks to a Signor Patrizu Nieddu. The instructions do not give a reason for the distribution." He held out another sheet. "This is the record of distributions. As you can see, Signor Nieddu has signed for every withdrawal."

Fontana glared at the manager. "That wasn't so difficult, was it?

All you have to do now is to come with us and repeat that to a magistrate." The manager opened his mouth to object until he glimpsed Nico standing rigidly straight and glowering at him.

The three men did not speak as they walked from the bank to the courtroom at Palazzo D'Accursio. The bank manager was already positioned at the witness stand when the nones hour arrived and Magistrate Pozzo entered the chamber. The vein pulsing in his neck showed that Pozzo was not happy.

When he reached the bench, Pozzo turned to the clerk and gestured to the water glass on the bench. He grumbled, "This water has been sitting here all day. Bring me a fresh glass." After being seated, he said brusquely, "Messer Fontana, I see that you managed to find your witness."

Fontana stood. "Honorable Magistrate, Signor Mancini is the manager of the Bardi Bank here in Bologna. He is prepared to testify to business arrangements made by Signor Ercole Strozzi."

"You may begin, signor bank manager. What information do you have regarding Ercole Strozzi?"

"Signor Strozzi established an account at the Bardi bank two months past. My understanding is that he established the account shortly after arriving in Bologna. One month past, he gave instructions to have twelve ducats withdrawn from his account and paid to Signor Patrizu Nieddu every two weeks." The manager held out a paper. "These are Signor Strozzi's instructions, including his affixed signature."

Pozzo gestured for the paper to be brought to him. The clerk raced to the witness stand, collected the sheet, and handed it to the magistrate. Pozzo read the sheet, then he grunted, looked up at the manager, and said in a firm voice, "Has the bank made payments to Signor Nieddu in accordance with these instructions?"

Not daring to look directly at the magistrate, the manager dropped his gaze to the floor and answered, "Yes, magistrate, three payments were made." The manager held out a second sheet. "This is the disposition record." Again, the clerk delivered the sheet to the magistrate.

"What is the extent of Signor Strozzi's account?" The manager appeared confused by the question, so Pozzo rephrased it. "How much money is in the account?"

"I'm sorry, but I don't have that information with me. I can have one of my clerks bring the account record from the bank."

Pozzo ignored the manager's offer and asked instead, "In what form was Signor Strozzi's initial deposit when he open the account, coins, or gold, or...."

"A letter of credit from the Bardi bank branch in Venice."

"Of course, a letter of credit. Coins, gold, letters of credit, all ways of transferring money while keeping it hidden from the eyes of tax collectors. Did Signor Strozzi retain his account in Venice?"

"I have no way of knowing that. Each Bardi bank branch keeps separate records."

Pozzo waved a hand to dismiss the manager; then he turned to the prosecutor. "Do you have other witnesses?"

When Fontana replied that he had no other witnesses, the magistrate instructed him to present his closing statement. "Honorable Magistrate, two witnesses have personally experienced Luigi Attendolo's brutality. Both witnesses testified that Luigi Attendolo and the mercenaries under his command have pillaged defenseless villages and abducted innocent children from their homes. The prosecution contends that Luigi Attendolo should be convicted of thievery and forcible abduction, both crimes under the laws of the Province of Bologna and the Papal States.

"Signor Nieddu has testified that he was employed by Ercole Strozzi to deliver payments to Luigi Attendolo for the purpose of organizing a mercenary army to overthrow the government of the Republic of Florence. Signor Mancini, the manager of the Bardi bank, has corroborated Nieddu's statements with records that show funds were withdrawn from Ercole Strozzi's account and paid to Signor Nieddu. The prosecution contends, therefore, that Ercole

Strozzi is complicit in the acts of pillaging and abduction conducted by Luigi Attendolo's mercenaries, and that, therefore, Ercole Strozzi should also be convicted of the crimes of thievery and forcible abduction."

Pozzo turned to the clerk. "Prepare a transcript of the prosecution's accusations and have it delivered to Signor Attendolo and Signor Strozzi or their representatives. Schedule time for the defendants to appear and present their rebuttals to the charges made against them." As he rose to leave, Pozzo declared, "This tribunal is in recess."

Nico and Fontana waited until the magistrate exited the chamber; then they went to the anteroom, where Gasparo and Marso Potuesi were sitting quietly. Fontana faced the two witnesses. "You both did well. The magistrate found your testimonies to be truthful and compelling."

Gasparo said, "It wasn't as frightening as I expected."

Nico smiled at Gasparo. "Now you can return home. You must miss your family. They will be proud of what you've done."

Nico's statement did not elicit the response he expected. Gasparo looked from Nico to Marso Potuesi, then back to Nico while searching for words. "I want to go home, but...."

Potuesi put a hand on Gasparo's shoulder. "I understand your hesitation. There comes a time when village life is not enough for a young man. I left my village when I was about your age. I missed my parents and my friends. Now that my son is gone, his mother and I miss him. We will always miss him, but we realize that he must make his own life. We pray that someday he will return if only for a visit. Perhaps your father can find an apprenticeship for you with someone who trades in the city. Then you can live in both worlds."

"I would like that," Gasparo said and smiled at Nico.

47

A sign proudly proclaiming the law office of Messer Baldo de'Rossi stretched over the doorway of a building in Piazza Santa Tecla. Upstanding clients used that entrance to meet with the person regarded by many to be Bologna's most notorious lawyer. At the rear of the building, a second entrance, this one an unmarked door in a narrow alley, was the portal used by de'Rossi's many paid informers who kept him a step ahead of his adversaries.

Callers who used the main entrance passed into an elegant office with stylish furnishings. They were received by a gracious notary and treated to snacks while they waited for their audience with Messer de'Rossi. Those who came through the rear entrance were greeted by a scraggy man called Male, who might have been one of the downtrodden souls in Dante's Inferno. De'Rossi had found Male near death, face down in filth, behind a tavern. The lawyer rescued the decrepit man and offered him a job. It wasn't a magnanimous act; de'Rossi was never magnanimous. Male filled de'Rossi's need for a lackey who would follow any orders without question and do so for pitifully low pay.

One of Male's tasks was to gather information from the tipsters.

Male had little education, but enough so that he could write down facts and deliver them to Messer de'Rossi. A cleaner of the courtrooms at Palazzo D'Accursio gave a lopsided grin that showed his missing teeth when Male answered a knock on the rear door. Cleaners and caretakers were de'Rossi's favorite sources of information. They were invisible, able to go anywhere and listen to any conversations without objection.

"Four witnesses were at the trial," the cleaner began. He looked down at notes he had written. "A boy named Gazper, a villager called Putisi or Potisi, a man called Naydo, and someone from the Bardi bank. I didn't hear the bank man's name." He handed the note to Male who rewarded him with a coin.

De'Rossi laughed when he saw the note and read the letters, "N A Y D O." That was the name he was looking for, Nieddu. The boy and the villager were of little consequence. They would have testified against the mercenary captain, not against his client. Mention of the Bardi bank was unexpected. He would have to ask Strozzi about that.

Later, when Ercole Strozzi walked through the main entrance, the notary knew better than to engage this client in conversation. Strozzi shunned idle chitchat. The notary escorted Strozzi directly to Baldo de'Rossi's private office, where the two men would plan Strozzi's defense. De'Rossi gestured for Strozzi to be seated, then poured two glasses of grappa, a hospitality reserved for his most wealthy clients. His flashy gold ring clinked against the bottle. Gold symbolized winning, and de'Rossi's clients wanted every assurance they were being represented by a winner.

Strozzi acknowledged the lawyer's hospitality by taking a sip of the grappa, a drink that was too strong for his taste. He set the glass down and asked, "Have you received a transcript of the accusations?"

"No, not yet. It will take time for the magistrate to review and approve the transcript before it is released. However, there are matters for us to discuss. You were mistaken in saying that Patrizu Nieddu would not testify. He did testify, although until I receive the transcript, I won't know how damaging his testimony is to your case."

"Damn that bastard!" Strozzi bellowed. He pounded a fist down onto de'Rossi's desk, nearly toppling the bottle of grappa. "Alfonso assured me he could find men to dispose of Nieddu. That damned priest is worthless," Strozzi fumed.

De'Rossi held out a hand to calm his client, but Strozzi would not relent. "He failed. He needs to pay for the pain that Nieddu's testimony could cause me. He's finished." Strozzi looked directly at the lawyer. "Have your clerk bring me paper and a pen."

The lawyer did so; then he waited while Strozzi penned a note and ordered the notary to deliver it. The notary eyed de'Rossi and waited for him to signal his approval before accepting the note. After the notary left the room, Strozzi took another drink of grappa, a large swig this time. The potent drink boosted Strozzi's rage. The lawyer refilled Strozzi's glass, then said, "There was another witness, someone from the Bardi bank. Do you have a connection with the Bardi bank?"

Strozzi's eyes narrowed. "I have an account there."

"Merely having an account at the bank is not a sufficient reason for Fontana to put a bank representative on the stand. There must be something more."

Strozzi gritted his teeth. "The bank has instructions from me to pay out money from that account to Nieddu. Nieddu delivers the payment to the mercenaries."

"Does the bank know that the payments are for the mercenaries?"

"No, they've only been told to make the funds available to Nieddu."

De'Rossi leaned back in his chair. "Ah, it's likely Nieddu testified that you are financing the mercenaries for the purpose of undermining the government of Florence. His testimony and the bank's corroboration of at least a portion of his testimony makes your case more difficult. I'll have to give some thought to the best approach for your defense." He thought for a moment, then asked, "Are all of your funds in that account?"

"No, I'd never feel secure with all my ducks in the same pond. My funds are spread in accounts from Venice to Genoa." Strozzi lifted an eyebrow. "Why do you ask? Should I be concerned about that account?"

"There is nothing that would let the courts in Bologna prevent you from accessing funds in your account; however, the Bardi bank is a Florentine institution. The Florentine Signoria has been known to find ways around the law when it suits them. There is no way to know what pressures the Signoria might exert on the bank. You should consider reducing your holdings in the Bardi bank."

∼

Matteo Fontana sat in his office reviewing case notes when a young man entered and held out a note. "Messer Baldo de'Rossi instructed me to deliver this message to you." It was most unusual for a defense lawyer to contact him directly during an ongoing trial. Fontana reached out slowly, took the note, and read, 'Father Alfonso, secretary to the Papal Legate, hired two men to attack Patrizu Nieddu in an attempt to prevent him from testifying.'

"Messer de'Rossi wrote this note?" Fontana asked.

The young man shrugged. "Messer de'Rossi didn't say who wrote the note. He only told me to deliver it to you."

"Unbelievable," Fontana muttered to himself. Unbelievable that a priest who is a respected member of the papal delegation in Bologna would do such a thing, and unbelievable that Baldo de'Rossi would reveal the offense to the prosecution lawyer.

Fontana walked to the office at the end of the corridor, entered, and handed the note to Cardinal Capranica. As usual, Father Alfonso was sitting at a small desk across the room. Capranica read the note and looked up at Fontana with a puzzled expression. "I just received the note. I have no explanation for it and nothing to add," Fontana said.

Capranica turned and handed the note to Alfonso. Color drained from the priest's face as he read the accusation. He shrank back in his chair, his shoulders slumped, and his gaze dropped to the floor. "Every day, Florentines are meddling more and more in Bologna. They're taking over businesses and telling us how to live. My cousin owned a silk business here. He worked hard trying to make his business a success, but he lost the business to a Florentine silk merchant. My cousin was overwhelmed. His small shop couldn't compete with the Florentines."

Alfonso's eyes filled with tears as he continued. "I just wanted the Florentines out of Bologna. Signor Strozzi said he could make it happen. He said that he could do it by removing the Medici government from power in Florence. I wanted to help him. He asked me for only little things at first, but as time passed, he asked me to do more. The men I hired were supposed to take Signor Nieddu away from Bologna, so he couldn't testify. That's all. They weren't supposed to hurt him."

Alfonso finally looked up at the cardinal. "But I shouldn't have trusted them because they disregarded my direction once before. I told them to convince the lawyer, Argenti, that he was interfering in the affairs of Bologna and should return to Florence. I expected them to approach the lawyer forcefully... but with words. They weren't told to beat him." Alfonso's head dropped forward into his hands. "I'm sorry. May God forgive me."

Capranica rose and went to stand next to Alfonso. He placed a hand on Alfonso's shoulder and recited a prayer in Latin.

～

Fontana returned to his office to find Nico standing in the corridor chatting with one of the prosecution notaries. When Nico saw Fontana approach, he ended the idle talk and said to Fontana, "You have experience with Magistrate Pozzo. Do you think he was persuaded by our witnesses?"

Fontana placed a hand on Nico's shoulder and escorted him into the office. "Before we discuss the trial, I have some astonishing news."

Fontana's words flowed in a continuous, rapid stream. "Moments ago, I received a message from Baldo de'Rossi's office."

Nico's eyes narrowed. "Strozzi's lawyer?"

"Yes, Strozzi's lawyer. The message said that Father Alfonso, the secretary to the Papal Legate, has been collaborating with Strozzi. I took the note to Cardinal Capranica, who made Father Alfonso read it. Alfonso admitted to aiding Strozzi. He also confessed to hiring the two thugs who beat you and attempted to dispose of Signor Nieddu."

"A priest wanted me beaten?" Nico muttered. "Why did the lawyer send the note?"

"Neither the note nor the person who delivered it explained why it was sent. I can only imagine that Alfonso did something that displeased Strozzi."

"What will happen to Father Alfonso?"

"Cardinal Capranica will decide Alfonso's fate. By his nature, the cardinal is a forgiving soul, but I'm sure that at the very least, he will revoke Alfonso's appointment as the legate's secretary."

Both men reflected in silence on how someone who held a trusted position in the church hierarchy could join with Ercole Strozzi. After a minute, Fontana said, "I've tried many cases before Magistrate Pozzo and I've never seen him as sympathetic as he was when listening to Gasparo. Gasparo's testimony alone might have been sufficient to gain a ruling against Attendolo. I'm confident that Gasparo's story, followed by the emotional words of Signor Potuesi, were convincing."

Fontana ran a hand through his hair. "However, the case against Strozzi is problematic. Pozzo was not receptive to Nieddu's embellishments. Thank the Holy Spirit that you thought of getting the bank manager to testify, but even his statement might not have been enough to secure a judgment against Strozzi. The verdict will depend on the strength of the defense presented by Strozzi's lawyer. There is none better than that devil de'Rossi for getting his clients acquitted.

48

Trial day 2: The Defense

Ercole Strozzi and his lawyer, Baldo de'Rossi, were already seated at the defense table when Nico and Matteo Fontana entered the courtroom. De'Rossi flashed a confident smile at Fontana, who returned the acknowledgment with a perfunctory nod. Fontana explained to Nico, "The smiling one with the paunch stretching his tunic is de'Rossi."

"Ah, then the taller one, who looks like he's just eaten a lemon, must be Ercole Strozzi," Nico concluded. "It will be interesting to hear their defense."

Fontana said, "De'Rossi can't merely let Strozzi testify that he isn't supporting the mercenaries, because magistrates rarely give credence to the unsubstantiated word of a defendant. De'Rossi has had three days since he received the transcripts of the accusations to prepare his defense. He could try to fabricate a defense by paying derelicts to testify on Strozzi's behalf. He's used that ploy before, but unfortunately for him, I know most of the scoundrels who are willing to perjure themselves for a few coins."

As the magistrate entered the chamber, Nico glanced at the empty second defense table that had been arranged for Captain Attendolo. True to his word, Attendolo had rebuffed the court's summons. Magistrate Pozzo glowered upon seeing the empty table and turned to the court notary. "Has Signor Luigi Attendolo been duly informed of the charges against him?"

"Yes, your honor. He's been so advised, and a copy of the transcript has been delivered to him."

Pozzo slapped his hand down onto the bench and announced, "It is the decision of this tribunal that Luigi Attendolo is a fugitive from justice." He turned again to the notary. "Inform the Papal Army of this judgment and order that he be apprehended." Pozzo and everyone else in the courtroom knew it would be impossible for the undersized army contingent in Bologna to take Attendolo into custody, but Pozzo wanted the indictment on record.

Pozzo turned to de'Rossi, who rose and said, "Honorable Magistrate. I am representing Signor Ercole Strozzi against the fallacious charges that have been brought against him. It has been alleged that Signor Strozzi supported a rogue band of mercenaries in their vile acts of pillaging villages and abducting young boys. Those libelous and unfounded claims were made by a disreputable person named Patrizu Nieddu."

Upon hearing Nieddu's name mentioned, Nico leaned close to Fontana. "How does he know about Nieddu? Witness names are not included in the transcript."

Fontana whispered, "De'Rossi is known in the Bolognese legal community as *il roditore affamato*, the hungry rodent, because he's willing to sift through garbage, if he must, to find any morsel he can use. He has a cadre of paid informants acting as his ears around the Palazzo D'Accursio. They listen for any tidbit that might help his cause."

De'Rossi continued his opening statement. "Nieddu's allegations against Signor Strozzi are preposterous. Signor Strozzi is a law-abiding and God-fearing individual who would never endorse such uncivil acts." One of De'Rossi's strengths was his ability to assess people. Pozzo's expression told him that the magistrate was growing impatient, so he ended his monologue. Eyeing the clerk, he said, "Bring in the witness."

The man who stepped into the witness box was familiar to Nico. He had seen the man before but couldn't recall where. His recollection returned when de'Rossi announced, "Signor Bertu Fenu can speak to the character of the accuser Patrizu Nieddu." The lawyer's smug expression revealed his delight in shocking the prosecution by calling upon an unexpected witness.

To Fenu, de'Rossi said, "Describe your relationship with Signor Nieddu."

Fenu grasped the sides of the witness stand with both hands and leaned forward, his eyes locked firmly on the magistrate. "I am the owner of a warehouse at the port of Cagliari in Sardinia. Nieddu was employed in my warehouse as a dockworker, loading and unloading cargo from ships. I tolerated his obnoxious behavior and excessive drinking because I needed workers. I tolerated him until I found him in the back of the warehouse, raping my precious daughter, Caderina. She was a sweet, innocent child and now her life is ruined." Fenu choked up as he continued saying, "The poor girl is ashamed to be seen in public; ashamed even to attend mass.

"May God forgive me, but I would have killed the bast... the devil, if he had not fled from the island. I followed him to Pisa and then to Florence. There, in Florence, I learned he was committing other despicable acts. He lied to government officials to gain a position at the orphanage, and once there, he sold poor helpless orphans and stole money from the orphanage." Pozzo leaned forward on the bench, listening intently to Fenu's account.

"When officials in Florence uncovered his crimes, he fled again, this time to Bologna. Nieddu is a rapist, a thief, and an abuser of children. He's an incessant liar who will say and do anything to further his own cause."

Strozzi maintained an impassive expression as his lawyer had instructed, but de'Rossi struggled to suppress a smile as he listened to

Fenu giving his testimony precisely as de'Rossi had schooled him. When Fenu finished, the notary escorted him out of the chamber; then de'Rossi rose to deliver his closing statement. "Honorable Magistrate, you have heard testimony that a mercenary band pillaged villages and took young boys from their homes. If those crimes were indeed committed, a conclusion not yet reached by this tribunal, they were perpetrated by Captain Luigi Attendolo, the leader of the mercenary band. No accusation has been offered, suggesting that Signor Ercole Strozzi condoned or was even aware that those crimes were being committed.

"You have heard testimony that my client, Signor Strozzi, provided financial support to the mercenaries, but I ask you to consider the sole source of that accusation, Signor Patrizu Nieddu. As you have just heard, Signor Nieddu is himself a criminal. He has already fled from two jurisdictions where he is wanted for committing vile acts. You have heard that Signor Nieddu will tell any lies to achieve his own ends. He even lied to officials of the Republic of Florence. In sum, no evidence has been presented to connect Signor Ercole Strozzi with any alleged crimes, and no reliable witness has connected Signor Strozzi with Captain Luigi Attendolo." De'Rossi sat and cast a self-satisfied grin toward the prosecution lawyers.

Pozzo announced, "I will deliberate on the testimony and evidence presented before rendering my verdict. This tribunal is in recess until that time."

∼

Nico joined Matteo Fontana in the prosecutor's office. "Where did de'Rossi find his witness... Fenu?" Fontana wondered aloud.

Nico said, "I encountered Bertu Fenu in Florence. He came up to me on the street. He was furious that Nieddu had damaged his daughter's honor, and he swore he wouldn't rest until he found Nieddu and made him pay. Fenu's statement in court today wasn't the same as what he told me in Florence. At that time, Fenu said his daughter was seduced by Nieddu; whereas today he testified that Nieddu had raped his daughter."

Fontana said, "De'Rossi is masterful at tuning the language of his witnesses and he did it effectively with Fenu. Pozzo absorbed his every word." Fontana's lips curled up in a smile. "I'm surprised that de'Rossi didn't know that the bank manager had testified. Very little escapes de'Rossi's informants.'

"You've prosecuted other cases before Magistrate Pozzo. Can you predict how he will rule?" Nico asked.

"I believe Strozzi knew that Attendolo was raiding villages and abducting boys, but the weakness in our case is that we cannot directly link Strozzi to those crimes. Nieddu could say only that Strozzi supported the mercenaries financially and, as de'Rossi pointed out, that is not a crime." Fontana huffed. "I suspect that Strozzi will be acquitted."

Nico let Fontana's conclusion hang for a moment, then asked, "What about Attendolo?"

Fontana relaxed. "The case against Attendolo is strong. Even if he had appeared at the tribunal and presented a defense, I feel certain that he would have been convicted. Failing to appear makes him subject to additional charges. Pozzo ordered the army to apprehend Attendolo, but I'm sure he knows that won't be possible until the full army detachment returns to Bologna. And no one can predict when that might be."

"So for now, Attendolo can continue unchecked?" Nico surmised.

Fontana bit his lip. "Yes." Then his outlook suddenly changed from discouragement to laughter. "Unless Attendolo believes your threat of bringing the Milanese Army against him."

Nico thought for a minute then said, "I admit that suggesting the Milanese Army could be called upon was a fanciful threat, but the loss of funding will put pressure on Attendolo. Neither he nor his men will work without pay for very long."

49

Bright sunshine and warm morning air boosted Nico's spirit as he walked out of the city to the farm owned by Matteo Fontana's cousin. Farmers bringing produce from their outlying farms had already made their daily trek to the markets of the city, so the road had little traffic. Nico inhaled deeply, relishing the pristine air free of the dust plumes that the farm carts always lofted in their wakes.

After the attack on Nieddu at his apartment, Fontana had arranged for him to stay at the farm to keep him safe from another possible attack. Massimo and Vittorio visited the farm each day to make sure that Nieddu behaved properly. The farm, tended only by Fontana's cousin, his wife, and their two sons, grew vegetables that were sold in the city's markets.

Stimulated by the long walk, Nico was singing a Neapolitan folk song—one Alessa enjoyed playing on her lute—when he reached the turnoff to the farmhouse. In the distance, Massimo and Vittorio were talking with the farmer's wife, who was gesturing toward a pile of logs alongside the barn. Their conversation paused, and they turned toward Nico as he approached. From the corner of his eye, Nico glimpsed Nieddu coming around the side of the house, carrying an axe over his shoulder. She saw Nico stiffen and called to him. "The axe is for chopping firewood. Signor Nieddu has been helping with chores around the farm."

Nieddu saw the three Florentines, but he did not alter his course: he continued walking toward the barn. The men got a brief account of Nieddu's conduct from the woman before she left them and resumed hanging clothes on a drying stand.

"The magistrate rendered his verdict," Nico said in a somber tone. "He found Strozzi not guilty. Our case wasn't strong enough to show that Strozzi had knowledge of Attendolo's crimes."

Massimo squeezed his hands into fists. "Damn! Does it mean Strozzi is free to continue plotting against Florence?"

"As far as the courts are concerned, Strozzi hasn't committed any crime, so they can take no action against him. The only way he can be stopped is if we find another way to pressure him."

Vittorio asked, "What about Attendolo? Has the army taken steps to apprehend him?"

"They've done nothing, and they probably won't until the full contingent returns to Bologna."

Vittorio growled, "And who knows where Attendolo will be by then... or what other crimes he will have committed?"

The men stood silent for a moment while Massimo and Vittorio absorbed Nico's disappointment; then they walked to the barn where Nieddu was pulling a log free from the wood pile. Sweat on his brow and soil on his hands proved he had been toiling for a time. Vittorio said, "I wouldn't have expected you to take to farm life."

Nieddu cackled. "I haven't taken to it. I could never be a farmer. These fools work constantly from when they step off their beds at daybreak until they drop onto their mattresses at night. They're worse off than slaves."

"Yet here you are chopping wood," Massimo said. Nieddu grunted.

Nico said, "You're getting wholesome food to eat, a comfortable bed, and a place to stay where you won't be beaten by Strozzi's thugs. It's good that you're helping with the chores as payback."

"Payback my ass. Sitting around here doing nothing is boring. If I didn't do something, I'd go mad."

"That's just what I would expect from you," Vittorio said bitterly.

Nico said, "The trial is over. The magistrate found Ercole Strozzi not guilty, so it's possible that you'll no longer be pursued by Strozzi's thugs. But you know Strozzi better than I do. In any case, you are free to go."

Nieddu's eyes widened. "You're not taking me back to Florence?"

"We agreed that if you testified against Strozzi, we wouldn't force you to return to Florence. However, the charges against you there will remain. If you ever do return to Florence, you will be prosecuted."

Nieddu set the axe down and wiped the wood flecks from his hands. "I have no interest in going back to Florence, but with that bastard Fenu looking for me, I can't stay in Bologna." He thought for a moment, then said, "I can get a job on the docks in any port, Ravenna or Venice or...." He paused another moment, grinned, and added, "until I find something more profitable."

50

Nico had passed Palazzo Bentivoglio many times as he traversed Via San Donato, one of the major roads extending out from the heart of Bologna. The palazzo was the home of Bologna's most influential families for the past four generations. The impressive arcade spanned the full width of the structure's façade and rose higher than the nearby two-level buildings. It drew the attention of every first-time visitor to the city. Five years after construction began, workers were still busy extending the sides of the building to create an enclosed courtyard. Nico approached a stonemason who was cleaning his tools. "I've walked past the front of this palazzo many times and always thought that the building was complete."

"The original part of the building was finished five years past, but when young Giovanni became the head of the family, he wanted the palazzo to be grander, so we are adding a new section. When we finish here, the palazzo's depth will be triple the width of its face," the mason replied.

"Incredible!" Nico exclaimed. *Florence has no buildings that big*, he thought.

"What is incredible to me," the mason laughed, "is that I'll be an old man by the time the work is finished."

Nico returned to the front of the building. A burly man with a horse-like face topped with thick black hair responded to Nico's pull on the announcement cord at the palazzo's main entrance. His military garb showed him to be a guard, not a house servant. Nico looked up at the man, who stood a head taller than himself, and said, "I have information of interest to Signor Bentivoglio."

In a deep, gravely voice, the guard asked, "Do you have an appointment?"

"No, but..."

Before Nico finished speaking, the man interrupted. "Signor Bentivoglio is a busy man. He doesn't see visitors without appointments."

Undeterred by the guard's statement, Nico said, "I am an envoy of the Republic of Florence." He held out his official letter of introduction from the Florentine Signoria.

The guard barely glanced at the letter, then reiterated. "You cannot see Signor Bentivoglio without an appointment."

"Then I wish to make an appointment," Nico insisted.

"Wait," the guard grumbled; he turned and entered the palazzo, closing the door behind him. Nico heard a click as the latch dropped into place.

After several minutes, Nico began to suspect that his request for an appointment had been dismissed when again he heard a click as the latch was released. The door opened and a different man filled the doorway. This one stood taller and wider than the last, but he was clean shaven, and his hair was pulled back neatly in a horsetail. "You're an official from Florence," he voiced as neither a statement nor a question.

"A Florentine envoy," Nico corrected. Again, he held out his letter of introduction.

This guard took time to read the letter. He ran a finger over the Signoria's wax seal. "Come with me," he said. Nico followed him into the palazzo, up to the second level, and into a sitting room. "Wait here," he said, then he left the room.

The well-appointed room had three couches in a cluster at the near end and a table surrounded by chairs at the far end, but Nico felt it would have been presumptuous for him to sit without invitation, so he remained standing. Each of the six portraits adorning the walls showed men with similar flat foreheads and small noses. One painting had clearly superior shadowing and color layering, so Nico judged it to be the newest of the group. As he studied the portrait, a voice behind him said, "You requested an appointment with Giovanni Bentivoglio."

Nico turned. He recognized Bentivoglio immediately, having seen him at the birthday celebration for his wife. At first, it appeared that he was short, but Nico quickly realized that the man seemed short only in comparison to the giant guards. The man had the same moon-round face and long chestnut brown hair as the men in the portraits. He was young, no older than Nico, and his eyes signaled his serious nature. Again Nico stated his purpose. "I am Nico Argenti, an envoy from Florence. I am here regarding a matter of concern to the Republic of Florence."

When Nico reached out for the third time to present his letter of introduction, Bentivoglio waved a hand dismissively. "The letter is not necessary." He had not met Nico at the birthday celebration, so he introduced himself to the stranger standing before him. "I am Giovanni Bentivoglio, so tell me what is of such concern to the rulers of Florence that they dispatched an envoy to Bologna."

Nico dipped his head slightly in deference to Bologna's most powerful citizen. "A band of mercenaries is roaming the hills of Bologna, recruiting members to increase their number."

"You are speaking of Luigi Attendolo and his followers. I'm aware of his activities and I know that charges have been brought against him by the Papal Prosecutor. If he is convicted, he will be punished. What I don't understand is why Attendolo's crimes are of interest to Florence and why you are bringing them to my attention."

"Attendolo is being funded by a wealthy Florentine exile named Ercole Strozzi, who intends to have Attendolo mount an attack against the Florentine Signoria," Nico explained.

Bentivoglio raised an eyebrow. He shouted into the corridor behind him. "Carlo, bring refreshments!" Then he stepped into the room, gestured for Nico to be seated on one couch, and seated himself on a facing couch. "The painting you were admiring is of my cousin, Santo. He lived many years in Florence and developed a great fondness for that city, which he passed on to me. I would not want any actions in Bologna to injure our relationship with Florence. However, I'm still unclear what you expect of me. As I'm sure you know, the Reformatori have jurisdiction for crimes within the city and those outside the city are the responsibility of the Papal Legate. Have you brought this matter to Cardinal Capranica?"

Nico nodded. "Yes, the cardinal shares our fear that rogue mercenaries from Bologna might mount an attack against Florence, but he is stymied because the Papal Army detachment is deployed in the south."

Bentivoglio paused while the servant placed a tray of fruit and cheese on a nearby table, then he said, "What would you have me do, send my own force against Attendolo?"

"Perhaps just an indication that you are considering such an action might be sufficient to dissuade the mercenary," Nico suggested diplomatically.

"I know Luigi Attendolo only by reputation, but I believe him to be a man who is not easily intimidated." Bentivoglio rose and paced slowly across the room in contemplation. He returned to where Nico was seated and looked down at the Florentine envoy. "It is also said that Attendolo's actions are driven by gold; therefore, another way to deter him would be to halt his funding by expelling his patron."

Nico said, "The Papal Prosecutor tried to make a case against Strozzi. He argued that by funding Attendolo, Ercole Strozzi is complicit in Attendolo's crimes. Unfortunately, the prosecutor was unable to make his case strong enough to convince the magistrate."

Bentivoglio grinned. "Laws and justice do not always coincide." Nico recalled an instance when he had expressed the same sentiment. "I can send men to speak with Ercole Strozzi. My men can be very persuasive. I'm certain they can convince Signor Strozzi that he is no longer welcome in the Province of Bologna."

∽

The following morning, Nico rapped on the prosecutor's door. "Matteo, your clerk came to the inn to tell me that you have new information."

"Yes, I do. Come in, Nico." Matteo Fontana glanced into the hallway behind Nico. "Your colleagues, Massimo and Vittorio, aren't with you."

Nico dropped into a chair. "They've been recalled to Florence. Chancellor Scala has another assignment for them. They left Bologna after the first day of the trial."

Fontana raised an eyebrow. "I hadn't realized there are so many threats against your republic that the Florentine Security Commission is kept busy constantly."

"Their assignment isn't a new condition; it's related to Ercole Strozzi. The chancellor discovered that Strozzi has an informant in Florence. Massimo and Vittorio have been tasked with finding him."

Fontana leaned back in his chair and stroked his chin. "Your commission is unusual. We prosecutors only become involved after crimes have been committed, whereas you and your colleagues hunt for people who are only suspected of violating laws."

Nico slowly straightened the sleeve of his tunic while he considered Fontana's comment. "I still believe the concept of our commission is sound, but I'm disappointed by our recent performance. Captain Attendolo defied the tribunal, Ercole Strozzi was acquitted, and I let Patrizu Nieddu avoid punishment in exchange for his testimony. By those measures, it seems that I've accomplished little."

"Perhaps your conclusion is premature, my friend. It appears that your petition to Signor Bentivoglio may have had the result you desired. One of Cardinal Capranica's sources reported that Ercole Strozzi is no longer at the Canneschi villa."

Nico looked up and asked expectantly, "Has he left Bologna?"

Fontana replied, "The cardinal's source spoke with a servant at the villa who said that Strozzi had gone, but the servant didn't know Strozzi's destination."

"So, Strozzi could still be in Bologna, in hiding."

"That's possible, but my other news is that Luigi Attendolo and his men are no longer in Bologna. When the payments from Strozzi ended, Attendolo wasted no time in searching for another lucrative arrangement. A Bolognese merchant doing business in Venice reported that Attendolo received a contract from the Venetians to help defend their colony in Dalmatia. The merchant saw Attendolo's men boarding a ship for the Dalmatian coast."

Nico rubbed his chin. "So, not only has Attendolo left Bologna, he's left the entire Italian peninsula."

Fontana watched Nico's expression brighten, then asked, "You were sent here to eliminate a mercenary threat. Now that Attendolo is gone and the threat no longer exists, will you be returning to Florence?"

"Yes, since the immediate threat has been eliminated, I will be returning home, but I won't be surprised if Strozzi finds another way to carry out his vendetta against Florence in the future. However, before I leave Bologna, I plan to attend the university's Founder's Day celebration. You are also an alumnus. Will you be at the celebration?"

"I never miss it," Matteo answered, smiling.

51

Nico had gone to Bologna with two goals. His primary purpose was to prevent the mercenaries who had been raiding Apennine Mountain villages from crossing into Florentine territory. His other objective, on behalf of the Florentine guild of notaries and lawyers, was to encourage gifted law student Gerhard Ritter to move to Florence upon graduation. The university's Founders' Day celebration gave Nico the opportunity to meet with Gerhard a final time before he left Bologna.

Unlike some other universities, the University of Bologna did not have a central campus. The different colleges met in various buildings around the city. Some classes were even held in the homes of professors. Founders' Day was the one time each year when all students came together for a festive celebration at taverns and restaurants near the city's main square, Piazza Maggiore.

Although students and professors wandered from one venue to another during the evening, each college had a preferred gathering place. For members of the law college, it was a tavern called *Le dodici tavole*, The Twelve Tables. The name referred not to pieces of furniture, but to the twelve stone tablets on which the ancient Romans had codified their first laws. Students had favored the venerable tavern ever since a respected law professor opened the establishment nearly two centuries past.

The boisterous celebration was already underway when Nico wove his way through the throngs of students filling the piazza. There was standing room only at The Twelve Tables. Beer mug wielding students filled the tavern's interior and spilled out into the streets. Gerhard Ritter huddled in a corner of the room with his fellow Austrian students. He spotted Nico working his way through the crowd to the bar. Gerhard joined Nico, and the two moved out of the noisy tavern to a quiet side street where they could talk.

Gerhard said, "I've decided to take your suggestion and find out what opportunities there might be for me in Florence after I graduate."

"I'm pleased to hear that, and I know the guild consuls will be pleased as well. You are making the right decision to investigate every possibility open to you. The guild will tell you about the many opportunities for lawyers in Florence, but you must also visit me when you come to the city, so I can show you the city's other attractions."

"How much longer will you be staying in Bologna?" Gerhard asked.

Nico gave Gerhard a friendly slap on the shoulder. "Now that you've agreed to come to Florence, my work here is finished. I'll be returning home in the morning."

They chatted for a while before Nico wished Gerhard success in his final term and the two men parted. Gerhard rejoined his friends, and Nico crossed the piazza to a more sedate tavern favored by the university faculty. Peering in through the window, he spotted Professor Allard, the philosophy professor who had told him about the mercenaries purchasing weapons from an armorer in Bologna. Allard was engaged in an animated conversation with another man. Both men gesticulated vigorously, nearly bumping into those around them. Finally, Allard threw up his hands, shook his head, and walked away from his associate. He mumbled a string of phrases in French as he exited the tavern. Nico fell in beside him, waited until the French rant ended, then said, "Professor, I couldn't help notice your squabble in the tavern."

"Ah, the Florentine envoy, Messer Argenti. It is good to see you again. Were you successful in routing the mercenaries?"

"Yes, I'm pleased to say they are no longer in Bologna."

"We are saved from them while others will suffer their wrath," Allard said cynically. Then, in a more pleasant tone, he said, "The disagreement you saw wasn't as fierce as it might have appeared. My fellow disputant is one of yours, a professor in the law college. He supports the current legal practice of having witnesses testify in secret, whereas I maintain that defendants should be allowed to question their accusers." Allard chuckled. "We argue out our differences whenever we meet. Thus far, neither one of us has succeeded in persuading the other."

Nico said, "I can see merit to both arguments."

"Bah, you're just being amicable. In the clash that you saw, I cited a case where a witness had knowledge of missing money, but his information was not heard because he couldn't be questioned by the defense. My argument would convince any tribunal, but my able colleague remains as stubborn as ever." Allard waved a hand dismissively. "Ah, maybe next time his mind will be open."

Allard escorted Nico to the tavern favored by philosophy students, where the two men shared a jug of wine. By observing the revelers, Nico concluded that wine was the favorite drink of philosophers and their celebrations consisted more of talking than drinking. Later, as he walked back to his room at the inn, Nico recalled the case the professor had cited and decided that it might light the way to finding where Strozzi had gone. Tomorrow he would pursue the money.

Nico had intended to depart for Florence early the next morning; instead, his insight the previous evening changed his plans. He stood in the street outside the Bardi bank, waiting for it to open. As soon as he heard the lock release, Nico rushed past the clerk who had unlocked the door and headed directly for the manager's office.

Paltroni, the manager, recognized Nico immediately. "Buon giorno, Messer Argenti," Paltroni said, smiling broadly. "I could tell myself that you are here to open an account, but I suspect that would be a delusion."

Nico returned Paltroni's smile. "You are perceptive, Signor Paltroni. It is the Ercole Strozzi matter that brings me here. I have reason to believe that Signor Strozzi may have left Bologna."

"I am usually unhappy to lose a customer... especially a wealthy customer, but Strozzi is an exception. Since I first met him... even before I met him, he made onerous demands. We endeavor to please all of our customers, but Signor Strozzi was impossible."

"Has he closed his account?"

"His account is not closed, in the sense that his account is hosted at our branch in Venice and that account is still open. However, all of his funds have been withdrawn from the bank here in Bologna."

"Were those funds returned to Venice?"

"No, we were directed to transfer the funds to the Norsa bank in Ferrara."

Nico's jaw clenched. "Ferrara," he echoed and thought, *a fertile place for Strozzi to continue his vendetta against Florence.*

EPILOGUE

Florence

Vittorio looked up from reading the dispatch sent by the Florentine embassy in Rome when Nico and Massimo entered the Florentine Security Commission office on the upper level of the Palazzo della Signoria.

"Were you able to find Ercole Strozzi's confidant here in Florence?" Massimo asked.

"Yes, I found him. The man's a merchant who travels frequently. He meets with Strozzi outside of Florence, and they exchange letters when he's here."

Nico asked, "How did you find him?"

"He's one of Strozzi's distant cousins. I researched all of Strozzi's relatives living in Florence until I found one who had criticized the Signoria."

Nico said, "Merely criticizing the Signoria isn't much of a reason to suspect him. He isn't the only person in Florence who is unhappy with the Signoria."

"True. I could have been wrong about him, but in my experience, intimidation often gets results. I merely accused him of conspiring with Strozzi and then I watched his reaction. Guilty and innocent people react differently to accusations. I knew immediately from the way he stammered and the way his face reddened that he was guilty. Then I kept pressing until he confessed, and it didn't take much pressure before the spineless cretin admitted his role."

"What is going to happen to him?" Nico asked.

"Nothing. Thus far, the fool did nothing illegal," Vittorio replied. "But he'll be monitored closely in the future. The chancery is going to intercept his letters, the ones he writes and the ones he receives."

Massimo said, "Since he's a merchant who travels outside of Florence, he could have secret meetings with Ercole."

"Whenever he travels, a chancery clerk will travel with him serving as his assistant. We'll know everyone he meets with and what they discuss."

Footsteps in the corridor drew the men's attention. A man whom Nico recognized as a server from the Uccello entered the room carrying a tray of *crostini*. "Compliments of Chancellor Scala," he said, as he placed the tray on a table and handed a note to Nico.

Massimo bent down to examine the delicacies. "Apricot! Who has apricots at this time of year?"

"Nico's cousin, Donato, got a shipment from Africa," the server replied.

Nico unfolded and read the note. *Once again, the Florentine Security Commission has proved its worth. All members of the Signoria are grateful for the work you men have done in eliminating the threat to our republic.*

Massimo said, "Chancellor Scala's note and the *crostini* are nice, but I appreciate even more his allowing us to take a five-day holiday. There's a woman in Prato who is missing her Massimo. And you, Nico, your soul must be missing Bianca."

"I'll be heading to Siena tomorrow morning at first light and I intend to spend all five days with her. But first, Donato and Joanna have planned a safe-return dinner for us at the Uccello. You are both invited."

"Will your sister be there?" Massimo asked.

"I suppose so, but I thought your mind was on the woman in Prato."

Massimo grinned, "Prato is tomorrow."

Vittorio said, "I appreciate the invitation, but I have other plans."

Nico and Massimo knew better than to probe their enigmatic colleague.

∽

Nico's cousin Donato had reserved one of the Uccello's private dining rooms for a dinner to celebrate Nico's safe return to Florence. Donato had the chef prepare one of Nico's favorites, wild boar stewed in wine sauce. Donato's wife met Nico as he entered the room and kissed him lightly on the cheek. "From your uncle Nunzio's vineyard," Joanna said as she handed him a glass of Sangiovese wine.

Massimo followed Nico into the room. His eyes brightened when he spotted Nico's sister, Alessa. After giving Joanna a quick hug, he moved to the table where Alessa was setting out artichoke appetizers. He withdrew a recorder from a small sack and held it out to Alessa. "I know you like music and play the lute, so I thought you might enjoy playing the recorder."

Alessa lifted the instrument to her lips and surprised everyone in the room by rendering the notes of a popular madrigal. "A friend of mine who plays the recorder taught me this tune." Alessa laughed. "It's the only tune I know, but now having my own instrument will let me learn some new ones. Thank you," she added as she pulled Massimo close in a hug.

As a guest of honor, Nico was seated at the head of the table. Massimo was offered the place at the opposite end, but he chose, instead, to sit next to Alessa. When all were seated, Donato raised his glass. "We thank the Lord for keeping you safe these past weeks." Donato gestured toward Massimo and added, "Both of you."

Nico tensed upon hearing Donato's words, but Joanna sensed his barely perceptible reaction. "Is there something you haven't told us, Nico?" she asked. Before Nico could answer, she turned to Massimo. "What is he withholding?"

Massimo raised a hand in a gesture of resignation. "He had a slight encounter with two thugs who didn't want him asking questions about the mercenaries."

"I knew it!" Alessa exclaimed. "I was carrying a basket of laundry when suddenly I got a cold chill and dropped the basket. It was the same feeling I had the last time you were injured. Wherever you are, I can always tell if something happens to you."

"It was just a minor incident," Nico interjected. "As you can see, I have no scars and no broken bones."

Alessa turned to Massimo and asked, "And you, Massimo? Did you encounter the same thugs?"

"They wouldn't trouble Massimo. He'd scare them away simply by growling," Nico jested.

Alessa waved a finger at Nico. "Don't make light of it. You need to stop putting yourself in danger."

While servers were removing the appetizer plates and refilling wine glasses, Alessa calmed herself and said, "Your letter mentioned that Vittorio succeeded in finding Signor Nieddu. Did he say what happened to Armando?"

Nico replied, "We learned from a source that Armando joined the mercenaries. It seems cruel for boys to be taken from the orphanage or from their homes, but many of the boys who were taken chose to stay with the mercenaries. They are lured by the excitement and adventure. From what we have seen, they are treated well. You need not worry about Armando."

Alessa looked doubtful as she asked, "Is Armando in Bologna?"

Nico said, "When the mercenaries lost their source of funding in Bologna, they contracted with Venice to defend one of the Venetian colonies in Dalmatia."

Massimo added, "That is the life of mercenaries. They never stay in the same place for very long."

The chef accompanied the servers when they brought the *cinghiale*, the wild boar roast, to the table. He sliced the roast and personally served each guest.

After dinner, while Nico and Donato were enjoying a *digestivo*, Donato said, "You told me earlier that Ercole Strozzi was funding the mercenaries in preparation for an attack on the Signoria. What is Strozzi doing, now that his plan has been disrupted?"

"Unfortunately, we were not able to prove that he had violated any laws, so he remains free. He was persuaded to leave Bologna and now has taken refuge in Ferrara. He still has control of his fortune and, if anything, his hatred of Florence and the Medicis has been heightened."

Donato said, "That doesn't bode well. Relations with Ferrara have been tense because Lord Este is no friend of Florence. Having a dissident like Ercole Strozzi in Ferrara will only exacerbate the tense relationship between Florence and Ferrara."

Nico nodded. "I agree. I don't believe we've heard the last of Ercole Strozzi."

Get the next book in the award winning Nico Argenti series, **Rebels in Pisa**, where Nico and his team find and stop smugglers before they resort to violence.

REBELS IN PISA - NICO'S NEXT ADVENTURE

Rumors of insurrection in Renaissance Pisa spur Florentine authorities to send young lawyer Nico Argenti to investigate. He and his team uncover more than expected: smuggling, abduction, and murder.

Renaissance Italy 1465: After six decades of domination by Florence, agitators in Pisa are taking action. They remember the past when Pisa was an independent State and they are impatient to regain that freedom. Rumors of an impending insurrection reach officials in Florence who dispatch Nico Argenti and his team to find and stop the troublemakers before they resort to violence.

The hunt turns urgent when the rebels show their resolve by abducting the provincial governor. Nico's team intensify their efforts to discover the source of the rebels' weapons which, surprisingly, leads them back to Florence. In Florence's highest court, Nico uses his legal skills to bring the traitorous arms dealer to justice.

NICO'S STORY

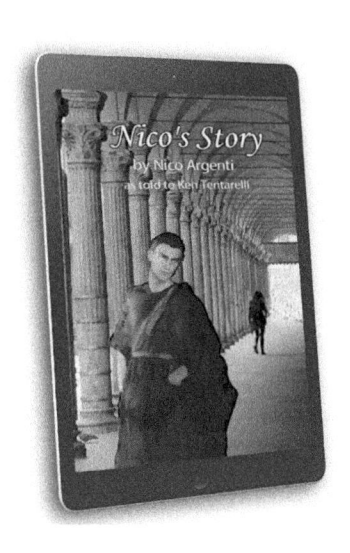

What was it like to be a student at a Renaissance university?

Sign up for our newsletter at KenTentarelli.com and download — FREE— *Nico's Story* in his own words.

ABOUT THE AUTHOR

Ken Tentarelli is a frequent visitor to Italy. In travels from the Alps to the southern coast of Sicily he developed a love for its history and its people. He has studied Italian culture and language in Rome and Perugia. At home he has taught courses in Italian history spanning time from the Etruscans to the Renaissance. When not traveling Ken and his wife live in New Hampshire.

ALSO BY KEN TENTARELLI

Also by Ken Tentarelli

The Laureate: Mystery in Renaissance Italy

(Nico Argenti series book 1)

Nico Argenti returns from the university to find Florence, his beloved city, gripped by power hungry aristocrats. He is drawn into the turmoil where he must uncover and thwart the conspirators before their assassin makes Nico the next victim.

The Advisor: Intrigue in Tuscany

(Nico Argenti series book 2)

Nico Argenti uses his legal training to help a small mountain town outwit a vindictive knight and win the town's independence. To gather the evidence he needs, Nico travels throughout Tuscany to locate documents and to interview displaced refugees before confronting the rogue knight. Will the knight accept the ruling of a Papal court, or will he turn against Nico?

Assignment Milan

(Nico Argenti series book 3)

Nico moves quickly when a Florentine banker mysteriously goes missing in Milan. When the disappearance turns into murder and conspiracy, he races to uncover the plot targeting the heart of the Florentine Republic.

Rebels in Pisa

(Nico Argenti series book 5)

Rumors of insurrection in Renaissance Pisa spur Florentine authorities to send your lawyer Nico Argenti to investigate. He and his team uncover more than expected: smuggling, abduction, and murder

Ingram Content Group UK Ltd.
Milton Keynes UK
UKHW010705130723
425033UK00018B/173/J